THE CHRISTMAS AGREEMENT

SHARON WOODS

For all the women waiting for someone who will never stop choosing them.

CHAPTER 1

GRACIE

"**I**'m freaking out."

"Why? A baby isn't a death sentence." I chuckle at Ava's strained voice through the phone. I can tell she is on the verge of crying. Something my friend barely does. One thing about Ava is, she isn't weak. She won't take shit from anyone. So, this fragile side is unnerving and, truthfully, I want my fiery friend back. Her strength helps me stay strong.

"But we aren't ready...we aren't married yet."

"You're engaged. That's the same bloody thing," I argue, trying to snap some sense into her.

"It's too soon," she mumbles.

"For who?"

She stays silent, then I hear a hiccup down the line.

"Listen, I know this is really about you. And—" I clear my throat, taking a breath through my now tightening airway. It always happens when I talk about the past. "You're not going to leave your baby."

That has her sobbing loudly, and I drop my chin. Clutching my phone tightly in my hand, I'm surprised it's not breaking. My eyes swell with tears threatening to sprinkle my cheeks at hearing her struggle.

"I can't do this."

"Well, it looks like you don't have an option. Have you told Josh yet?" I ask.

"No," she splutters through a sob. "What's he going to think?"

"I'm not a mind reader, but if I had to guess, I'd say he's going to be fucking ecstatic. The guy worships the ground you walk on. If he wasn't serious about a future with you, he wouldn't have proposed, and you wouldn't be planning your dream wedding."

"But a baby...it's a big fucking deal."

I wonder what it would be like to have someone like that...

Someone who truly loves me. Who won't leave me. Adores me.

I shake my head at the ridiculous thought. Every day at work, I see more shit guys than good. It would take a lot for me to settle down. I'm happy to hookup for relief and a good time, but it's always no strings attached, and so far, I've never wanted more.

"It is, but you have Josh and me—" A beep in my ear has me pulling my phone away to see who the other caller is.

"Someone's trying to call you. I should let you go." She splutters.

Sandra flashes across the screen. I hesitate. Should I let it go to voicemail?

My stomach hardens at the thought of hanging up, so instead, I say, "It's Sandra. I can call her back. But, Ava"—I wait until she says "yeah" before continuing—"you will make an amazing mom. "

She sniffs and says, "Thanks. I don't know what I'd do without you. But answer Sandra, she wouldn't call unless it was important. I'm fine. Call me tomorrow."

I smile, feeling that way too. She is my ride or die, the friend who you can always count on to always be there for you in the good or bad times. I'd do anything for her.

"Ditto. I really have to take Sandra's call before she hangs up, but I'll pop in tomorrow to see you, and we can talk this out properly."

"Sounds good. Bye." She sniffs once more before I hang up.

I quickly accept the incoming call, catching it on the last ring.

"Hello, Sandra?" I say with a frown, wondering why she is calling.

"Hi. Could you possibly come in and help tonight? It's hectic with the Christmas crowd, and I need your experience."

My frown deepens at her question, and I run my hand through my freshly washed hair, not wanting to get it ruined from the smoke.

"But didn't we roster staff for every shift?" I ask.

"I know, and I'm sorry to even ask this of you."

I have worked every day this week, and tonight was my night off.

"You wouldn't unless you were desperate," I mumble, closing my eyes and lying back on my couch.

"I'm sorry."

Me too.

I open my eyes and look down at my tartan flannel pajamas, knowing they are about to be replaced by a Santa skirt and crop top.

The thought of how cold it is outside makes me shiver. But no matter the weather, I do my best to make tips on every shift, and that requires the scantily clad look. It doesn't mean I like it, but the more tips, the quicker I can save for bigger and better things.

I sigh. "I'll get ready and come as soon as I can."

"Thank you! You're the best. I owe you!"

A laugh slips, and I say, "Don't thank me yet. I'm not even there. I could totally stand you up."

"You never let me down."

I smile, grateful she notices that I'm reliable, a quality I take pride in myself for. I work hard and care for others, and I'll always feel indebted to Sandra for giving me a job and a restart in life.

"I'll see you soon," I say, then hang up, tossing the phone to my side before getting ready for another busy night.

Only a couple of hours in, and it's been nonstop. I have been directing newer staff on what to do, as well as making drinks and doing rounds of the room to make sure no one is misbehaving. Which, so far, thankfully, they aren't. That would mean me having to kick them out, or worse—call the cops.

I'm too tired for that shit tonight, so everyone better stay on their best behavior.

"Can I have another rum and Coke, darling?"

My skin crawls at the sexual tone, and I turn from my position at the fridge, where I'm neatly restocking bottles of pre-mixed alcohol. Looking around the Christmas decorations, I plaster the biggest fakest smile I can muster at the white-haired man pushing late sixties, wearing a flannel shirt and torn jeans, and a matching white overgrown beard.

He's a regular.

"Kevin, I thought I told you not to call me darling. It makes me feel old."

I don't get up from my position and his glossy half-closed eyes spring open, looking me up and down. I internally roll my eyes. *Gross*.

Where is the vomit bucket when you need one?

I turn and finish unpacking the drinks.

He speaks again. "You are definitely not old, Gracieee."

This time of year, the bar is always busy, being the holiday season. But Kevin here comes by every week. Since his wife died, he religiously saunters in, taking a seat right at the bar, drooling all over me and offering to pay me for sex. Which, I'm sorry, no matter how much money he was to offer, I just can't do it. Drunk or sober, there is just no fucking way.

The money, I'm not going to lie, would be amazing, and help me reach my goal of becoming an architect faster. But allowing him into my bed takes on a whole level of low. I'd rather build my savings the old fashion way—by working hard.

And I'm happy to work. But Christmas has to be one of the saddest times for me. Most nights I leave here, I'm alone, dreaming of a bright future that involves a career earning good money, a house in the city, and a family. I want the whole husband and the white picket fence, but one goal at a time. The real kicker was that it was a Christmas week when I left home in search of a better life.

I finish restocking and then stand to pour Kevin his rum and Coke, placing it in front of him. He pays me, and as usual, tips me well. Putting on my best fake smile, I say my "Thank you" and hurry back to cleaning, trying to keep my distance.

But before I can get too far, *his* voice cuts through the Christmas carols playing, making me pause. "Excuse me."

It's the voice of someone I've thought about more than I'd care to admit, even though we've never really spoken more than a couple of words to each other.

Swallowing roughly, I look down the bar until I locate him. Our gazes lock, and his piercing brown eyes, olive skin, and tousled brown-black hair send a tingle through my limbs.

This alluring man has only been in a few times, and every one of those times, I turn to jelly. I can't string two fucking words together. His looks cause my brain to turn to mush, and I have to take a minute to recover from his presence.

Say something tonight, I beg myself. Looking briefly up at the mistletoe.

I'm never tongue-tied or struggling for words. Normally, you can't shut me up, but this man has me shaky on my knees.

I finally step over to him, running my hands over my skimpy Santa clothes and my eyes over his white shirt that's rolled up at the sleeves, showcasing his muscled forearms dusted with dark hair. He must've pulled at his tie because it's loose around his neck.

It's like he has just left work. On Christmas Eve?

CHAPTER 2

MARCO

I hate Christmas. It's the worst holiday of the year, when everyone plays pretend happy family. I'm on my way back to New York City, but I needed to see her for some reason. I knew she could make Christmas more bearable and looking at her hazel lust-filled eyes staring back at me now, makes me glad I stopped by.

A place like this isn't one you'd typically find me in, but I stay down at the end of the bar to keep off other patrons' radars while I'm here. I don't want to be spoken to by anyone while I'm here...except her.

I watch her move like an angel. She wears the brightest red lipstick, only enhancing the shine of her brilliant white smile. And her small sexy santa outfit including her thigh high socks are causing me to swallow a growl. The way these men look at her makes me sick. I stumbled into this bar once when my car broke down on a work trip, and I have only been back since to get a glance at her.

I sip my drink slowly, admiring her beauty, and I wonder every time what her story is...why is she working here?

She looks to be mid-twenties and seems to have a good head on her shoulders, but she works here, in this old town bar. Is this a part-time job? Is she in school? If so, that'd mean she's starting late? Or maybe she's gone back for additional studies? Maybe instead of thinking about every possibility, I could make this a lot simpler and talk to the woman.

All these questions come to me, but every time I have come in here, I haven't been able to ask. I'm speechless by her beauty, but also, I know I'm too old for her. Heck, I'm a thirty-eight-year-old who can't talk to a woman. I bet my friends would have a field day with that. So, when she comes over, standing in front of me, her hands gripped to the counter, and her angelic voice says, "Hi," it's no surprise that I respond so lamely.

I smile and say, "Hi."

"Would you like the usual?" she asks with a wide grin and a sparkle in her eye. My heart skips a beat at the adorable way she is staring at me right now. When she looks at me like that, I wonder for a brief second if she does that with everyone, or if it's saved just for me.

Hell, I hope it's the latter.

"Please," I say with a small nod. The corner of my lip twitches.

"Gotcha. I'll be right back." She pushes off the bar and moves effortlessly to make my scotch on the rocks before dropping it in front of me and pausing. Her hands are leaning on the counter again, seemingly waiting for me.

"Thanks." I hand over my money and my usual generous tip.

She takes it from me, and when our hands graze, it sends my heart hammering.

What was that?

Pushing that feeling aside, I decide I need to take this opportunity to talk to her. Finally.

"So—"

"Did you—"

But she has the same idea, and it makes us both laugh.

"You go." She lifts her hand toward me.

I shake my head. "Ladies first."

"Did you, uh, just finish work?" she stumbles, and I smile wider. Glad I'm not the only one affected. I run my gaze over her hand to check—but no ring still.

Good. Real fucking good.

"Uh-huh," I mumble as I sip the drink, welcoming the burn down my throat. Licking my lips, I'm unable to remove my eyes from her high cheekbones, bowing pouty lips, and heart-shaped face as she continues to multitask, indulging in her magnificence as she stacks a pile of glasses on a dish rack.

I shouldn't be asking, but I need to know. Speaking loudly to be heard over the music and chatter, I ask, "Do you have a b—?"

But I'm cut off by a drunk customer waving her down, cutting off others as if he's more important than anyone else waiting at the bar. "Excuse me!" he yells again, and I grind my teeth.

As I turn to her, she offers me a strained smile and dips her head, moving to serve him. Watching him smile at her with dopey eyes makes my blood boil. I need to walk away from him and cool down. It's getting under my skin. Heck, anything to do with her gets under my skin. *But why?*

Who fucking knows.

I pick up my glass and drain it before moving to the dingy hallway to seek out the restroom. I don't miss the way her eyes skim over me as I do, sending a silent thrill through me.

As I come back down the hallway, I have never appreciated the warm, dim lighting except for right now. My eyes connect with her, and the way it hits her pink flushed cheeks enhances her beauty. Illuminates her, as I watch her ass move around the tables, refreshing drinks, and taking orders. The way she works tells me she has been doing this for a while.

And that gets me thinking she couldn't have a boyfriend, surely. What kind of man would sit back and watch an old man crack on to her and not want to punch the shit out of him? Well, if she was with me, she wouldn't work here.

My phone chimes in my pocket, pulling me from my thoughts, and I lean against the wall to check it. I see a notification from my assistant.

Cassie: Flight's delayed by two hours.

I squeeze my eyes shut. Fuck. I'm going to be more tired tomorrow, and even less thrilled to be dealing with the family for Christmas lunch.

I suck in a long breath through my nose and try to be positive.

Walking back to the bar, I'm stopped dead in my tracks when I see her wiping down the counter, her skirt pulled up from the simple task, showing me her toned legs. I wonder if she likes to work out as much as I do.

I'm an early riser who runs or hits the gym in my penthouse before work every day.

I can't help but notice all the other patrons' eyes ogling her too, and my jaw clenches. Nope, I definitely don't like the size of her skirt for work now.

It's not her fault she's getting so much attention. She is beautiful, stunningly so, with the hourglass figure that every man in this room wants to have between their palms. But it doesn't change how protective I'm being all of a sudden.

What is it about her that makes me like this?

I never come back to see the same woman, but with her, I have this need to visit this bar every time I'm in town.

She walks out of sight, so I shake off my wandering thoughts and return to my seat at the high counter. I need another drink stat, to deal with both the flight delay and these men drooling over her. Maybe I need some food too.

"What's your name?" I ask when she comes to the beer taps to refill a drink. I don't know why, I need to know it right this minute. Like it matters to me. It's not like I'm interested in her or anything. I've seen her multiple times now and have yet to open that door.

"Sandy," a woman beside me slurs, sliding her arm over my shoulder. I stiffen, hating the contact even more as I look into her hooded, glassy eyes. Glancing at the woman I was actually asking, I see she is biting her lip until she pops it, and it turns into a cheeky grin. The tension in me dissipates a little, loving her face while wearing humor—it's sexy.

Just like her.

"I'm not talking to you. I'm asking her." I tilt my chin.

She opens her mouth, but Sandy interrupts, saying, "Gracie. But she is twenty-six, so a little young for you, don't you think?"

What is this lady talking about? I've only asked for a name, not a hand in marriage. Fuck, this is getting out of control.

Gracie's face falls, and as she grabs my empty glass, I cover her hand with mine. She stills under my touch.

Our gazes lock, and I say, "I think it's her choice."

Gracie's face softens. I would say she agrees.

Sandy squeezes my shoulder, whispering not so quietly in my ear, "If you say so, but I think I'm closer to your age and much better suited."

She's trying to be seductive, but this woman is vile, and I wish she would simply fuck off. She is saying everything right in front of Gracie, who, right now, I'm sure, is insulted. And I don't want anyone hurting or upsetting her.

My hand is still on hers, and really, I should remove it, but I can't seem to make myself.

I've had enough, and my blood is pumping harder in my ears. I speak through gritted teeth. "That's untrue, and if you don't mind, I'd like to be left alone."

Sandy huffs before pushing out her chest and storming off, probably to annoy some other fucker for the night. But maybe with their beer goggles, she will be more appealing.

I return to face Gracie, who smiles at me before slipping her hand out from under mine so she can return to work. A flash of disappointment hits me from the loss of contact, feeling cold and empty.

The question I tried to ask earlier enters my mind once more, and I am desperate to know. I lean forward, lacing my fingers before me on the counter. Watching the way she peeks up at me from under her dark lashes and the way she bites her plump lip has me shifting in my seat, and fuck it. "Do you have a boyfriend?" I ask, keeping my voice low and firm away from prying patrons.

Her eyes widen as she peers around with a slackened mouth before returning to my gaze, and she responds with a knowing smile, "No."

A hum vibrates through my chest at her answer.

This woman is piquing my interest, but should her age deter me? Twenty-six is an age that she knows what she wants, but there are still twelve years between us, so maybe it's too much. Why am I even thinking this way? I never said I would act on my desire. Even with the way my body reacts to her, I won't give in. I just came in for an hour and planned to watch her from afar and have a brief conversation before I leave again.

But tonight is the first time I have stayed longer than usual. And it seems I chose a busy night, with the bartenders moving nonstop. A noise in front of me brings my attention back just as she lowers another drink down in front of me, and she smiles before moving to serve another customer.

"Gracie," I say.

She turns to me, and I smirk, loving the sound of her name rolling off my tongue. Her brow raises in question.

"Could I order some food? My flight's delayed." I should be more upset by this turn of events, as usually it would piss me off, but having more time with her is a secret blessing. It's only two hours, so what's the harm? And with that time, I can ask her more questions and watch her move in that little outfit.

"I'm sorry to hear that." The way she looks at me and her genuine sadness causes my dick to twitch.

"I'm not. At least I'll have great company." My smirk widens when I see the wheels turning in her head.

"You will. Where were you headed?" She leans over the counter, and I can't help but run my gaze over her sinful curves again, her full breasts taunting me. I drop my gaze lower, admiring the dips in her waist, and then slowly make my way to her exquisite face again. She gives me a wide grin and an appreciative look of her own. I've never worried about what a woman thinks of me, but I hope she likes what she sees.

She seems more relaxed and confident around me now, giving me a side I haven't seen yet. I want to get to know more.

"New York," I reply.

"Is that where you live?" she gushes with a beaming expression.

"It is."

She pushes off the counter. "Oh, I need to grab you a menu. At this hour, it's bar food only, sorry."

"I'll take anything."

She reaches down and hands me a menu.

"Can you recommend anything?" I ask as I scan it over.

She leans forward and points to the nachos and hot wings.

"These are crowd favorites."

I stare at her finger, noting her red painted nails. They'd look great leaving scratch marks on my back.

Scanning the rest of the menu before looking back up, I say, "I can't go past the crowd favorite, can I? I'll get the nachos and hot wings." And hopefully, I won't get food poisoning, except it might be a good way out of lunch with my ex tomorrow.

"Good choice. Are you going to eat them here or at a table?"

I pay and look around. A bit of the crowd has cleared and there is a table near the TV, but wanting to watch her more wins out, so I decide to stay where I am, and hope Sandy doesn't come back.

"I'll stay right here," I say, and she bites her lip to stop a broad smile from forming.

Chapter 3

GRACIE

I'm serving the rowdy crowd, and a bead of sweat runs down my back from the nonstop night. I chance a peek at him in the corner, munching on the pretzels, then get back to work. He's so damn handsome.

No one else has come over to bother him since Sandy, and I can't help but smirk at the memory. His horrified expression was priceless. She is thirty-nine and very attractive, so to watch him become so repulsed by her made me feel lighter. And the way he said it was my choice...I don't know exactly how old he is, but age is just a number. I've dated guys my age, and yes, it's fun, but the electricity I have with him is different. I want to find out his name now. He knows mine, so it's only fair.

The way he spoke and acted gave me the confidence boost I needed to let my guard down. I can't help but remember the subtle hand squeeze and smile just for me, showing me his interest in me too. I want to do something about it, but I don't know what. He's more sophisticated than the men I've been with before; in a league of his own.

He hasn't left the spot at the bar, which I'm secretly humbled about. And I've refilled his drink a couple of times now. It's a nice excuse to check in with him, and we exchange flirty smiles. I wish I had longer to stop and talk to him, since I know he'll be gone soon, but the crowd is still large, and I'm too busy to have a long chat.

I'm restocking the limes when, from the corner of my eye, I see a young man slip something into a drink. I snatch the glass from the bar before he can reach for it, narrowing my eyes and saying, "Don't fucking bother."

I know his name, so I'm going to report him.

"Give it to me," he sneers.

"No, you spiked it."

The woman standing near him gasps and covers her mouth, looking totally bewildered, and I feel sorry for her as what I said sinks in. But what I wasn't expecting was for her to pour the drink over him and yell, "How dare you? You creep. I'm going to the cops."

She storms off in the exit's direction, and I stand there, proud of her. Her speaking up at the disgusting act is impressive. Spiking isn't a usual occurrence here, but it's still an unfortunate reality. Every time I've found women passed out or slurring their words when I know they weren't drunk, it causes me to dislike men as a whole.

I watch him look around, embarrassed at being caught. *Piece of trash.* As I walk over to the phone to report him, his face pales.

"Please don't. It won't happen again." He leans over the bar, his expression one of desperation.

"Not a chance in hell," I spit, my body vibrating in anger.

The bouncer grabs him and takes him away.

After I make the call, I return to work, but I'm a little shaken.

"Are you okay?" The sexy stranger asks, his voice cutting across my wandering thoughts.

"Yeah," I mumble, not wanting to expose to him how rattled I really am. I just want to push it aside and go back to the fun, flirty night.

"That happens often?" he asks, and the deep tone of concern in his voice has me looking up.

His head is tilted, and he's holding strong eye contact with me. When I stay silent, a deep frown settles between his brows. "Gracie?"

I sigh. "Thankfully not. I don't understand why they do it."

His eyes darken, and he rubs his chin with his hand as he speaks. "Baffles me. Consent is huge for me."

My pulse skips a beat.

"Same. And don't they want the woman to enjoy it?" I shake my head.

"I guess not. Which doesn't make any sense, since that's the best part."

I swallow hard, knowing what he's implying.

I'm about to respond when he pulls his phone out, pinching the bridge of his nose as he grumbles, "Fuck."

"Is everything all right?" I ask.

He runs his hand through his hair before cradling his drink again. Lifting it to his lips, he drains half the glass. His eyes flick up to me and he says, "My flight's canceled."

I wait, but nothing else comes. He's rubbing his lip with his finger and staring at his phone, clearly upset. "Do you need any help?"

"Gracie!" a customer shouts, and I hate that I'm being interrupted. I want to help him even though I don't even know how I could possibly do that. I just want to remove that stress from his face.

He stares at me and then looks away and then back at me. I smile softly in apology, and he offers one in return before looking at his phone once again as I'm pulled back to serve more customers.

A little bit later, his food is ready, so I bring it over, but his back is to me. He's standing with his hand buried deep in his pocket, showing me his tight ass in his gray pants, his other clutching the phone to his ear.

I lower the food down carefully, trying not to make a noise. I want to hear his conversation and perv on him a little longer without him knowing.

"You need to find me a new flight. I must get home tonight."

My brows knit. He can't get home at all? And who's at home waiting for him? I look at his left hand, but I don't see a ring, but maybe there is a girlfriend.

My stomach hardens in disappointment. Of course, he would have someone. He's handsome, intelligent, and he probably sees me in the way every other guy in here does.

But then why did he flirt with me all night if he had someone? There is something undeniable that's shared between us. Surely, I haven't been reading all the signals wrong? Hell, *he* asked me if I had a boyfriend. He instigated that, not me.

No, I shake my head. I'm not delusional.

Tonight, before he leaves, I'm going to find out if this is all a fantasy I've made up in my head, or something I should let myself indulge in...even just for the night.

CHAPTER 4

MARCO

I 'm sipping another drink and by now the burn isn't there, it's numb.

I need to get home to my daughter and ex-wife for Christmas lunch, but I'm stuck here. I'm scrolling my phone, looking at every stupid motel around here, but either they have no vacancies, or the places look like bed bugs come as part of the room.

I'm at a loss about what to do.

Slumping over the counter, I rub my forehead and scroll until my phone dies. I squeeze my eyes tight. *Fuck*. Seriously?

My phone is dead and I'm in a bar far from home, with no place to sleep tonight. Taking a deep breath, I notice how quiet the bar is. I lower my phone and peer up to see there are only a few customers left.

"You have been here all night," Gracie says with a cute smile. Her red lipstick has worn off and now her naturally pink lips are visible.

"Yeah, I sure have." I can't help but grin at her. I am welcoming her presence to cut through the bad mood I've found myself in.

"This is the longest you've ever been here." Her face lights up in a mischievous look. That single look breaks through the dull headache that's now forming behind my brow.

"Yeah, well, a flight cancellation and no rooms anywhere." I bark out a laugh, even though it's the least bit funny. "And to top it off...my phone just died."

I lift the phone to show her a black screen.

She winces. "Ouch. Today isn't your day, huh?"

I shake my head. "Nope, I pissed in someone's Wheaties."

She giggles, and it's the lightest, prettiest sound. It makes me laugh along with her.

"Well, I have a charger you can borrow, but that won't help your sleeping situation."

"I'll take what I can get. The charger would be great."

She nods and retrieves the charger from a back room, bringing it over to me.

"There is an outlet over there, next to the booth." I follow where she is pointing. Nodding, I slide off the stool, my ass officially dead from the lack of circulation after sitting for so long.

"Have a seat there. I'll bring you a fresh drink and join you."

My mouth falls open, and I do a double take. I see her panic at my reaction, and she quickly waves a hand around. "Or I'll leave you be. I don't want to bother you."

My face morphs into a wide smile. "Oh, no. I'd love it if you'd join me. Just...don't you have somewhere else to be?" Surely, she doesn't want to babysit me.

"No. I'm closing up tonight."

"But it's Christmas Eve."

She shrugs. "Someone has to do it." Her voice is flat with her response, and it causes my gut to twist, telling me something isn't adding up. But I don't push her.

I nod. "Okay, I'll be waiting over there." I smile and take off to the booth.

She comes after a while carrying two glasses. Sliding one across the wooden table to me, she sits on the opposite side.

I pick up the glass and hold it out to cheers. "Thanks for this."

"Bye, Gracie!" a patron calls out.

She waves and watches them leave before returning to face me, clinking her glass with mine and taking a sip. Staring at me over her glass, she lowers it to the table, and an unreadable expression appears on her face.

"What's your name?" she asks.

I smirk as I answer, "Marc."

"Marc," she repeats, and it's like a purr, or at least that's how it sounds to me. My pulse races, and I swear I see interest flash across her face. I wonder if she's attracted to me too.

Nah, she is just trying to be nice. Probably feels sorry for me being stranded here.

I nod, watching her as I drink. "Am I your last customer?" I ask, checking my watch and glancing at the time, shocked to see its one thirty in the morning.

It's fucking Christmas.

"Mm-hmm."

"Now I feel worse," I say with a groan.

"Don't. It's not like you asked for this to happen?"

"Definitely not." I scoff.

"Well, now that you're here, we may as well get to know each other," she says with a shrug.

"Really?" This is too good to be true.

She lifts her glass to her lips, taking a decent drink. When she lowers it back to the table, she licks the residue off her lips. Her pink tongue gliding over her plump bottom lip is taunting, and the alcohol running through my veins hasn't slowed down my desire. If anything, spending more time around her tonight has increased it tenfold.

I clutch the glass in my hand like a lifeline.

She nods and asks, "How old are you, Marc?"

God, the sound of my name coming from her throat is stirring me up.

I need to stay focused and try to keep my mind from drifting into dangerous territory.

"Older than you," I say with a smirk.

She rolls her eyes playfully. "Tell me, it won't scare me," she whispers.

I stare at her, and I know it won't. She already knows I'm older, and it hasn't had her running away. Instead, it seems to attract her more.

"Thirty-eight," I reply, watching her face to see what her reaction is.

"You're younger than I thought."

A deep chuckle leaves me at her answer. "Yeah, not too old, you reckon?"

"Not an old man just yet." She swats my hand with a giggle.

Silence falls between us, and when she smiles, it causes me to frown in confusion.

"Why are you smiling?"

"It wasn't that hard, was it?"

I chuckle. The only hard thing is my cock between my legs. It's growing and making me spread my thighs under the table.

Keeping those thoughts to myself, I say, "No."

"Do you want to play a game?" she asks, looking like she needs liquid courage as she takes another sip.

"I don't play games," I say honestly.

"Come on. It's Christmas and you're stuck here. Let's have some fun." There's a twinkle in her eye I'm not sure I can deny.

I squint, trying to read where she is going with this. "What are you thinking?" I ask, still mulling over her words.

"Truth or Dare."

I haven't played this game since I was young. It seems stupid and dangerous. Playing Truth or Dare with her could lead to trouble. Serious fucking trouble.

"I'm a thirty-eight-year-old man, and you want me to play Truth or Dare?" I shake my head.

"You're not dead." She winks, and I let out a groan, rubbing my jaw.

"Come on, live a little. Or are you too scared I'll have you eating a spoonful of hot sauce when you choose dare?" She wiggles her eyebrows, and the humor is back, and fuck if she isn't tempting. As she brings her drink to her lips again, I'm suddenly jealous of the glass, wishing that perfect mouth was pressed against mine or full of my cock.

I used to be young and carefree like Gracie is now. I used to be the guy that actually lived his life and had fun, then things changed when work took over and effectively ruined my life a bit.

The issues with my ex-wife only arose because all I did was work. It broke my family and caused my divorce, but I couldn't give it up. Work is my life—it consumes me.

And now, here I am, unable to work. So why shouldn't I live a little? Indulge in the temptation that sits across from me…because I don't see this game ending with me letting her walk away untouched unless she doesn't want it. Her hungry eyes keep suggesting things that I doubt I'm wrong about.

"I'm in," I say with a lift of my brow. "But no fucking hot sauce, deal?"

She tips her head back, laughing, before sitting up and clapping excitedly. And I can't help but roll my eyes with a grin.

"Truth or dare?" she asks.

"Truth."

I'm not game to try dare yet. I don't know where her head is at.

She stares at me for a minute, and my pulse rises, wondering what the first question will be.

"Are you married?" she asks, and I let out the breath I was holding.

Easy.

"No," I answer and watch as she bites down on her lip, hiding a smile, but the gleam in her eyes gives away how happy she is. I can't help but grin stupidly at her before asking, "Truth or dare?"

"Truth."

Good. I was hoping to get to know her more.

"Do you have a girlfriend? Or are you seeing anyone at all?"

"Hey! That was two questions, Mister!"

I smirk. Knowing I totally did, but not on purpose.

I hold my hand up in surrender. "Sorry, honest mistake. I promise."

She narrows her eyes, as if reading my face to see if I'm lying. I can't help but laugh. She shakes her head, laughing too, before answering, "No to both, cheater."

Perfect.

I nod and sit back in the booth and wait for her.

"Truth or dare."

"Truth."

"Are you single? Like, not seeing anyone at all?"

I chuckle darkly before saying, "I'm completely single. There is no one." I say every word slowly, so she gets it before asking her, "Truth or dare?"

"Truth."

"Are you attracted to me?"

She blinks rapidly at my direct question, and I pick up my glass and drain it. I hide my grin, knowing I caught her off guard.

"Yes," she says unevenly. And I feel anything but even. Her admitting exactly what I wanted to hear causes my mouth to suddenly dry. I take a long sip of my drink whilst she asks me the next question.

"Truth or dare."

"Truth."

"Are you attracted to me?"

My gaze stays locked on hers. "Obviously, yes."

She bites down on her lip and blushes, and my mind pictures her under me. Completely naked, except for her sexy thigh high socks and heels. Her luscious body writhing in pleasure, and those tempting pink lips I'm currently staring at, calling out my name. But my daydream is cut short by her husky voice. "Truth or dare?"

I clear my throat. Needing a minute to get my head on straight, I decide to change the direction of the game.

"I dare you to make me a drink that describes you."

"That's not how you play the game. You clearly haven't played in a while."

"Are you calling me old?" I ask, smirking.

"You might be showing your age now."

"Ouch." I lay a hand on my chest, pretending to be hurt.

She giggles before draining her glass and sliding out of the booth. Reaching over to grab my glass, our hands touch, and it sends a spark through me.

"Maybe another drink will remind you how to play." She holds my gaze before she sashays off to the bar. Her hips have me transfixed.

Yeah, I definitely needed a second. Her effect on me is unlike anything I've experienced.

"I might lock up first."

"But I need somewhere to stay tonight!" I call out, wondering what I'm going to do. I still haven't figured out a backup plan, therefore, I need the bar to stay open until I do.

"Do you?" she calls, and I swear I've heard wrong. Surely, she isn't insinuating...

Nah...she's just playing with me.

But it doesn't stop this unfamiliar feeling of hope. That maybe someone will want me again.

"Let's just enjoy Christmas. You definitely need—"

"Are we back to the live a little speech? I heard that loud and clear," I tease.

"Good, you heard me. I'm checking on your old age; you still clean your ears."

I chuckle. This woman kills me...in the best way.

I don't bother discussing the issue of where I'm sleeping tonight. I'll deal with it later. I just want to enjoy this...simply...enjoy her.

Be present in this moment, right here, right now.

Sensible Marc can return tomorrow back in New York, where work and reality are waiting for me.

"Is there anything you're allergic to or don't like?" she calls out over her shoulder, while my eyes stay glued to her. I love those hips...curves...they are making me sweat.

"Marc," she prompts.

Fuck, focus. "Ah, no, I eat and drink everything."

She lifts her head up slowly, meeting my gaze. Nodding, she walks behind the bar, cutting off my view. I'm curious to see what she is doing with the drink, so I slip out of the brown booth and walk over, leaning over the bar to take a peek.

"Nuh-uh, you can't see what it is."

I chuckle and say, "Well, let me use the restroom, and then I'll meet you back in the booth."

"Okay."

I go to the restroom and then return to my seat and see a plate of Christmas sugar cookies. She must've dropped them off, so I grab one and munch on it, until she comes around carrying two drinks.

Watching her lower one glass in front of me, she takes her seat, cradling hers. I try to focus on something else other than her petite shape and how perfect she would feel between my hands. So, I look down at what she made.

"What is it?" I ask, picking up the pale-yellow drink that has a foam top to inspect it before sipping, enjoying the sugar, citrus, and spirit flavors.

Licking my lips slowly, I catch her watching the movement with intensity. My chest tightens and when she licks her own lips, I struggle to hold myself back from leaning over this table and kissing the shit out of her, running my tongue over her delicious lips. Instead, I sit back and clutch the glass tightly as she answers.

"Whiskey sour."

I chuckle and ask, "You describe yourself as sour?"

She laughs, and when she recovers, she says, "The name is stupid, but I love the taste and think it's me."

I take another sip and describe it. "Rich, smooth, with a hint of tart."

"Oh, shit. Rich is not me; I wish."

That has me thinking of what I was asking myself earlier.

"Why do you work here?" I ask.

She pops a brow. "Are you forgetting the rules?"

I run my tongue over my teeth. Her sassiness tonight is fucking turning me on.

"No. I just want to know more about you." Our eyes are locked with an intense stare, and we hold it for a moment before she speaks huskily.

"We are playing, remember, but I'll choose the truth, so you get the answer." She winks and then sips her drink. "I go to college, so I'm here paying for that until I can get a traineeship."

I smile, loving how she is working to better herself and not living off her parents, or waiting for a man to rescue her. She is working for what she wants. And that to me is fucking sexy.

"So, working here is just temporary, not a chosen career?"

"Why? What's wrong with working in a bar?" she asks, furrowing her brow.

"Nothing at all if that's what you want to do, but as I have gotten to know you, I see more potential."

"Oh, really?"

"Yes, you're very good here. I have seen you and you're on top of everything, including the dick tonight who slipped drugs into the girl's drink. The way you caught him and reported him speaks volumes. You're on the ball and very hardworking."

Her mouth is partly open before she swallows and asks. "You could see all that?"

"Yes, *Bella*," I say with a frown.

Why can't she believe it?

CHAPTER 5

GRACIE

He called me *Bella*.

The only "Bella" I know is for the word *beautiful* in Italian. But did he really just call me that? I know for certain I heard it. I bite my lip, hiding my smile. The warmth spreading over my chest just from the name is moving to my cheeks.

Not only does he call me *Bella*, but he sees my potential? How does this stranger feel so connected to me? I haven't even gotten my biological parents thinking that way. No, they see me as worthless and unlovable. But as I stare at Marc, there is a genuine warmth coming from him, and I believe him. At this moment, I have no reason not to.

Other than my fill-in parents and my friends, I stay low key. But tonight, with him, I'm relaxed—I'm me. And it's refreshing to have someone else to talk to.

"What are your plans for tomorrow. I mean today?" he asks.

Not wanting to discuss my family dynamics right now, I keep it short and simple. "I'm having Christmas lunch with family, and then I'll see my best friend for dinner. How about you?"

A lock of hair falls on his face, so without thought, I shift forward in my seat. But as I lift my hand, he pushes it back with his fingers, and I can see his heated gaze staring back at me. As the night has worn on, he's undone a button and pushed his shirt sleeves up, definitely becoming more relaxed too.

"If I get out of here, I'll be having Christmas lunch with my family," he says with a lopsided grin that creases his eyes and sends heat to my core.

"And dinner?" Call me curious, but I'm trying to soak up as much information as I can get from him.

"No plans. I'll probably work or sleep." He shrugs, but continues to stare at me before asking, "Do you have brothers or sisters?"

Nausea rolls in my stomach thinking about it. But it's sweet he is asking me personal questions. This is what makes him different. Other guys don't give a shit. "No. What about you?"

"Yeah, three brothers, but I'm the eldest."

"Your poor mom."

He chuckles. "Oh yeah, we were a wild bunch. Growing up, the pranks we pulled on her." He shudders, and I can't help but grin. I love hearing these types of stories, even if it pains me that it wasn't what I had.

"I don't believe you. I haven't met your brothers, so I can't comment on them, but you don't seem the type to put a foot out of line," I tease, imagining him as a young boy.

His eyes gleam at that before saying, "I wasn't always so"—he rubs the back of his neck before continuing—"stiff."

"I like stiff." I pinch my lips together to hold back a laugh before I give him a wide, open smile.

He smirks, knowing exactly where my mind has gone.

"Probably the wrong word to use. Let's try that again. Rule abiding."

I smile, but I've had enough family talk for the evening. I want to bring his young Marc out and have some fun. He's been on my mind so many times, and this is the first time I've been able to act on it, and hell, I deserve to live a little too.

To just once kiss those lips I've been dreaming of tasting; grab onto his muscles I've been twitching to touch, and feel the warmth of his skin against mine.

Yeah, I need this with him...now.

"Truth or dare?" I ask.

He leans back, narrowing his eyes at me. His smoldering look is making my belly swarm with nerves and excitement.

"Dare." He sips his drink, staring into my soul over his glass. Getting to know each other seems to have made the electricity between us hit another level. Maybe it's that we both admitted that we are attracted to each other, but either way, I need to think of a dare; I wasn't expecting that.

As moments pass, I try to get some air into my lungs. They seem to be constricted.

"I dare you to..." All the dares I'm thinking of involve me in some way.

Take a tequila shot from my stomach and suck the lime slice from my mouth.

Take an ice cube between your lips and run it over my body, starting at my lips.

Pour your drink all over my chest and use your tongue to clean me up.

Yeah, my mind has gone way off track.

He smirks, as if reading my flustered thoughts. I simply can't think of a dare without me.

My brain is all misfiring about how much I want to lean over and capture his lips. I wonder what they would feel like and what he would taste like. His hands tighten around his glass as he watches me. They would have the power to destroy me, and fuck, I can't lie. I want that so fucking much. His hands on me and me getting lost in his toned body for the night, ridding my bad memories of Christmas. Could he replace the pain, or would he leave me aching for him? Exchanging one heartbreak for another?

I sip my drink before lowering it to the wooden table and cradling it in my hands.

"I can't think of one..." I say with a soft shake of my head.

He raises a brow. "Hmm, well, how about the truth?"

It doesn't help, but I ask the first thing that pops into my mind. "What are you thinking?"

"Right now?"

"Mm-hmm."

His gaze drops to my lips, and I hadn't realized I was nibbling them until now. I let go of my lip, and his eyes meet mine again.

He clears his throat and says, "How much I want to kiss you."

"Oh."

Yes, please.

He smirks seductively at me, and I tingle.

I want that too.

It's silent and I don't know what to do, so I sit still and luckily, he interrupts the awkwardness. "Truth or dare?"

"Truth," I say.

"What are you thinking right now?"

I blink and think about it for a second before I decide to take what I can get from this moment.

I want this.

I want him to kiss me.

"How much I want that too," I say.

He sucks in a sharp breath, lowering his glass to the table, and then he's suddenly standing. I look up at him, neither one of our gazes wavering, both of us knowing what is happening between us right now.

Stepping over to me, he holds out his hand. I put my hand in his, and he helps me stand before him. We are toe to toe, my heart thundering inside my rib cage.

I'm having to remind myself to breathe.

"Can I kiss you?"

I nod.

"Words, *Bella*. I need to hear the words."

Hearing that endearment again sends the warmth back, but this time not just through my chest, but into my sex. I like when he calls me that. I like it a lot.

I gulp, and say, "Yes, kiss me. Please."

He doesn't wait another second. He closes the distance between us, and when his lips hit mine, I sigh. All the tension in me leaves. I raise my arms and link them behind his head, pulling him down and making our bodies flush against each other. His warm, powerful body holds me up, and I feel safe and protected in his arms.

I have never felt this way. His power, control, and confidence oozing from his pores and onto me is causing me to soften in his embrace and kiss him back without any doubts or holding back. His tongue hits my lips, seeking entry, so I part them, our tongues sliding along each other's in a perfect rhythm. I enjoy his rum and masculine taste, savoring him.

I don't want this to end.

When I suck on his tongue, he groans into my mouth. The sound makes me shiver as I hold back a smile and do it again. His hand on my back tightens. He likes that. I do it once more, and another growl rumbles from his chest, vibrating through me.

Wanting to see what else he likes; I pull my tongue from his and move my lips to his bottom one, sucking, and he moans again. This is fun. The power is in my hands, and how I respond to what's happening now. It's my decision.

And right now, I want him. All of him.

Kissing me harder, his hands glide over my lower back, and I want to beg him to lower them to my ass and squeeze, but I don't want to appear desperate.

Pulling back, he looks down at me, speaking in a gravelly voice. "I have wanted to do that every time I've come to this bar."

"Why didn't you?" I whisper against his lips.

"I figured you would think of me as an old man, or you had a boyfriend, and I thought...well, I was only flying in, so I can't offer you anything long term."

I won't lie; I'm happy he has been thinking of kissing me, but I'm confused about the last part, so I ask, "Why?"

"Because I don't live here," he says and kisses me again.

I nod my understanding, remembering he told me earlier he lives in New York. But inside, I'm disappointed, wishing he lived closer. I guess this really is a one-night agreement.

He pecks me again before pulling me into his chest and hugging me. I've never thought much about hugging because I've simply never had it. I haven't been held or cuddled since I was a baby. I've had one serious boyfriend, and he wasn't affectionate after sex. So, this is strange, but comfortable. The beating of his heart under my ear has a calming effect on me and makes me want to stay like this forever.

"Why are you here, then?" I ask.

"Work."

"What do you do?"

"Design."

I suck in his scent, which is spicy and earthy. It's exactly like him, sexy and tantalizing.

I'm about to ask him what type of design he works in, but he distracts me when his hand moves up and down my back, stoking it with care. With nowhere to go, I don't move, soaking up every second. Yeah, I can ask that question later.

The feel of his toned body wrapped around me has me wanting to explore him further. One night suits me. If that's all I can have with him, then that's what I want. "I'm okay with just the night."

He shifts, and it causes me to lift my head off his chest so I can peer up at him. He kisses my forehead and whispers, "You don't have to."

"I know, but I want you."

He smiles, and it makes my heart race.

"I want you too." He moves to kiss my lips this time. A slow, long kiss that has my toes curling.

When we pull apart, he says, "I need to move for a sec. Hold on."

I look at him, puzzled.

"I need my phone to message my assistant. She can find us somewhere to stay tonight."

I shake my head. "No need. There is an empty bedroom upstairs. Just stay until you can get a flight out of here."

His face lights up with a wide grin before he kisses me softly. "Sounds perfect. But I'll message her anyway, because I need her to organize a new flight."

He has an assistant. Well, his work in design must be higher up. I could tell from his designer clothes and shoes he wasn't average but having your own assistant—that's fancy shit.

I pull away reluctantly, wishing I didn't have to stop touching him. He grabs his phone and texts while I admire him before I shake it off and walk back to the bar to refill our drinks. But on the way to turn down the lights, leaving a soft warm glow over us, changing the music to a soft hum as I do.

I'm lost in the cocktail mix and swaying of my hips when I look up and freeze. He walks around the counter to join me behind the bar, stopping right next to me with an intense stare.

His brown eyes are now darker and hooded. A new determination.

"So, you agree, then?"

"To what?" I ask, totally confused.

"One night."

Ah, I get it.

I nod.

"The words, *Bella*."

I swallow the lump in my throat but roll my shoulders back and put my game face on. This is what I want. I want him, and I'm about to have him.

"Yes, captain, show me what you've got."

His eyebrow quirks, and his face softens. "Captain?" His tone sends a shiver down my spine.

Then he's lifting me up and setting me down on the bar counter. A high-pitched squeak leaves my mouth, and my heart feels like it's in my stomach with anticipation.

"Open your legs," he commands. I follow his order, but he growls, "Wider."

Fuck me.

I'm already throbbing.

I do just that, but he isn't happy, so he pushes them as wide as I can physically handle. I lean back on my hands, my movement pushing aside the clutter of cups and plates on the wooden bar top. The counter is sticky from alcohol, but I don't dare stop the moment to clean any of it. The way he's watching me has my sex clenching, and I quickly forget all about the mess.

The warm lights hit his face, and I watch him hungrily.

He lifts my top, so I sit up and help him take it off. I drop my arms and catch his gaze flicking between my pushed-up tits. He mumbles, "Exquisite. Red is my favorite color." Before I have any time to think or help him with taking it off, he has reached behind my back and unbuckled the bra swiftly.

Experienced.

He stands back and stares at my now heavy breasts, letting out an appreciative growl. "Fucking perfect."

The cool air and his tone send my nipples into stiff peaks, begging for attention. I push out my chest in a silent offer. He stands straight and grabs my chin roughly, capturing my lips in a passionate kiss. His warm, wet tongue feels perfect with mine. We massage and feel each other, and when he pulls back, I peel my eyes open and peek at him from under my lashes.

He is looking at me with an unreadable expression as he rubs my bottom lip and then runs his finger over my top, grunting, "Swollen, pink, and beautiful." He pecks before moving his lips to my ear. "I bet your pussy is just the same."

I moan. Fuck, this man and his dirty words. My pussy is aching and becoming wetter with every touch and every kiss.

He runs his five-o'clock shadow and lips over my neck, trailing slowly down over my collarbone. Teasing me with soft kisses and then bites, followed by licks to soothe.

I'm breathing quickly from the anticipation, my breasts heaving with every inhale and exhale.

Moving his mouth to between my breasts, he repeats the bites and kisses over to my right nipple. The moment he claims my nipple in his mouth, sucking so hard it causes me to moan louder, I see stars. I'm trying to grab the counter under me, but there isn't anywhere to grip. I move my right hand into his brown locks and pull, leaving the other behind me to hold my body up. His hands rest at my sides, his thumbs stroking under my breasts.

He bites the sensitive flesh before popping off to kiss his way across the center of my chest to the left nipple, capturing that one in his mouth and repeating the actions.

Kissing along my stomach, he drops his hands to grab the sides of my ass that's squashed on the counter. No time to worry about what I may look like to him because I don't think he minds the cellulite or my stretch marks from my teenage years. He is kissing along the top of my skirt, and I'm about to rip it off just to have his mouth on me faster.

He pushes my skirt up, and hisses, "*Bella*, you're so wet."

He drops to his knees, and I need to be able to see.

"Wait."

He pulls back instantly and asks, "Is everything okay? Is this too much?"

"No, I want this. I want you, but I need to watch you eat my pussy."

His face softens before a wicked grin twists on his mouth.

Within moments, my skirt is off and he steps forward, ripping off his tie, and tossing it to the side. He kneels and grabs my inner thighs, and they quiver from his touch.

I'm sucking in breaths, trying to calm my overheated body, but it's not working. He leans forward, and I expect to feel his mouth, but a gush of cold air hits my center and I shiver. My legs try to close from the sensation as I mumble, "Oh my God."

"You're going to drip onto the counter. I figured I'd help dry you up."

"Fuckin' hell," I breathe, closing my eyes.

When I look at him again, his eyes are dancing with humor. He knows exactly what he is doing to me, and it's driving me wild.

He does it again, and even though I expect it this time, it doesn't lessen my shiver. Sitting up, I grab onto his hair, directing him to my pussy. "Please, Marc."

He answers me by putting his mouth over my clit and sucking me hard, all the while staring up at me. I curl my hand in his hair and moan. "Yes!"

Needing more friction, I move my hips to rub myself over his face. His five-o'clock shadow feels so good with each move he makes.

As he hums against me, I feel the vibration, making me moan again. He uses his tongue with strong, slow licks before sliding inside and pulling it out, repeating this over and over, fucking me with his tongue. His hands grip my thighs tightly and keep me stretched wide for him.

I can't believe I'm here right now, with this six-foot-four man on his knees for me, eating my pussy like he could for hours.

And I wouldn't fucking protest if he did just that; I'd fucking encourage it.

I tense at the incoming orgasm as he twirls his tongue around my clit, grazing his teeth around it as he does.

It isn't long before I'm grinding my hips harder over his face, over and over, until I'm quivering uncontrollably and screaming his name so loudly it echoes off the walls. "Marc!" It's an out-of-body experience; I have never in my whole life screamed from an orgasm, and I'm slightly embarrassed.

But after the most intense release I've ever had, that thought doesn't last long.

CHAPTER 6

MARCO

I'm so fucking hard from watching her orgasm; I'm barely keeping my own at bay. The way she screamed my name almost did me in.

As I stand and move to the sink, grabbing the sprayer, I turn to face her with a wicked grin. I wish I could read her mind.

"Lean back and put both feet on the counter," I demand, trying to suck in slow, deep breaths through my nose to control the raging desire inside me. I want her to enjoy herself, so I need to take my time.

"Why?" she asks, tilting her head with the most relaxed post-orgasmic face.

"Trust me to make you feel good." I lean forward to kiss her inner thigh, and it quakes under my lips. Pulling back, I see her watching me with droopy lips and a wide smile.

"I just orgasmed so hard, I'm surprised I can still speak; I don't think you can top that."

I raise a brow at the challenge, and she giggles. "Oh, I know you have more than that to give me. I'll have you coming until you're so spent, all you want to do is hug me and rest your delectable body."

Her mouth drops open briefly before closing, and though she swallows roughly, she doesn't argue.

Stepping closer, I hand her the sprayer and say, "Lean back, open wide. I want you to spray your pussy until you come again."

"What will you do?" she asks, scrunching up her nose.

"Watch," I answer with a smirk.

Her pretty eyes widen in shock. "Oh."

But then she's reaching out and grabbing the sprayer, with not an ounce of embarrassment. No. The way her eyes glint and the twist on her lips tell me I'm going to enjoy the show.

From where I'm positioned, her pink core is swollen and wet and every bit ready for more. My hands are twitching, so I have to shove them in my pockets to stop myself from going over there and touching her. I'm using every ounce of my restraint because it will be worth every second if I stay here. My eyes are heavy with desire, and when she leans back and positions the sprayer on herself, I can't help but let out a low, long groan.

She's so fucking perfect.

She presses down until it's spraying water directly onto her clit, and that's all it takes to have her moaning. My dick pulses with excitement.

"How does it feel?" I ask.

"Mmmmm...so good." Her head rolls back on her shoulders, and she tips her chin up to the ceiling so I can no longer see her eyes. And I *need* to see her eyes when she comes.

"Look at me as you pleasure yourself. I want to see what you look like getting yourself off."

She lifts her head up and slowly peels her eyes open, and her hazels heavy with lust and desire stare back at me. I suck in a breath as I lean against the back of the bar, right between her legs, getting the perfect view of her dripping pussy on display for me.

I'm a lucky fucking bastard.

Movement catches my gaze, so I glance down and watch her bring the water up over her clit. She shudders, before moving the spray farther down, repeating that sequence again, but faster.

"Slower." I know she is getting closer because her chest is rising and falling quicker now. The way her perky breasts move with each breath is teasing me. I am desperate to move and take one of her buds in my mouth and suck it hard, but she needs to come again first.

"How does it feel?" I ask.

"Good," she pants, before adding. "But I—I need more."

"Use your other hand and finger yourself."

She sits up and tries, but she struggles to find the right angle. I wait and watch to see if she can work it out before I step in. But after a minute, she huffs and I ask with a grin, "Do you want me to help?"

"Yes. God, yes!"

I chuckle and push off the counter, taking the few steps to her. I stand between her legs, the water getting all over me, but I can't complain with the way the cold water relieves my overheated skin.

I run my hands lightly up her legs, causing her body to break out in goosebumps. Her soft skin in my rough hands feels so good. When I make my way to her thighs, I squeeze, digging my thumbs in and gripping, and she lets out a sexy moan of approval at the possessive touch. It causes her to drop the sprayer, the water hitting her thighs instead of her core.

"Keep the spray on your clit," I growl.

She follows my order, and I edge closer to her pussy. My hands skim her legs in an up and down motion until I've had enough playing. Lifting one hand off her but keeping the other locked on her inner thigh to keep her wide and still, I slowly enter a finger into her hot, wet pussy and she arches into me. I hiss at the feel of her tight core. It's so warm and perfect, just like her.

"You're soaking wet, and so goddamn tight. I can't want to fuck this pussy."

"Oh shit, Marc."

I curl my finger and pull it down, causing a long moan from her. When she is used to one finger, I enter a second finger with the next stroke, pushing up, and suddenly her skin feels feverish and her face transforms from pleasure. The desperate look is causing my own breathing to pick up, and I've widened my stance to accommodate my painfully hard dick.

"You're so fucking sexy."

"Mmm," is all she mutters back, and I love how she is struggling to even answer me. She's so responsive to my touch.

"You're close."

Again, she mumbles incoherently. I thrust my fingers in and out faster, trying to edge her closer to climax. This time when she tilts her head back and arches, clearly chasing her orgasm, I let her. She looks completely and utterly lost in the wave of pleasure racking through her sexy body, and I feel her walls tightening around my fingers when I put them in as deep as I can.

"Such a perfect greedy pussy," I grunt, more affected by this than I could have ever imagined. She's turning me on more by the second. I didn't even know that was possible. When was the last time I came in my pants without a woman's touch?

Never.

Fucking never.

But now? Right here...

She owns me, and she doesn't even know it.

I pause on her G-spot and curl my fingers again, pulling down, watching her convulse in my hands as she comes. I continue stroking, knowing she has more. "Give it all to me."

She lets go of the nozzle to stop the water spray, letting it drop to the floor. Not caring about anything other than trying to suck more air into her lungs as one last moan leaves her chest.

I remove my fingers gently, and she shudders in after-shocks. When she recovers, she flutters her eyes open, and a cheeky grin appears on her face.

I'm running my hands up and down her thighs, unable to keep them off her.

A strand of wet hair sticks to her forehead, so I push it back, and she leans in, capturing my mouth with hers unexpectedly in a kiss that has me ready to explode.

Pulling back an inch, her warm breath hits my lips. "I want to taste you."

I open my eyes and lift my head away from hers, seeing the biggest shit-eating grin. My dick is throbbing from her words.

"You don't have to. I'm having enough fun just touching you," I say, running my hand to the back of her neck and holding it to stare into her gaze.

"I know, but I want to."

I squeeze my eyes shut for a moment to collect myself. "Fuck."

How can I deny her?

It's not that I don't want it. Because I do. But I also want her to come again.

Carrying her effortlessly up the stairs, following her directions, I pass the mess and make a mental note to come down later and clean up for her when she falls asleep. I'm not someone who sleeps much anyway.

Our lips still touch with every step I take, because I need it. I need her. I haven't felt this way for a very long time. We fit perfectly together.

She pulls away from my lips and whispers, "The room on the right."

I don't answer. I just kiss her again and she kisses me harder, our teeth clashing in the frenzy. Entering a room, I only disconnecting our lips to lower her onto the bed. With her sprawled before me, I trail more kisses over her body, knowing I need to get my fill of her taste and scent.

"Are you ready to come again?" I ask between kisses.

"Well, weren't you the one who said, and I quote, 'I'll have you coming until you're so spent...'"

I chuckle against her throat and mumble, "Don't be cheeky, *Bella*."

"I'm not. But I can still move, and I'm not ready to sleep yet."

"Well, then you definitely need to come more."

She nods eagerly, an infectious smile on her face.

"But don't forget, I want you in my mouth."

I pinch my lips together.

This woman!

"And I want that too. There is nothing that sounds more perfect than having those pink pretty lips wrapped around me. But I want you to come again, okay?"

I hover over her, my hands on either side of her head, watching as lust takes over her expression. She bites her lips and nods, and before I can tell her to speak, she says, "Yes."

"Good girl."

Pushing back, I get off the bed to remove my soaked shirt. She leans on her elbows, her hooded eyes locked on me, her mouth parted and breasts rising and falling with each breath. She looks ravishing as she watches me, captivated by every pop of a button. I shrug the shirt off my shoulders, and she sucks in an audible gasp.

"You know how to make a man feel good," I say.

"I've never met a man that looks that good. You're going to wreck me for all other men."

"Precisely," I say with a smug grin. Loving that she will always remember this between us.

"I'm already ruined," she mumbles.

Smirking, she pushes herself off the bed, dropping to her knees, making me stumble back a step.

I hiss from the sight. "You look good on your knees."

She looks up at me, begging in a hungry manner with only her eyes, and I know I'm a goner. I want to feel her warm mouth on me too. And I don't want to wait.

She's all smiles, and I swallow hard, trying to calm the crazy rhythm my heart has found itself in. She's peering up at me with parted lips, and fuck, she is delectable, naked before me and eager to suck me dry.

She unbuttons my pants and pulls my erection out, grabbing me at the base. I jerk at the sudden contact, my hips moving forward on their own as she tries to wrap her hand around me.

"You're so big. I can't put my hands all the way around you."

I groan. "It's okay. Take as much as you can."

But I need to shut her up. Her words are killing me. I'm barely hanging on; my balls are heavy and growing tighter with every word out of her mouth. I'm going to blow my load all over her face if she doesn't stop.

"Take me into your sweet mouth." I thrust forward, and she opens her mouth when my tip hits her lips. But she doesn't take me in, instead she licks her tongue over my slit to taste my pre-cum, and I tremble.

Swirling her tongue around the head, her eyes stay closed, loving every fucking second of this. And so am I. I just need to hold on for as long as I can and at least enjoy this for more than a minute before blowing down her throat. Just when I thought I couldn't handle any more, I watch her wrap her pink lips around my cock, sucking me in, and I groan again. She pulls me into her mouth as far as she can, and I feel lightheaded at the feel of her. Her hot, wet mouth is impeccable, and I reach out and run my hands through her soft brown hair, needing to hold on to her for stability. She moves her other hand to grip my hip, bobbing her head up and down my dick with little grunts each time it hits the back of her throat.

"Shit," I say, holding her hair back tighter now so I can watch her take me all the way in as far as she can, then slowly withdraw and repeat it again.

"So good," she mumbles around me.

The vibrations from her words cause me to grow harder.

"Don't stop," I grunt. No, I want to shoot down her throat and watch her swallow it all up.

Her eyes stay closed as she continues to work me over, and I don't ask her to look up just yet. But as soon as my balls tighten, and she must feel me thicken, she pulls me tighter and sucks me harder, peering up at me with a small smile on her face.

She is into it, and so am I. And damn if that doesn't make it even better.

Closing my eyes, I enjoy the lapping of her tongue, her saliva, and her suction. But I'm surprised when I feel her touch my balls. I thrust my cock farther, making her gag, and grip her hair, stilling her.

"Fuck, *Bella*. I'm gonna come, but you have to join me."

She mumbles, "Come?" and looks at me with a pinched expression.

"Yes. I want us to come together." I suck in a deep breath, trying to calm myself down. "Touch yourself. I can imagine you're wet and achy from sucking me."

She nods and mumbles, "Very," moving her hand between her thighs.

Good girl.

"Slide two fingers in and rub your clit with your thumb."

I see her arm moving before she sucks me back in, but deeper this time. And I just hope I can hold back long enough for her to come with me.

"I bet you're wet and ready to take me."

She moans around my cock, the vibrations killing me, but I control my breathing and focus on her.

"Go faster and push down harder on your clit."

She not only goes faster on herself, but me too, and shit, I'm not going to be able to hold back for much longer. And just before I'm going to come, I rasp, "Look at me. I'm going to come. So, you need to come too."

The moment her hazel eyes hit mine, I come so fucking hard, and she swallows every fucking drop. She follows me and comes with a shudder, mumbling around my dick. And by far, that's the hottest fucking experience of my life.

Hands down, she is the most beautiful woman I've ever met.

I'm gasping for air, but I stroke her hair as she releases me, my pulse beating in my ears.

I open my eyes and see her looking up at me with a dazed smile. She sits back on her heels, about to wipe her mouth where a small bit of cum has trickled out. I lean down and run my thumb to clean it up, and she grabs my hand before I can take it away, shaking her head, putting my thumb in her mouth, and sucking.

"Do you know how fucking sexy you are?" I growl.

My brain is fizzling. She is better than any fantasy, and I'm incoherent because of it.

She smirks and pops my thumb out. "Nope."

Taking in her naked body and the sated look on her face, all I want is to have her in my arms, so I grab her hands and help her stand.

"Well, you are the sexiest woman I've ever laid eyes on."

She looks away before looking back at me. "Thanks. You're not so bad yourself."

Then I grab the sides of her head in my palms, and I kiss her passionately, enjoying the taste of me mixed with her on my tongue.

"Okay, better than not so bad. But I just didn't want your head to be bigger than it already is. I want to do that again."

I chuckle and pull back to get a good look at her. "I'm spent." I murmur, laying another kiss on her lips, this one tender and lingering, and she kisses me back. "Thank you," I whisper against her mouth.

"And thank you." She smiles warmly up at me. With her cheeks now flushed, she looks even more breathtaking.

As I pick her up in my arms, she goes lax, welcoming the unexpected help.

Breathing her in and holding her tight, the only thought running through my mind is how I don't want to let go, not even for a second.

CHAPTER 7

MARCO

The heaviness in my chest from being with her is not simmering down.

We've been lying here together, recovering, for a few minutes. Her head rests on my chest as I draw lazy circles on her back, her arm wrapped around my middle and one of her legs draped over mine. This warm entanglement and closeness are foreign, but so welcomed. This here right now isn't usual; holding a woman in my arms after sex isn't something I do. But with Gracie, I need it. I need her close to me, to feel her skin touching mine.

The warmth of her seeps into me, and I'm struggling to breathe, so I pull back and lock my gaze with hers. With the way she is looking at me right now, the whole world fades, and all there's left is us. The reality that I'm going to be leaving her and the playful Marc behind in just a matter of hours isn't something I want to acknowledge. So, I don't. I soak up this time with her instead.

My finger trails down to her hip, dusting it up to her breast, then up and down again. She shivers beneath my touch, and a crooked smile forms on my lips. Turning her head, she looks up at me. Her gaze shimmers with desire, and my cock hardens in response. Just one look from her, and it's all I need to be ready again. She is wickedly dangerous, and I need to be inside of her.

Grabbing her hand from my middle, I shift us so I can kneel between her legs, and her teeth sink deep into her bottom lip as she watches me. I lean forward and kiss her, but as our tongues dance, she sucks my tongue again, making me hiss. I've never had a woman do that to me, but now that she has, I want it every time she kisses me.

"You like that?"

"Sure do."

I peck her again, then pull away, leaning back to glance between her legs. My cock is painfully hard, aching, as I see her core glistening with desire. I can't hold back my growl.

"You're wet again, *Bella*."

She was serious about doing it again; it obviously turns her on. Fuck me, if she wasn't already trying to kill me, I think she is now.

She nods and says, "Sucking you made me horny."

This new flame of confidence is making her a whole lot sexier. The cute, shy woman I first met drew me in, and this side of her is just an unexpected surprise in the best way. She has me insatiable for each version of her.

"I see. I better work on rectifying that and make you spent like I promised."

A wicked grin takes over her face. "I'm ready, captain."

"Are you sure?" My eyes hold hers, waiting for her answer. I don't want to hurt her.

"Definitely." She smiles and with that, I get off the bed and grab a condom from my wallet, tearing the packet and rolling it on before crawling onto the bed and positioning myself between her parted legs.

Grabbing her hips, I angle her just right to line myself up with her opening. As I do, she sucks in a breath, and I dip my hips to enter her. I hiss, "Fuck, you're tight," closing my eyes at the feeling, and push farther into her before pausing and saying, "I'll go slow."

"Don't. Please." She writhes under me.

My eyes open and see her watching me with hazy, lust-filled eyes.

The beat of my heart is begging me to take my time and enjoy this, but my head is loving what she is saying and screaming at me to thrust in. Take her. Claim her.

"I don't want to break you. I want to pleasure you. Treasure you, remember you."

"Oh. You are, but I want to come." She smiles, her hips lifting ever so slightly to welcome me.

I inch in a little more at her movement, her walls warm, and I wait for her to adjust to me before thrusting.

"Please. Give me more. I want all of you," she says around a moan, pulling a matching one from my chest as her pussy clamps around me.

As I lean forward, her arms wrap around my shoulders. Her eyes fall closed, and I whisper, "I know, and I got you."

I thrust all the way in, stretching her completely. And her reaction is perfection. Her back arches, her breasts pointed at the ceiling, a raspy gasp leaving her mouth and turning into a long moan.

I groan, loving the way she fits around me like a vice, snuggling tightly around my cock. I want to move so badly, but I need to wait for her body to relax, until I know she has loosened to the feel of me.

She kicks her feet up onto my ass, instructing me to move. I smirk, loving the little commands she's giving me.

"Open your eyes," I say and watch her flutter her lashes open.

I want to see her as we come together. Keeping our gazes locked, I pull out of her and thrust back inside to the hilt. The sensation causes a spasm to run through me, my cock already feeling heavy and ready for release.

As I continue to thrust at a pace to draw out her pleasure, her walls tighten around me, and her nails claw at my shoulders, digging in, silently begging me to let her come.

"Your tight pussy is milking my cock. Do you feel how good we fit together?"

She moans loudly, but I don't get an answer.

"This pussy is mine."

"Yes. *God*. Yes, Marc."

Those words are music to my ears, but I'm not ready for her to orgasm yet. I want to join her. So, I simply say, "No."

I pump my hips harder, deeper, craving every scrape from her nails. I want her to leave marks as memories of this perfect night.

My body is perspiring, and I'm puffing with every thrust, not from exertion but restraint. I'm struggling to hold on, and as her walls keep tightening around me and her moans get louder, I'm not sure I can hold back much longer.

"Marc. So close...Yes."

She lets out a frustrated groan, but holds back, her walls squeezing harder on my cock. I feel like I'm about to blow again.

"Are you ready?" I grunt. Needing her to be.

"Y-yesss," she stammers.

Thank fuck.

"Come. Now."

As the wave of orgasm rips through her, causing her body to arch and shake beneath me, her screams of my name are my last moment of sanity. I'm done for. My balls tighten, and I spill into her with a roar, continuing to move until we are both finished and breathing heavily. As I pull out, she quivers under me, pulling me closer. I drop my forehead to hers, pressing a soft kiss to her lips before collecting myself and inching back to discard the condom.

I bring a washcloth back with me, and her brows pinch together as she asks, "What are you doing?"

"Cleaning you up."

She shakes her head, and her cheeks flushed from her orgasm have now turned crimson.

"Please, let me. I want to look after you."

Her mouth drops open, and she tries to speak, but when she can't, I gently wipe her clean before discarding the cloth in the bathroom and coming back to the bed.

"Come, *Bella*." I strip back the covers and lie down, pulling her close. I want to hold her for as long as possible...*before I leave*.

She crawls over and joins me under the blanket, and I bring her flush against me, wrapping my arms around her.

"That was amazing, thank you," she says sweetly, peering up at me.

I smile. "No, thank you. You're every bit of the word—*Bella*."

A slow smile forms, and she turns her head to rest on my chest again. I move my hand up to stroke her hair, loving the feel of her silky strands between my fingers.

Our breathing becomes slow and in sync, neither of us speaking, just enjoying holding each other. I feel myself becoming tired, so I know it won't be long before I'm fast asleep. She's a wonderful blanket.

As we lie here, she whispers, "I've never cuddled after sex before."

What?

I blink. Now I'm awake. Surely, she can't be serious. "Are you kidding me?"

"No." I stare down at her, my brow furrowed, and she lifts her head again to look at me.

"Why?" I ask.

She shrugs, biting her lip. I know she doesn't want to tell me, but I can't help but try one more time.

"Come on, why?"

"They have never wanted to."

Her words are spoken so quietly, but I heard them loud and clear, and fuck...it wrecks me. How could they not want her luscious body curled around them? What idiots to not realize she's a fucking gift.

"It's their loss, because I'm not letting you out of my arms all night, *Bella*."

Her eyes gloss over, and she smiles bashfully. Leaning forward, I kiss her delicately, wanting to show her the side I don't show most—the soft side.

The side kept just for her.

CHAPTER 8

GRACIE

He's sleeping soundly under me, my hand resting on top of his abs, his skin warm and soft but toned. I move a hand up his chiseled chest and turn to rest my chin on it to soak him in while he sleeps. The dusting of dark hair under my hand reminds me of how much of a man he is.

I'm staring at his profile wrapped in a lust bubble when I hear...

"Gracie?"

It's Sandra.

Oh my God, this can't be happening.

I squeeze my eyes shut, but when I reopen them, I'm still in bed, tangled up naked with Marc. I lift my head up, looking around in a frantic moment of *how the fuck am I going to get out of this one?*

No idea, but please let me figure it out. Quickly.

I don't want to wake him, but I also don't want Sandra coming in here. Not that she has ever barged into my old room, but still, today could be the day.

"Gracie?" she calls again.

I peel myself off him, slowly and carefully, and *very* reluctantly. As I watch him stir, I hold my breath and stay frozen to the spot. He rolls over to his side, breathing deeply.

And I breathe easy again.

I don't want to explain anything right now. There is no time for that. I have to find Sandra and tell her I'm here.

How does she know I stayed here tonight?

My car is in the parking lot—of course.

I grab a sweater and some sweat pants that are stored in the cupboard for emergency sleepovers and tiptoe out of the room. Gently opening the door, I close it softly behind me and then take the stairs down.

"Sandra," I say.

Her head pops out from the bar. I jump on the spot and feel my pulse rise from the shock.

"Shit, you scared me," I say, knowing I'm edgy because I'm hiding a sexy man in my bed, and even though she might not care, I do. This would be so damn embarrassing if she knew.

And to admit it's a hookup—even worse.

"Sorry, love. I'm tidying up. You must have had a busy night for you not to clean up afterward."

She frowns as she looks around, and as I do too, I swallow hard. Yep, I officially left a trail of mess in the whole fucking bar, including cups, food bowls, stains, and water... water everywhere.

I hope to God that there is no evidence of *me* from the bar. I still need to scrub it. Which I plan to do right fucking now.

"Yeah, it was a wild bunch last night," I lie. Well, kind of.

"Well, Merry Christmas, Gracie. I was grabbing some wine for lunch today, but I can stay and help clean up."

"Oh no, it's fine. I've got this. You go and organize lunch. And Merry Christmas to you too." I smile.

I'm not affectionate, and I love how Sandra has always given me my space. Allowed me to be me and not try to push the physical niceties, like hugs and cheek kisses. Marc cuddling me all night was a huge deal; it took a while for me to accept he wasn't going to peel away and sneak out. But no, he stuck to his promise, and it was wonderful.

"Let me just help with the tables and then grab the wine. And don't forget the pudding."

"Okay," I say and move behind the bar, wincing at the mess we made. I don't regret it. I just wish I did this last night.

I'm almost finished scrubbing everything down, and she has finished tidying the tables, when I feel a hand on my stomach. He's standing behind me. I tense and glance around at Sandra clearing tables with wide eyes. What the fuck is he doing? And why didn't I see or hear him come down the stairs?

"Shhh," he whispers in my ear. "Stay quiet."

I nod, adrenaline pumping through my veins. And I don't have any time to think about anything else because he drops behind me, and I feel his hand inside my pants, reaching around to rub my clit, using hard, purposeful strokes. My body hums in response, liking every way he touches me. I widen my stance and grip the counter as I feel a finger slip inside my pussy, and I have to swallow back a moan. This is so much harder than I ever thought possible.

The thought of getting caught by Sandra is sending me into a tailspin. I have sweat forming on my back and my heart is racing with nerves, but the feeling of an incoming climax washes through me regardless. He slips in a second finger, pumping in and out in perfect rhythm, making my thighs clench around his hand. I can hear my wetness, and usually that would make me blush, but I'm past being embarrassed around him. I'm just too eager for release.

"Don't make a sound, or she might hear you."

I gulp and nod.

He is about to bring me to orgasm, and I'm not allowed to make a sound. This isn't fucking fair.

I turn my head so I can look at him. He pauses his fingers, and I'm about to protest, but I remember he will leave me here hanging until I answer him with words.

"I promise to not make a sound," I whisper under my breath.

He stands to whisper behind me, "*Bella, Bella, Bella,* after last night...I don't think that's true."

"Please," I beg. I'm not someone who begs, but with him, I do, and right now, I need this. I need him. I'll do anything to orgasm.

"You're so sexy when you beg."

Shut the fuck up, and fuck me with your fingers, is what I want to say, but the words don't leave my throat. Luckily for me, he drops down and enters me again. I push back on his fingers, loving the friction of us working together.

"All right, love, I got the wine. I'll see you later, okay?"

I pop open my eyes as I try not to convulse in front of her. Fuck, I'm so going to get busted. She walks closer to the counter, and I'm shaking from the panic of her catching us, but thankfully, she keeps walking past and waves with her free hand, the other one holding the bottle of wine.

The shaking intensifies, and I'm wobbling on my knees as I wave back.

He hasn't stopped fingering me the whole time, and I'm so, so close. He enters a third, and the stretch and sting are enough for me to close my eyes and slump forward, coming apart and calling out his name. And just like he said, I couldn't be quiet. There is something about him that has me unhinged. He continues to pump me to draw out my release.

When I have come down, and there is no more orgasm left, he removes his fingers and I lift my pants back into place, turning around and watching him stand before me. He brings his hand up to his face and begins licking the fingers coated in me. He is devious and delicious, looking like the best, dirtiest Christmas present I've ever had the pleasure of receiving.

"I'm sorry for not cleaning up. I planned to do it once you fell asleep, but I ended up having the best sleep I've had in years. I never sleep through the night..." He frowns, as if not able to believe it happened. "But with you...I did."

I bite my lip, hiding my smile. My stomach swarms with butterflies, and I can't help but feel giddy from hearing that.

"It's okay, I won't complain."

He presses a kiss on my lips.

"Merry Christmas, *Bella*." He smirks.

"Merry Christmas, Marc. Now I need to give you a present before you leave."

He frowns and turns his head, asking, "What present?"

I grab his dick through his suit pants and say, "This. I need it once more."

I bite my lip as he stares at me with wide eyes, in total shock. I don't hesitate any further, though. This is my last time with him. So, I push my pants down, and he lifts me onto the counter, shoving his own pants down and pulling out his heavy thick cock.

He goes to grab a condom from his wallet, but I interrupt this time. "I'm on the pill."

He nods. And I lean back on my hands, eager for him. The sight of his thick cock with pre-cum dripping from the tip has my sex aching and needy.

"Are you ready?" he asks with a sexy grin.

"Yes, I've never been more ready."

He slips his fingers through my folds and says, "Seems you are."

And then he moves those fingers to my lips, and I take them into my mouth, closing my eyes as I taste myself. He grunts in pleasure, pulling them out, causing me to snap my eyes open.

Smirking, he shakes his head. Then he's grabbing his cock in one hand and my ass cheek in the other, lining himself up, and before I have time to think, he is entering me in one thrust. I moan from the pain and pleasure, wrapping my legs around his middle, tilting my pelvis up, and the friction is glorious. He moves faster now, and I lean back on my hands, meeting his thrusts to chase my orgasm.

He must feel my thighs quake because he grunts, "Don't come yet."

"Please," I beg.

"Not yet."

He continues to thrust into me.

I don't know how long I can hold on for. The tingle running down my spine is telling me he is running out of time.

"Come, *Bella*."

And come I do. I feel his release by his jerking and bruising squeeze on my ass. Opening my eyes to take him in, it's so sexy to see him come undone.

When he finishes pulsing, we both stare at each other, heaving as we try to capture our breaths. I'm about to lean in to kiss him, but he drops to his knees again. Pulling me to the edge, he licks up my cum that's mixed with his.

How am I meant to be with anyone else after this? One moment, he is fucking me, and the next, he is tenderly holding me in ways I have never experienced. I think he has wrecked me, and I can only hope it does the same to him.

But he is leaving today for New York and this fairy-tale is over.

He groans as he licks every drop before pulling back, his chin glistening from our desire. I swallow the lump that's formed in my throat and watch him from under my hooded eyes as he rises. As I sit up, he grabs the back of my head and kisses me. His tongue hits mine, and it's a unique taste to what I'm used to, but it's ridiculously hot, and if I wasn't spent, I'd be begging for another round.

But...he has to leave. Speaking of...

"What time is your flight?" I ask.

"I don't know. I need to grab my phone off the charger and check."

I nod and look over at the phone sitting in the corner, and I wonder if Sandra saw it. Nothing I can do about it now, so I shrug it off and watch him as he pulls his pants up, pecks me on the lips, and heads over to his phone.

"A couple of hours."

"Okay, well, did you want a shower?"

He nods and says, "Please."

I hop off the counter and pull my sweats up, grabbing his hand and walking him back up the stairs.

We shower together, then get dressed, before heading back downstairs for something to eat. "I have my car here. Did you want a lift to the airport?"

"That would have been nice, but my assistant scheduled a car for me already."

Of course, they did.

And reality is really hitting me now.

Pushing it aside, I say, "That's okay," and step into his arms, holding him to me, trying to enjoy every minute I have with him before he walks out those bar doors and out of my life for good. Right now, I don't know how I'm going to feel when he leaves.

"Thanks for everything last night. You were incredible," he says into my hair.

I pull back, still clutching to him like a lifeline, staring into his mesmerizing eyes. His hands stay on my lower back, holding me close. Standing on my tiptoes, I bring my lips to his to take one last passionate kiss. One to save in my memory.

When he steps back, he says, "I'm going to miss you."

I sigh. "Same."

"I've got to go."

"I wish you didn't have to leave," I say as we pull apart.

I wrap my arms around myself to prevent myself from begging him to stay.

"Me too, but I have to."

He grabs my face and holds it, locking my eyes with his, and then presses his lips to mine in a knee-weakening kiss.

Why does this have to be a one-night thing?

But it is.

I sigh and nod, understanding that work is waiting for him back in New York.

And then I watch him turn and leave the bar forever.

When he exits the doors, I stand still in the hope he will barge back through and sweep me off my feet.

But when I realize he isn't coming back, I trudge up the stairs with a sting behind my eyes and an ache in my throat. I don't cry over anyone, so what is this weird sensation?

I don't need to cry. There is no reason to. We both agreed on one night, right? I didn't even get a last name, so where would I even start to look for him?

When I walk back into the room we just shared, I fall face first onto the bed, smelling his scent immediately. I groan and smack the sheets in frustration.

My hand hits a piece of paper as I do. I scramble to sit up, resting back on my heels as I grab the paper and read it.

I smile stupidly.

It's a letter from him.

His handwriting is perfect cursive, like the professional he is. He must have done this when I was in the shower, and I didn't notice because we walked straight downstairs.

My smile broadens from the anticipation of what he could have written.

Bella,

Thank you for an incredible night. You were perfect. Those few times I came into the bar and simply watched you from afar, I knew you were different. Everything I had imagined was not even close to how amazing last night was. You're a strong, beautiful young woman, and I'm honored to have met you and shared the night with you. Merry Christmas and take care. You're truly something special, and I'm so glad last night happened.

Marc

P.S. Here is my address and number, in case you ever find yourself in New York.

CHAPTER 9

MARCO

A **Month Later**

I'm drowning in work. I've been sitting here for two hours, staring at the monitor with a new client's contract. So, when my phone rings, I welcome the distraction.

"Mr. Giordano, I have your mail," Cassie, my personal assistant, says, pulling me out of my thoughts.

"Bring them in," I tell her quickly before hanging up.

She knocks a minute later and enters. I turn in my chair to face her, my hand already out and waiting. It feels like she is walking from the ground floor instead of just outside my office.

When she hands them to me, I thank her, and wait until she leaves, before I flick through each one with eagerness, but a deep sigh leaves me once again. Not one letter is anything of importance.

I lower the pile to my desk and return to completing the design and spec sheet. Just when I'm finishing up the billing, I check my calendar and see there is another meeting with HR, followed by the board. I run my hands over my face, my eyes stinging from staring at the screen for so long, but I pull myself up and head down to the HR department, with a deep, centering breath.

HR runs overtime because I'm scanning all the applicants chosen for the interview stage. I'm not required to be this hands-on, but I like to be involved and trust each staff member I hire.

I run back to my office before the meeting with the board. As I enter my floor, Cassie hands me my afternoon coffee and fires a bunch of questions to me as quickly as she can, knowing I'm on a time crunch. Checking my watch, I have exactly five minutes, and I just want to sit down and breathe for a second.

Once she's asked everything she needed to, I'm alone in my office. I ease back into the leather chair and drink my warm coffee, finally feeling a bit more relaxed. Today has wiped me, but as my phone vibrates, my spine straightens, and I wonder if it's her?

Sitting up, I dig my phone out of my pocket and sigh when I see Romeo sending me some dumb video of a guy spewing on a bartender. I roll my eyes at the video and put the phone away. I think he sent it to me by mistake because he doesn't normally send stuff like that to me. Which, right now, after watching the disgusting video, I'm glad.

The bar, though, has my mind wandering back to a sexy brunette who, since I left her on Christmas Day, almost a month ago, still hasn't contacted me. I left my details on a note, but she hasn't used them. I don't know what's wrong with me. Back then, I had to stop myself from sprinting back inside the bar and begging her to come to New York with me.

How stupid would I have looked if I had done that when she's clearly not interested?

Yet I still stupidly hold on to a flicker of hope...that just maybe she will contact me. Then, every day that passes with no text or person knocking on my home door who is Gracie, I continue to be disappointed.

Her name is seared into my brain, never to be forgotten.

I run a hand through my hair and return to my computer, leaving all thoughts of her where they belong, in my dreams.

Two hours later, the board meeting is over and my stomach churns in on itself from hunger I'm unable to ignore anymore. I rise and step around my desk, but pause, my phone buzzing in my pocket. I pull it out, thinking it's Romeo again, but when I read the unknown number, I frown. My brows pull in further when I read *Marc* not *Marco*.

I rub my jaw, because only a select few calls me Marc. But none of my friends or family would send me a text from an unknown number. Not wasting another second, I open it and begin reading.

A broad smile hits me, taking over my entire face. Suddenly my stomach isn't grumbling anymore, instead it's flipping with excitement. I stroll back to my chair, eager to sit and read it.

> **Gracie:** Hi, Marc. Hope you're well. I figured if I was still thinking of you a month later, then I needed to text you. You left me your address and number for a reason...well, here is me using one.

I can't help but read it slowly a second, then a third time. I shake my head at myself. Needing to write something back instead of staring at the phone like a dumbass. I can't even stop the stupid wide grin that sits on my face as my thumb hovers over the screen. I give her an honest response not wasting anymore time.

> **Marc:** *Bella*, I'm great now that you've texted me. How are you? I'm surprised and thrilled to hear from you today. It's what I hoped would happen with my contact details I left for you. I won't lie though, you had me sweating for a month.

> **Gracie:** I'm good too. I'm sorry to have left you sweating, but I couldn't be texting you straight away. I didn't want to appear desperate. ;)

I can't help but laugh to myself at the fact she says she's doesn't want to appear desperate because I've been feeling more desperate and needy than I ever have.

> **Marc:** You wouldn't have seemed desperate considering I have been eagerly waiting for this text. How is life in Chicago?

Gracie: Same old. Work is still the same, but I can't lie...I couldn't look Sandra in the face for a week. I've scrubbed the bar so many times, I'm sure it's never been so clean.

I really let out a deep chuckle this time. Before guilt hits me, making my chest heavy.

Marc: Sorry, I really should have cleaned it up that night.

Gracie: Oh, don't worry. I don't regret it, not one bit. If anything, it's just had me wishing you didn't live in New York, and you lived here in Chicago. Even though our agreement was a one night only thing...;)

I sit back in my office chair, running a hand down my neck, squeezing the tension that's building. The emotions swirling in me are pulling me in a bunch of different directions, and I don't know how to feel.

> **Marc:** I haven't planned another trip back to Chicago because that job ended. I hoped to come visit you but, since being back, work has been hectic. That's the only reason I haven't been back. I want to see your beautiful face again and talk over a whiskey sour.

I hit send but then add a follow up one quickly.

> **Marc:** I wish I could do that right now, *Bella*. And I'm not sure this is really a one-night thing...if you're still on my mind.

> **Gracie:** I miss you.

I grin like an idiot at those three words. Words that make my chest tighten and I'm about to text back, but I get another text from her before I have a chance.

> **Gracie:** I need you to know that I'm never this sappy, but you seem to bring out this needy and annoying version of me.

I feel this too. It's uncanny.

Marc: It's okay. You're definitely not annoying, and I'm never sappy either. There isn't a soul in New York who would believe that, so I'll keep your secret if you keep mine. ;)

Gracie: Your secret is safe with me :)

Marc: To be honest, I don't care that I'm a sap toward you. I'm more than happy to tell you how your smile brightens up my darkest days and how hollow I feel from being states apart. I hope I can get back to you soon, but if not, just know that I miss you too. And because I'm honest with you, I can tell you...I'll be checking my phone a little too much from now until we meet again. :)

Gracie: Life isn't the same now, and I will happily annoy you regularly if you promise to text me too. I just need to hear from you, because I don't want to be the only one texting.

Marc: Now that I have your number, expect me to annoy you.

Gracie: You could never annoy me...but I need to get ready for work. Sorry to cut this short. I promise to talk soon.

Gripping my phone a little harder, I take a deep breath and try to keep my unexpected jealousy at bay. Knowing what her outfit looks like and the way her customers hit on her causes my blood pressure to rise. I just remember the strong woman I met that night and know she doesn't need my protection. But I can't help wishing she was able to chase her dreams sooner than later.

On Wednesday, I had a meeting across town with a new contract for a joint venture on a skyscraper. The offer is lucrative, and even though I prefer my company to work solely on a project, this client is a well-known name. I've never had the opportunity to work with them on any project, so I'm willing to hear their terms and conditions and any ideas they have. At least for the company's portfolio, working with another successful company is a selling point.

After my driver rushes across town, I exit the car and make my way to the boardroom. A smiling woman greets me and ushers me into an office where I meet the other company I'm working with.

"I hope you weren't waiting on me?" I ask, readjusting my grip on my briefcase. Traffic was a nightmare trying to get across town.

She shakes her head. "No, you're fine. The client isn't here yet. They had some emergency at the job site they had to leave for. They shouldn't be much longer."

I sigh and scrub at my freshly shaved jaw. Thank Fuck. I'd hate to make a bad impression and lose the opportunity to work with them.

"Okay, great."

She steps aside. My mouth quirks up seeing Mason, who is representing the company I'll be working closely with.

"Mason. So glad to see you," I say, walking up to him and offering him a handshake.

He shakes it back. "Marco, it's also nice to see you. I'm relieved to see it's you I'll be working with."

"Same. I better get settled but talk to me while I do. What's happening over in your land?"

I step inside the office, moving to the opposite side of the wooden desk and lay my briefcase, unpacking my contract and notes before closing it and putting the case on the floor.

I look across at Mason, who's representing the other architect company in this joint venture. "We are busy at the moment. It's a lot of work, so we have a new intern starting. So that should be of help."

"Yeah, we are pumped as well, but there is no need to hire for this project, however..." I trail off, raising my brow at him with a smirk on my face.

He shakes his head with a laugh. "No, I'm not leaving Nora to come to you."

"Damn it. Worth a shot."

He takes a seat and I copy, leaning back and adjusting my tie.

"The trainee will follow me with this project."

"Where is he?" I ask, frowning.

"*She* is moving states."

I nod. "Ah, okay. Well, I'll have to meet her next meeting if it all goes according to plan. Is this your first time working with them too?"

He looks at the door before responding. "Yeah, and I'm pumped. This is a huge opportunity for all three companies."

"Exactly." I move my papers, when my phone vibrates. Checking who it is, I freeze at seeing her name. I quickly open it and scan it for anything urgent.

> **Gracie:** I really am sorry I made you sweat, but I hope it was worth it. Even though I feel stupid saying this, I'm telling you anyway, I had a dream about us, and I'm kinda bummed it isn't real...

My fingers are itching to respond and ask her if I was fucking her senseless, but it'll have to wait because the client walks in, and I have to put Marco back in the room. "Morning, sorry I'm late, but I had an emergency meeting on site." He peers at his watch before continuing. "I only have a couple of minutes to run through this before I have to get to another meeting."

My mind is elsewhere, but the client talking pulls me from my lack of concentration.

"I'll have weekly meetings scheduled for us, where we will work on one floor at a time and designs will be discussed. If I require changes, I expect them to be made and presented by the next meeting. First official design meeting is scheduled for next week. This was just an introduction and for me to meet you both and give you contracts. Are there any questions?"

"No. I look forward to next week."

He nods. I scan the contract before saying goodbye to Mason and rushing off to another meeting. As soon as I get into the car on the way back to my office, I pull out my phone and text Gracie back.

> **Marc:** Sorry I haven't replied sooner, but I had back to back meetings. Now tell me all about this dream.

> **Gracie:** No laughing. But I had this list of things to do with you on a piece of paper. Remember, this is just a silly dream!!!

Now I'm even more keen to know all about this.

> **Marc:** Now tell me what this list is...

Gracie: It may surprise you, but it was all very PG.

-Wake up cuddling and watch the sunrise

-Hold your hand

-Watch the sunset

-Go to the movies

-Get coffee

-A long walk

-Share a meal together

-Dance

Marc: I'd love to do all those things with you...and more, so much more.

I hit send and I don't get anything back. I try to distract myself by returning to work for the rest of the day. And later, when I finally get home, I take a quick shower and jump in my car because I'm due to meet my friends, Leo and Max, at our local spot for a drink.

"Anyone here pique your interest?" Max asks.

I raise my gaze from my tumbler of whiskey and scan the room. "No," I deadpan.

"Are you sure?" Leo nudges me to turn around.

Following his direction, I see the redhead talking with a friend, but I shake my head when my body is silent. Not a single thud, beat, or flip occurring when I look at her.

Returning to face the boys, I take a sip of my drink and welcome the burn. The only real heat I'm feeling tonight. Which is fucking sad it's from alcohol.

"Fine, if you won't go for her, maybe I will," Leo says as he looks over in her direction.

"Go for it." I mumble.

Max looks at me, skeptical.

"I hope she doesn't mind athletes."

"You won't know unless you ask," I say, flicking my gaze to her and back to Leo.

"Well, it's better to meet a woman in person and away from fans," Leo says with a shrug. "They all stand waiting after the game, and when you first get drafted, it's all fun and games. But when you realize they want fame and not you, it fades pretty quick."

"No difference for me when they find out I'm a CEO of a successful company."

Max snorts. "That would require you to talk to a woman."

Leo nods in agreement. "I have to agree. How long has it been since you spoke to a woman with an interest in being with her?"

"You two suck. It's none of your business," I argue, shaking my head.

I keep my bar escapade with Gracie to myself because I don't need them teasing me for pursuing a woman who lives in another state. It's just my luck to finally want to see where things could go with someone and she is a flight away.

"You need to get back out there. Aren't you sick of having blue balls?" Leo teases, and he and Max high five each other. I really wonder when they will grow up.

I roll my eyes at them and ask, "How am I friends with you two?"

"Because without us, you'd be lonely and bored," Max says with a proud grin.

"I beg to differ," I mutter under my breath and take another sip of my drink.

"I bet you'd work even more," Max says.

I shrug, knowing that's exactly what I'd do because outside of work, all I have is my daughter. But sharing time with her mother over the years, I've had to prioritize the time when she's with me. Leaving the rest to work, work, work. Wanting to leave Aria as much in her trust as I can, to know when I'm gone, she is well looked after.

I don't want them to judge me or make stupid comments, so I don't tell them that. They don't have kids;

they are NHL players, single and have never been married. The complete opposite of me. The only time I've ever not thought about work was my night with Gracie. And it has me wondering if we were together would work continue to consume me, or would she?

CHAPTER 10

GRACIE

"Are you sure this is a good idea?" Ava asks, sitting on my bed and watching me pack clothes into my case.

I peer over at her, meeting her glossed over eyes. She looks like she is ready to burst out crying. Sitting beside her on my unmade bed, I grab her hands and hold them on my lap.

"I know this is hard. Hell, it is for me too. This was a massive decision and step for me. It involves leaving my comfort zone, of you, the bar, my parents, Chicago, all to chase a dream. And when I need someone, I can't just come over. I have to call. But I have to do this." I offer her a sad smile, looking down at our joined hands, and then back up into her glossy eyes.

She nods. "I know, and I'm a selfish asshole. It's just...we've been together since we were teenagers, and I feel like you're breaking up with me."

I laugh, but then turn serious again. "You're my rock. My family. But I need to take this opportunity the professor helped me get, because it won't come my way again. I've worked so hard for it. College, worked over time, the saving, it's all for this."

"I know it's one of the top companies, and you'll make a wonderful trainee."

"If I get to finish," I say, sharing a fear of mine with her.

"You will. You're not allowed to leave me for nothing. It must be worth it," she says, narrowing her eyes at me.

"I promise to video and call you often."

"You better." She squeezes my hands.

I smile and scoot off the bed, breaking our connection to continue packing. She doesn't move, just watches.

"If you're not going to help, can you pour me some wine?" I tease with a warm smile.

"Wine sounds like a great idea. But I can't, so I'll just have some water."

I chuckle. "Yes, no wine for you, Momma, and not too much. I don't have enough time. I need to finish packing."

She grumbles, and I snigger. She is acting like a child throwing a tantrum.

She grabs our drinks and some snacks and returns to watching me pack.

"What's your new apartment like?" she asks as she stuffs her mouth full of chips and chews, waiting for me to answer.

"It's not modern. It's a little old, but not like falling apart," I clarify when her face turns horrified. "More like unique."

"That doesn't sound any better to me."

"I'll be fine. Stop trying to find ways to deter me from going."

I pause packing my clothes to sip my wine, welcoming the cold, fruity Moscato.

"I'm not. I promise. I'm just worried that it will be awful."

I grab a salty chip and chew before answering her. "I'll be fine, and remember, James helped me find it. Without him and his contacts, I'm sure I would have ended up in a dodgy area with a very average apartment."

She mumbles her agreement and nods. "This is true."

"I'm in a safe area. Close to work and the park."

"Maybe you will take up running. I heard it's good around Central Park."

I snort. "Me and running sound like a disaster. I've never exercised a day in my life. Bar work was my cardio."

"Maybe a walk, then. Meet some nice people," she says with a tone that has me looking up to meet her gaze.

I shake my head with a laugh. "I'm not meeting a fitness freak in Central Park."

"Come on," she begs.

"No."

"Maybe a long walk?" she asks, and as I think about her suggestion, Marc's text pops into my mind.

That's the only person I want to meet on a walk, and soon I'll be so close to him, our to-do list will be checked off.

"If I bump into Marc, maybe I'll go for a walk, but definitely not a run."

Talking about him causes a warmth to spread through my chest.

"Marc, the famous hookup." She narrows her eyes at me, but the smirk on her face tells me she is happy.

"I wouldn't say famous. But definitely a good time." I don't want her overthinking or getting ahead of herself like she will, so I downplay it a bit, even if it was the best sex of my life.

"Well, you better be walking with him. If he can make your face light up like that, then you need to find him. I want that look on you permanently."

"What look?" I ask as I touch my face, trying to understand what's telling all my secrets.

"That twinkle in your eye. You don't have to say a word, and I know how you feel. Remember, I had that look when I first met Josh."

I do remember the stupid look on her face, but it was also so adorable how smitten my tough friend was.

I finish the last drawer, zipping the case and picking up my wine. "Come on, let's watch some trash TV before you have to leave."

"Changing the subject, something else I was good at."

I shake my head. "I'm not. There just isn't anything else to say. I will keep you updated, I promise, but for now, I don't have anything."

I can't tell her about the texts because they are too personal. They are just between him and me, not for anyone else. But I can't help but smile at the thought of seeing him in New York soon and tackling our to-do list.

When she leaves, I'm not tired. If anything, I'm more wired and jittery with excitement. I haven't been able to stop thinking of Marc since we spoke about him, so I want to respond to his text from earlier, before the moving craziness makes me forget.

> **Gracie:** I have some exciting news to share. Guess who's preparing to move? Me! I managed to score a traineeship, and it starts soon, so I've been organizing college and a new

place. If I'm a little distant, don't think it's because I'm avoiding you.

I want to tell him I'm moving to New York, but would he think I'm following him? I don't want to scare him or him think of me as a stalker. Simply an opportunity of a lifetime arose, and I took this as a sign.

So, for now, I think it's best I wait.

Marc: Congratulations! I'm happy for you! And this would mean there's no more bar work?

Gracie: You will be happy to know I have left bar work forever. So, if you were planning to go to the bar, you won't find me. I'm a little sad because I'm leaving so many good memories behind, like...us.

Marc: I know change can be scary, but you are ready for more. You're smart, warm, and kind. As an employee, you're dedicated. Except maybe cleaning up, but I'm partially to blame.

Gracie: LOL that is definitely not normal behavior for me. A one off...well, unless you want a repeat.

Marc: Don't tempt me...

Gracie: I have to get going, even though I just want to keep talking to you. Boo :(

Marc: I'm always here. A text or call and I'm yours.

The warm air of New York hits me straight in the face as I hang my head out of the window like a dog. As I look around, the biggest grin stretches across my cheeks. I'm in awe of the buildings and atmosphere.

The driver is glancing at me in the side-view mirror with a pinched expression.

I sit back down to explain. "I have never been to New York."

He nods. "Where are you from?"

"Chicago."

"Nice, and you're on vacation?" he asks nonchalantly.

"No. I'm moving to New York for a traineeship."

"Congratulations," he says with a smile.

I can't help but beam. I'm proud of myself for getting here because I never thought this day would happen. And I'm not going to waste a second of it.

"Thanks. I'm excited."

He nods again but doesn't say anything. I'm grateful for the silence so I don't have to make small talk and go back to absorbing everything on the drive.

I prop myself back out the window until the driver tells me we've arrived.

I practically jump out of the car, with my two cases.

"You traveled light." He comments.

"Yeah, I didn't want to bring too much." I swallow hard, not wanting to tell him I don't own a lot of belongings because I was always careful with my money.

He grumbles something I can't understand before driving off. I shrug off the awkward exchange, too busy digesting the fact I'm standing on the sidewalk of my new rental.

Home sweet home, I breathe.

The brown brick building with black accents is better looking in person than in the photos that James emailed me. I skip up the three steps, pulling my cases with me, and get my keys out to open the door.

Holy shit.

My mouth drops open as I take in the place. I owe James big time. It's a bit older than most in the area, but I love the character the age of the place gives. I gave James a strict budget based on my salary, and he definitely got me the best place my money could afford.

I run my hand on the hallway table and drop my keys, leaving my cases in the entryway as I walk through slowly, taking it all in. Moving through to the back, the kitchen and living room are spacious, and there is a cute gray couch already in place, which is perfect to curl up on after a long day at work.

I pull my phone out and video call Ava, knowing she will be waiting for me to give her an update.

"Hello. You're there?" She smiles into the camera.

"Hey. I'm here, and oh my God, you have to see this place."

"Show me," she says, matching my excitement. But I've already hit the phone to flip the camera around.

I take her to the kitchen and living room before I walk into the bedroom. "It's super quirky."

"Right," she agrees. "I can't wait to come over and have wine in there."

The comment makes me giddy, and a big grin appears on my face. "Yes, please. But maybe wait until I've settled in."

"I'm not waiting that long to see my best friend."

"Well, make sure you get your doctor's clearance." I say flipping the camera back to me.

She rolls her eyes. "Yes, Mom."

"Shut up. I just want you to be careful."

"I know. I know. But Josh smothers me enough."

I smile and sit down on the couch, and it feels like heaven. I could fall asleep, and I just may do that after I hang up with Ava.

"So, what are you doing on your day off?" I ask.

"Not much. Since it's Saturday, Josh went to the gym with James. He's been gone a while, actually."

"Are you complaining?" I laugh.

"Not at all. I get to watch whatever I want on Netflix in peace. I love him, but I hate his commentary when I'm watching my shows."

I smile. "Exactly. Enjoy the time alone."

"Are you ready for tomorrow?" she asks.

The thought makes my stomach churn. But it also could be because I need to find some food.

"I'm a little nervous, to be honest. This is a big step, and I just hope the people here are nice."

"You'll be fine. You are such a people person; you will fit in straight away. I have no doubts."

I know what she is saying is true. The bar made me talk to all different people, but it still didn't calm my nerves.

"I hope you're right," I mumble.

"I am."

My stomach growls, solidifying the need to eat something. I haven't had a decent meal today. "Well, I think I might go grab some food. I'm starving, and I have nothing in this place yet."

"Fair enough. Make sure you call me tomorrow. I want to know how your first day is." Ava smiles and waves at me through the camera.

I wave back. "I will."

I hang up from Ava and reluctantly get out of this sunken couch in the hunt for some food. And tomorrow, I'll go in search of Marc.

CHAPTER 11

GRACIE

I follow the directions I have for Marc's address. As I stroll, I try to calm my beating heart with slow breaths of New York City air. The nerves pulsating through my veins are higher the closer I walk to him. Turning down his street, I'm actually trembling. Why am I so nervous? I've met him before. Heck, I've slept with him. And to date, we've been communicating every day since my first text.

There is no need to be this shaken.

But I am.

There is no way I'd be in New York if we hadn't hooked up that night. He left an imprint on me that was slowly burning every day. Motivating me to try to find a way forward. And when it came, I took it with both hands. And having him with me now is going to be a dream.

Locating his house, I pause to stand on the opposite side of the road, giving the brown brick building a once over. With nondescript, black-framed windows and doors, it doesn't tell me anything about him.

I push away my nerves knowing I decided to surprise him. So, I suck in a deep breath and roll my shoulders back before deciding it's time to make my move. But, as I take a step forward to cross the street, a woman and a girl walk to the door, and he greets them immediately. My lungs are burning for the air that I'm depriving them of at seeing him again after all this time. I'm still more affected by him than I could have imagined. He wraps his arms around the girl, who looks to be a young teen, then smiles at the woman. My back tingles with unease as I wait for him to kiss her.

Standing here, watching, I should be worried I'm coming off as a creep, but I can't drag myself away. My eyes are glued to them. I must watch the whole exchange in case I'm wrong.

I hope I'm fucking wrong.

The backs of my eyes sting with threatened tears, but I refuse to let them fall. Even if the evidence is right here, I need to see for myself if anything happens between him and her. But regardless, this means he slept with me when he had a child, and he never mentioned having a kid. I try to think back, and I guess we spoke about everything other than that. He said he wasn't married, and he didn't have a girlfriend.

Then who is she?

Looking them over, the woman has long, blonde curly hair, and she's wearing what looks to be a designer navy jacket with blue jeans and heels. The girl has the same blonde hair but straight, and she's wearing an equally put-together outfit minus the heels. I look down at my clothes, and I'm happy I didn't wear sweats like I was going to.

As I'm assessing my own appearance, movement happens out of the corner of my eye, and I look up and watch as they all go into his house. He's holding the girls hand.

I stand unmoving for a while, not knowing what I should do now. I expected to come here and want him to open his arms out to me?

How stupid.

I blink the tears away. Maybe this was a sign, and I need to see it for what it is. He wasn't the one for me. I just wish my silly body wouldn't react the way it does whenever I see him.

With no other reason to stand here as people walk past, I dip my chin and turn to leave. I still take in the neighborhood and stop at a shop I find along the way. Inside the convenience store, I grab a bottle of wine and some crackers and dips.

I have zero desire to cook tonight. I just want to drink wine and eat while watching a girly movie.

Should I call Ava?

I shake my head. No. I need some more alone time to process.

I step through the doors on wobbly feet. I barely slept last night. One, because it's not the bed that I'm used to, and two, I was overthinking today and all the scenarios that could happen to me at this new job.

Today is a big deal. It's the start of a new chapter. The start where I leave my *past* of my family and Marc behind. Unfortunately, he lives here, so it's not as easy to forget him as much as family.

While I loved Chicago for some people, the memories still live there.

I smooth down my new black suit, courtesy of Ava, who helped find me new work attire before leaving. Much more appropriate for a New York office and not a Chicago bar.

I love the way it hugs my curves and how much I feel like I fit right in, even if I've never been to New York, or even worked in an office before.

I've tied my hair into a bun that I learned off YouTube, in an attempt to try to give today everything I could.

Coming to a halt at the reception desk, I check in with her before following her directions and head to the elevator and hitting the button to the twenty-first floor.

I wish it were higher because my teeth are chattering with the nervous vibrations.

The doors open, and I push myself to move. Entering my office, I sit down and look around. I turn the computer on and begin searching to familiarize myself.

I hear a throat being cleared, and it makes me sit up.

"Hi, sorry. I didn't mean to startle you. I was just introducing myself." The guy walks forward with a friendly smile.

"It's okay. I was looking around, and I didn't hear you," I say, nibbling my lip.

"Okay, but did you need help? A tour maybe?"

I get the sense of calm from him right away, and I don't want to be caught snooping where I don't belong, so I say, "Ah, sure. That would be great."

"Sorry, I never introduced myself. My name is Mason, and I work here. My office is just next door." He laughs, and I feel the tension in my back slowly dissipate.

I smile and release the breath I was holding. "Nice to meet you. My name is Gracie."

He nods with a warm smile, and I stand and leave the office, taking my bag with me.

"The breakroom's here. The boardroom there. Bathroom there." He points out every room as we stroll along the floor. "I'm right next door if you need help, but I'm sure Nora will be around soon to get you situated."

"I'm good for now, but I'll be sure to ask. Thanks for the tour; it would have taken me a long time to figure out where everything was otherwise."

"Anytime. I better get back to my office. I have an early design meeting with a client."

I nod and watch Mason turn to leave before I return to my office. Sitting back down, I'm still a little unsure of what to do, but I don't wait long before Nora walks in.

"Hi, Gracie. Nora."

I stand abruptly and smile. "Hi, Nora."

"It's lovely to meet you in person. Have you just arrived?"

"Yes, just a couple of minutes ago."

She nods. "Okay, well, I'll give you a tour." She turns to leave, but my stomach does a little flip, and I say, "Um. Mason already did."

"Wonderful. You will work with Mason closely, so I'm glad you two have already met. So, I guess let's run through some work."

I nod excitedly. Yes, I need to do something. Sitting here looking at books and a computer I don't understand isn't helping.

"I won't have you working on projects by yourself, so don't worry. It will be a slow process."

"I'm happy with anything you decide."

"After Mason's meeting, I have allocated him time to show you this new project. It will be a good one to start, as we don't get too many, but they require teamwork. I think when you start at a new company, that's always number one to get right."

I nod. I wonder how many people will work on this project and what that means for me...and what's this team-work?

My head pounds from overthinking. Again.

I need to stop.

Lack of sleep and food, mixed with stress, is a recipe for an incoming bed-ridden migraine.

Nora's phone rings, and she smiles and grabs it to read the name. "I'm sorry, I must get this. I'll be back in a couple of hours, but if you hit the button on the phone, it is a direct line to me. Please use it if Mason isn't around. I want you to settle in. I know moving is intimidating, as I've done it, but look at me now. It was the best thing I've ever done, and I haven't regretted it."

A warm smile spreads on my face. This is exactly what I want to hear. "Thank you, Nora, I appreciate it. To be honest, I've been a bit nervous, but I'm doing this for me, and I need to remember that. My career will further myself."

"Exactly." Her phone rings again. "Persistent, aren't they?" She smiles. "You've got this. I'll speak to you later."

I wave and take a seat, and just as I do, she turns and shuffles over to me. My brows pinch, wondering what she is doing.

"I forgot this. Here, read this while you wait for Mason. He will be in soon."

I nod and watch her leave, admiring her navy suit and stilettos and her bouncy red hair. The girl-boss attitude is giving me major Ava vibes, and I already know that we will get along famously.

An hour later, I'm flicking through the building paper-work that Nora gave me. I'm trying to understand it all, but a lot of it is going over my head. There is just way too much here.

And on top of that, it's more involved than anything I could read about online.

I'm deep into reading the design spec sheet when Mason steps in my doorway, knocking. My gaze shifts to his, and he smiles, asking, "Are you ready?"

I stand and scoop the papers into a pile on my desk. "Yes."

Grateful for the interruption, I hope he can help me understand this without being a burden.

"Let's go into the boardroom. We have space to lay everything out and use the whiteboard. Tomorrow morn-ing, we have a meeting with the client and the other com-pany."

I frown. "Other company?"

I'm assuming he means other colleagues, but the way he said it has me not so sure.

"Oh, sorry. I forgot you're new for a second and this is not a regular job. Take a seat anywhere, and I'll explain."

"Thanks," I say and pull out a black office chair from the brown wooden table, and as I sit, he sits beside me. We spin to face each other.

"So, this project will have two companies combined to produce the designs. It's called a joint venture. It will take a lot of back and forth for every piece and sometimes underwear gets knotted and chests puff out, thinking theirs is better, but ultimately, they settle with the client and can produce some really innovative and cool builds."

"Wow, I have never heard of this, even in my research, but I think they got the company name wrong. It had another company's name beside it."

He chuckles. "Yes, there is no error in the contract, but let's run you through tomorrow's first meeting. Because you will sit back and watch, and I'm sure it will be nice to understand what we are talking about."

I smile broadly and dip my chin. "Definitely, and I'll take some notes in case I need to ask you anything afterwards."

He leans back in his chair. "Good thinking."

"Well, the first thing to note is that there is always one speaker for each company. So, if anyone from our group has anything to say, they speak to me, and then I'll ask or speak it during the meeting."

"Does it get awkward when people don't like the same things?"

"Not really. We get stubborn and set in our ways, to be honest. Because both groups think their vision is the best."

He leans forward to spin and face the desk, so I follow. Then he runs me through more basics, and before I know it, we're packing up and leaving for a break.

"Did you want to grab coffee?" Mason asks.

I figure I will be sitting and eating by myself in the break room, or I could join him. And he was fun to be around, so it's an easy decision. "Coffee sounds great."

"Oh, it seems I caught you two at the best time," Nora says.

I look up and smile. "Hi, Nora."

"How was it?"

"Really interesting. The two companies working together on a joint venture will be fun."

"And a lot of testosterone," she says and winks at me.

"Hey, we aren't that bad," Mason calls out from his office.

Grabbing my bag, I stand next to Nora, pinching my lips together to prevent a smile.

"We may do a little sparring to make a point, but it's not the whole time."

"Mm-hmm," Nora says with a raised brow and an amused expression. Her arms fold over her chest.

Mason joins us in the hall, and we leave for the elevator together.

Inside, I stay quiet and just watch the floors light up, then on the ground floor we exit, and stroll to the nearest cafe. We place our orders quickly, find a spare table, and take a seat.

"Did you find a place okay?" Nora asks me. "I think the last time we spoke, you hadn't finalized anything."

I nod. "I did. It's not far from here, and it's perfect."

"That's wonderful."

"If you hadn't found somewhere, you could have crashed on my couch until you did. My roommate and I wouldn't have minded." Mason says with a kind smile.

I'm mixed between flattery and something else. The lack of trust in people rears its big ugly head. The sincere way he looks at me and the way Nora is looking at me tells me he isn't going to hurt me, though.

But living with someone again isn't something I ever want to do. Having my safe place involves having it all to myself.

"Thanks, that's kind of you," I say and peer out the window, freezing at who catches my eye.

It's Marc walking past on the phone, with a back briefcase in hand.

Where is he going?

Where does he work?

The flutters in my stomach are back, and as I look at his profile, I sigh. Remembering his sloped nose, sculpted jaw covered in his five-o'clock shadow, and his brown hair, the perfect length to tug. My cheeks tingle from the flush that the thoughts are giving me.

"Gracie." I hear my name being called. It sounds far away, and I quickly spin when I realize it's Mason letting me know the waitress is dropping off my drink.

"Ah. Thanks," I say and accidentally knock it over. As I rush to pick it up, she grabs a paper towel to dry it.

"I'm sorry. It was my fault. I seem to be a bit jerky," I say, choking on a pretend laugh and wiping the liquid that spilled onto my black pants. Even though I'm feeling anything but funny.

"Are you okay?" Nora asks.

"Yeah, sorry, I was distracted. I thought I saw someone I used to know."

A lump forms in my throat at the words *used to know*.

Is that it for us?

Yes.

I said that was it, because I have to remember he has a family.

I'm not a home-wrecker.

Never have and never will be one.

"Oh, I hate that feeling. Because it's like is it, or is it not?" Mason says.

I take a sip of my drink, welcoming the warm coffee on my tongue. It's definitely him, all right. His face is permanently fixed into my brain. There is no way I'd get him wrong, not when he was the only man to ever hold me.

No, I couldn't forget that face even if my heart aches for what can't be.

Chapter 12

Marco

"It's time to get up, sweetheart."

No answer.

I stare down at Aria's body coiled up under the blankets, her unruly blonde hair peeking out, while the rest of her stays hidden.

"Come on, you need to get to school, and I need to get to work," I call out, louder this time.

I missed my morning workout because Aria wanted to sleep at my house. My ex-wife dropped her off last night, and we had a movie night in the cinema room, watching a tween movie I can't remember the name of. I just soak up my time with her while she still wants to know me. It's also a good time for me to be without work mode on.

"Seriously, Aria, you must get up. I have to get to work. I have back-to-back meetings."

I check my watch, and I have five minutes for her to get up, eat, dress, and get out the door. I don't like my chances, especially when she pulls the blanket over her head as I walk closer.

Leaning over her bed, I grab the blanket and pull it off her head. "Now, sweetheart. I won't ask you again."

There is more grumbling, but she rolls out of bed this time.

Victory!

"I'll make you breakfast. Just please get dressed." I walk out of her room and into the kitchen to fix her up with some cereal.

She shuffles into the kitchen just a few moments later, propping herself onto a stool. "I hate school. Why do you and Mom make me go?"

I push the bowl and spoon in front of her and say, "Eat. And you go to school to get an education, so you can get a job when you're older."

"I guess I have to, if I'm going to be a doctor."

"You're too young to figure out your career, but you can go to school and learn."

She puts a spoonful into her mouth and chews, and I rub my brow, thinking how I can hurry her up.

I send a quick email to Cassie to tell her I'll be late getting in, and she will need to handle everything until then.

Pulling out my wallet, I slide some lunch money to her because I can't do packed lunches. My housekeeper would do it, but it feels wasteful when I remember as a kid, whatever food my parents made, I threw out. I'd rather not waste anyone's time and give her money instead, then at least I know she'll get something she likes.

She picks it up and stuffs it into her pocket, continuing to eat much too slowly. I stand at the counter, going through the morning emails, but when she pushes the food away and slides off the stool, I close the browser and glance up at her and ask, "Are you ready?"

"Yeah, let me get my bag."

I finally drop Aria off at school and get to work. A little wired from being an hour behind for a workday, but it's okay.

"Morning, Cassie. I need a coffee, please."

She smiles. "Sure thing, boss. I've got a couple of things to run past you first."

"Sure. Fire away," I say as I walk to my desk and let her get me up to speed with what I need to know. Cassie is a lifesaver; I couldn't function without her help. She organizes my work life and even my personal life sometimes too.

When she finishes talking to me, I begin working while she grabs me a coffee. The first project is a meeting I have...

Oh, shit.

In half an hour.

I pull up the designs and spend the next couple of minutes working on them. My stomach rumbles, reminding me I haven't eaten. And now it won't be for another couple of hours.

I sip my coffee on my way to the client's office. I have ten minutes to set up and prepare. Opening my case, I get back to work. When I finish writing on the whiteboard, I take a breath and turn around to double check my information.

And that's when I see none other than Gracie, like a vision from my dreams. She lets out an audible gasp at the sight of me.

I can only stand here, completely stunned, staring back at her. When I recover from the initial shock, I blink. What is she doing here? And when my brain catches up that it really is her, and that my mind isn't playing tricks, I run my gaze over her from head to toe. Oh my, she looks incredible. The way she wears a figure-hugging black suit and heels has me feeling a little hot under the collar. I tug on it a bit, trying to cool myself down.

I would love to have this boardroom alone so I could have my wicked way with her. I enjoy the view of her way too much to get through this meeting without distraction.

A throat clearing makes me flinch, and I remember where I am. Shaking my head, I move to my seat and take a sip of water, trying to focus on my notes. She has taken her seat opposite Mason, and I grind my teeth together.

Why didn't she mention this to me? I would have been interested to hear her story about wanting to become an architect too; another thing to have me all the more intrigued by her. I don't like this surprise, and I definitely don't like the fact she works for them. If she was interested in an architect traineeship, I would have...what? What would I have done? It would be a conflict of interest to have her working under me.

Does she plan to stay in New York? Or is it only a twelve-month contract? Why wouldn't she tell me this is where she was moving during one of our many text exchanges?

I take a glance at her any opportunity I can. Sometimes our eyes catch, and we hold them before one of us looks away. She has notes out, but Mason is the talker and surprisingly, I normally like the guy. But right now, I'm jealous of him working with her. Or, hell, is he teaching her? This bubbling in my veins is the green-eyed monster, and I can't believe it's happening here. I've never struggled to concentrate like this at work, but I've never slept with anyone in this field either.

"Are we ready to start?" the client asks, his eyes drifting to me and Mason.

"Yes," I answer, and Mason does too.

"Right, well, let's start at the top and work through the design options you both have for me. Talk me through them and their prices."

"Marco, you first."

I glance over and see her mouth parted and her eyes as wide as saucers. Fuck, she found out my real name, and now she will probably search for me without giving me a chance to explain.

"Marco?" the client asks again.

Get your head in the game.

I need to snap out of this obsession with the woman who is staring at me.

Standing, I move to the screen, clicking the remote to move slides. I feel her eyes on me, watching me present. I wonder what she thinks of me at work. It's heating me up, the thought of impressing her because I love my job, even if it's caused me pain in the past.

I manage to talk through my ideas. All the reasons why this is the best option. This pitch is for the client, so I always bring my gaze to them, even though I want to just hold hers.

When I finish, I hear the start of a clap, and I peer up and see it's Gracie, but she quickly stops and keeps her chin down. The way she is nibbling her lip tells me she's embarrassed, and God, I just want to hug her and tell her she can clap for me any day. I wear a grin but focus on collecting my papers before taking a seat so Mason can now present.

My eyes wander to her again, and we hold gazes before she looks away once more. I watch him present their idea designs. Now and then, I flick my gaze to her and catch her writing notes, and it makes my heart swell. She really is trying, and I'm proud. Not only is she beautiful, but she has the brains, and the fact she wants to work in a similar field to me is alluring. She couldn't be more tempting if she tried.

After we've both presented, the client thanks us both for coming, but says they want time to think everything over before discussing their decision in next week's meeting. My heart thuds.

I will see her again.

But I need her before then.

Fuck, I need to talk to her right now.

As I put my papers in my briefcase, I walk over to her side, but she is almost at the elevators. As if she is avoiding me? She hasn't acted like she wants to talk to me at all.

What's going on?

Have I missed something?

I watch the elevator doors close, and as our gazes lock, my chest heaves with increased breaths. I'm rattled and unnerved that she doesn't want to talk to me. This hasn't happened to me before. And after our connection...our texts.

What the fuck is going on?

It doesn't seem like embarrassment for oversharing how we feel, instead, it's like she's avoiding me. And I need to find out why.

"Marco?"

I turn to the voice, and it's pulling me from my thoughts.

"Yeah?" I say, raising my brow.

"Is everything okay? You seem a little...distracted." The client, Jason, narrows his eyes, as if trying to read me, but my stony expression is on. Work is work, and I appreciate the concern, but I won't indulge.

"I'm fine. Just thinking about the design meeting today, and wondering where your head is at," I lie.

"Yeah, I bet you'd love to know. Only one week, and you'll know."

"You give nothing away," I say.

And speaking of giving nothing away. The woman across from me did the same thing, and that's the only head I care about right now.

I grab some lunch from the deli, picking up my usual turkey sandwich and salad.

On my walk back to the building, I swear I see Gracie on the same street ahead. I walk a little faster, trying to catch her, but I get stuck at the lights, and she disappears with the crowd.

But was it her or is my imagination playing tricks on me?

I never received a text with her new address.

My phone buzzing in my pocket brings my attention back. It's my brother, Mateo. "Mat," I answer.

"Where are you?"

"Just grabbed some lunch. Why?"

"I'm in your office. I came to see you."

"I'll be back in a sec. I'm just across the street."

"You're grabbing your own lunch." He snorts. "This I would like to see."

I tsk. "I grab my own lunch...sometimes."

He laughs.

It may not be often, but I have done it before. I don't need to announce it to everyone just so they know I'm competent.

"If you say so. I'll see you soon."

"Yeah. A couple of minutes," I say and hang up, picking up my pace.

Even though Mat and I like to poke fun at each other, he picked the perfect time to drop in. I want to pick his brain on Gracie. Women are so hard to read, and Mat is really good with the ladies, so I'm sure he can help me figure out what to do.

A few minutes later, I pass Cassie, who tells me Mateo's waiting for me.

Entering my office, I close the door behind me, and Mat helps himself to whiskey from my drink trolley.

I raise a brow. "It's only lunchtime, and you're drinking hard liquor. What's up?" I ask.

"Romeo's giving me grief," he says.

"What's our little brother doing now?"

"He had a woman accusing him of getting her pregnant."

I lower my bag to the desk and take a seat, looking up at Mat with wide eyes. "You serious?"

"Deadly."

"And it's not his?" I ask.

"I'm in the process of sorting it out."

I smirk and open the bag, pulling out my food. "The fun of being the lawyer in the family."

He grumbles. "It's times like these I wish I had a different profession."

Opening my food, I take a bite and chew before saying. "You're a good lawyer. I don't know what else you could be. Nothing else would suit you."

"If the boys could behave, that would make my life easier. I spend half my time doing freebies for those two idiots."

I chuckle. "They are definitely the rebels of the family."

Romeo and Lorenzo are twins and are always up to no good. Between my parents and Mat, they are lucky they haven't ended up in jail or court. Sometimes I envy their carefree attitude. Like the time with Gracie at the bar, when I was just doing something for once without thinking about work or anyone else. I lived in the moment, and it felt good, freeing. The lightness was a world away from the heaviness I carry from my day-to-day life here with work and Aria.

I don't regret or dislike where I am in life. I guess it would be nice to have a bit of balance. Have a little bit of spark rather than having the same routine every day.

"Rebels or idiots," he grumbles.

"Both, but they're family."

He nods and sits down opposite me, leaning back as I bite more of my sandwich.

"Did you want a drink? I forgot to ask." Taking a sip from his glass, he raises it in my direction.

I shake my head as I chew, swallowing before I answer. "No thanks, my day has been bad, but I don't think that will help."

I get up and grab water, drinking some of it and returning to my seat.

"What happened today?" Mat asks, watching me curiously over his glass.

I lower the bottle and scrub my face with my hands, contemplating how far into it I should get with Mat. But he is the only brother I can get real advice from; the other two lunatics are playboys, hence the paternity issue. I think for a minute...

Fuck it.

"So it started at Christmas—"

"Christmas?" he interrupts.

"Shh. Let me speak, Mat."

"Sorry, go on."

I lean back in my chair and look at him. "Last Christmas, I was finishing up a job in Chicago, and I had a delayed flight. I popped into a bar that's not far from the job while waiting for the next flight. And then my flight was canceled, and I ended up hooking up with this hot bartender I've had a bit of a crush on."

At that exact moment, Mat sprays me with his drink.

I stand, cursing, "Fuck, Mat," dusting the residue off my shirt and jacket.

He lowers the glass down onto my desk. "I'm sorry, but you just said *you* hooked up with someone."

I clench my teeth together. Why is he making a big deal of this? So what if it's the first one in a while? "So?"

"You don't say those things. You're the sensible brother. Listen, this isn't bad. I'm happy for you. I'm just shocked."

"Can I finish my story?" I ask, annoyed.

"Go for it."

I sit back down. "So anyway, I stayed with her for the night and the next day I left her my digits and address. And a month later, she sent me a text. We've been texting back and forth since."

He's nodding, but not saying a word, which I'm grateful for.

"She must have got a traineeship with one of my competitors. She hasn't texted me this week, and she avoided me during and after the meeting. She practically took off. I'm so confused."

"What was the last text from her like?"

"Like normal. Sweet, nice, nothing bad."

"If she is new, maybe she didn't want to make a bad impression by talking to you?"

"Hmm...maybe. It just felt off. I can't put my finger on it. It's just a gut feeling."

"Do you have any other way of contacting her?"

I shake my head. "No, just her phone number. But she isn't answering my calls or texts."

Which is unusual.

"Will you see her for work again?"

"Actually, yes, next week we have another meeting with the client."

"Well, see how she acts then. Maybe call her name out and ask to have a minute."

"Yeah, I'll try that," I say and take another bite of my lunch.

"You are different with this one, brother."

I don't answer, because really, what's the point in denying how I feel about her? I haven't been consumed by a woman in years. The way I can't go a minute without my mind drifting to thoughts of her, and not focusing on work, it's the only sign I need to tell me that there is something about Gracie, something that I need.

Chapter 13

Gracie

Entering my apartment after work with McDonald's in tow, I hit the couch and dig into the fries and burger while they're hot. The sweet and salty taste is the perfect combination for my shattered mind. I don't like cooking normally, and the fact I've had an emotional day means I needed greasy takeout.

I sip the remaining soda, and afterward, I pick up my phone from the table and lie back on the couch to call Ava. I need to check in to see what's happening with the pregnancy and tell her what's happened with the new job and Marc.

Even saying his name makes me sad; it's as if I'm being punished for something.

I just don't know what.

"Hello," she answers after a couple of rings.

"Hi, it's just me," I say with some more excitement than I had a minute ago. Just hearing her familiar voice makes me feel comforted.

"What are you doing?" I ask.

"I'm just sorting out dinner. You?"

"I'm having McDonald's. What's your dinner? Do you have cravings yet?"

She chuckles. "Nachos. But yes, I have cravings all the time."

"Really. Like what?" I ask, intrigued.

"Cheese is mainly what I want right now."

I laugh. "That isn't something I would have guessed, but are you doing okay otherwise?"

"Yeah. I'm still coming to terms with it, but most of the time I'm happy."

I can understand her hesitation. Growing up after she lost her parents, then running away from her aunt and uncle, would make her scared about the type of parent she'll be and whether she'll be good enough.

I know the feeling because it's my fear too.

"Good, you deserve to be happy. And Josh, how is he?" I ask.

"Josh is thrilled. To be honest, he's way too fucking excited."

I giggle. I'm happy he's excited. Having that energy around her will rub off on her, and she will be happier soon enough too. He'll be doting on her more than ever, and I couldn't be more thrilled for my friend. She deserves this.

"How was your first day?" Ava asks, changing the subject.

"It was good. The people are surprisingly really welcoming and nice."

"I knew you would love it."

"I will, but there is a lot to learn." I sigh at how many notes I took in the meeting today.

"Of course, but that's part of the job. It won't be long, and you will know all the ropes."

I sigh. "I hope so."

"Yeah, and any other news?" she asks curiously. "Any Marc updates?"

My throat constricts at the thought. "Ah...yeah. Kinda a lot."

She gasps. "What? Spill."

"So first, last night, I went for a walk to his address, expecting to knock on his door and surprise him—"

"Oh, good idea," she interrupts.

I snort. "Not so much. I was about to cross the road when a woman and a girl knocked on his door. He grabbed the girl's hand, and they all went inside."

She gasps. "No way. And you've never asked if he had children?"

"Uh-huh. No. It never once crossed my mind. But I swear, I was gutted right there on the sidewalk. Like we hooked up at Christmas, and I guess it wasn't the place for him to say, 'Hey, I have a wife, or girlfriend, and teenage daughter,' but it would have been nice not to see that, especially after he said he wasn't married or seeing anyone."

"I bet. I'm so sorry, Gracie. What a dirty dog."

I laugh. "Oh, I haven't finished with the story yet."

"What? No."

"Mm-hmm. So I met the team, and like I said, they're amazing. I couldn't have asked for a nicer workplace. I go to a meeting with Mason, and guess who is at the meeting?"

"Fuck off."

I chuckle. "Right! Crazy. He works for the opposition, and both my company and his are working together on a joint venture for this client."

"Did you talk to him?"

"No. He kept looking over at me during the meeting, but I didn't want to speak to him. What could I say? I was working. I left afterwards as quickly as possible. I didn't want to make a bad impression in the first week."

"Yeah, good call. But now what? Will you see him again?"

"Yep, for another meeting next week. He presented today, and I had to watch him and act all professional while he looked hot and intelligent, talking all this shit I didn't understand, and I had to keep taking notes to make sure I was listening to everything. He makes it so hard to concentrate."

She snickers. "Hot and intelligent are a lethal mix."

"And good in bed," I mumble.

"Even hotter. Damn it, why did he have to go and be a dick?"

"Because that's men, right?"

"Don't be like that. He is just one guy. There are some really good ones that you can trust."

I trusted him. That's the problem. I finally let someone in and was sharing feelings, and it blew up in my face. I don't know if I want to do that again. And right now, I have no intentions of dating or seeing anyone. It's bad enough I'll have to see Marc next week.

"Oh, and his real name is Marco Giordano. He clearly didn't want me to find out his real name."

"Hmm, you sure? It could be a nickname. Like, Marc is better than Marco. I couldn't blame him for not wanting to be called Marco."

"Maybe, but now I have zero trust in him."

"Fair, but maybe it would be good to talk to him and ask him everything in person."

I've thought about this all day, but I keep coming back to the same thing. "I don't know if I could date a man with a child."

"Oh."

I swallow at the admission. I feel bad for being honest about this when she is pregnant, but I need her to get an idea of the turmoil running through me.

"It's just never crossed my mind that I would date a guy with a child. Hell, I'm not wise enough to parent."

"It's only one," she argues.

"A teenager. Remember, we were wild. I can't see how they would be easy to take on and accept me being a step-parent."

The word stepparent sends my stomach into a flutter of uneasiness.

"Yeah, they can be tough, but I think once you crack them and get them to warm to you, it would be kind of fun."

I scrunch up my nose at the idea. "I don't see how kids are fun. And anyway, are you forgetting the woman I saw enter his home?"

"Are you sure it was a wife or girlfriend? Did you see a ring?"

"No, I was across the street, staring like a freak. I couldn't move my feet that were glued to the sidewalk."

She chuckles. "And they didn't see you?"

"Nope, totally oblivious."

"Umm...well, I still say talk to him. This could all be a misunderstanding."

"Yeah, I know. I just don't want to do it before or after a meeting. I don't want Mason or Nora to catch on that he and I have hooked up. I want to make a good impression and sleeping with the competition isn't going to win me any favors."

"Yeah, that's fair enough. Well, whatever happens, you better keep me updated. This is the best gossip I've heard in a long time."

"I'm glad I can be your entertainment. Even if it's at my expense."

"No, but in all seriousness. Just follow your gut and do what feels right."

I have been and look where that led me. Maybe it's time I followed my head.

I'm sitting with Mason in his office, running through another design change that the client requested via email.

"Is this a good sign?" I ask Mason, wondering if this means our company's design beat *his*.

Speaking of Marc, today is another meeting where we will bump into each other and pretend we haven't fucked.

"Not necessarily. They change their minds constantly, so we never read into any change requests because you'll only be disappointed. We just need to keep fulfilling their changes to the best of our ability and hope they prefer our drafted design in the end. After they choose, both companies work together on the final design and build."

"Who gets the profit?" I ask.

"It's shared between both companies."

"So, what's the importance of who the client chooses?"

"Ego." He shrugs with a shit-eating grin.

I laugh.

"It's also important to be able to list our winning jobs to future clients. Makes us more appealing, and we can charge a higher amount."

I nod. "That makes sense."

"Anyway, let's make this a little grayer and two centimeters thicker, and see what it looks like."

"How about we add some blue into the gray? I think it might complement the building," I suggest. I hope I don't overstep, but I want to feel like I can contribute even a little bit.

"We can definitely try it. The more options, the better."

Spinning around, he types away on his computer. After a couple more versions with a few new shades of blue and gray options, he says, "Let's show Nora and then grab some lunch. I'm starving."

I smile, thinking I could do with a coffee and some food. We show Nora our new variations, and she has a suggestion that we run back to the office to try to attach them to the new file. And then finally, we hit the deli across the street.

Mason opens the door, and I'm about to step through the doorway when I gasp. I stand toe to toe with Marc, my gaze hitting his solid chest even through his white shirt. I remember the dark hair and tanned muscles that lie underneath. My fingers tingle with the need to touch him again. His chest rising and falling, I tip my head back, and his deep brown eyes stare down at me warmly. We stand in place, holding each other's gaze, and I can't speak a word. Totally lost in this moment.

"Gracie," Marc says deeply, and it trails down my spine. He can feel the sparks bouncing between us too.

We are so close, and the last time we were was at the bar...

"Marc. How are you, man?" Mason says from behind me.

Marc's eyes leave mine, and I blink, but I'm unable to tear my gaze from his handsome face. This close up, I can take in his dark lashes and chiseled nose, and moving down, I watch his tempting mouth as he answers Mason, showing peeks of his tongue. I can help but quiver from the memories of it in my mouth, colliding with mine, and between my legs on top of the bar.

I've never come as hard as I did that night with him.

"I'm good, Mase," Marc says, smiling at him. "How are you?"

"Yeah, same, same. Just grabbing some lunch with the new trainee, Gracie." The moment Mason says my name, Marc's face moves to me again, and my breath hitches. "You saw her at last week's meeting."

"I sure did," Marc says it with a slight purr, and it's like he's whispering it just to me. His voice is so smooth and velvety.

"Ah. Yeah. Hi," I say breathily. I'm still struggling to take a full, deep breath.

"Nice to meet you," Marc adds, but his lips perk up with a grin. As if knowing he's affecting me.

I clear my throat, trying to sound the opposite. "You too."

"You want to join us for lunch?" Mason asks, and my eyes widen. I turn my head to look at him, and then back at Marc, who flicks his gaze from Mason to me.

"I'd love to." His grin spreads across his face, and I want to point out that he already got his lunch, since he's holding a takeout bag. But instead, I stay silent.

"Come, let's catch up," Mason says.

I have so many questions, but I can't ask any with Mason around.

Marc turns, and I take a deep breath and follow. Mason's hot on my tail, not realizing the emotions brewing inside me.

I turn to speak to Mason. "I'm going to use the bathroom quickly."

"Do you want me to order you something?" he asks.

Marc is a few steps ahead, moving toward one of the empty tables.

"No, I'll order after I have a look at the menu. I'll be there in a couple of minutes," I say.

"All right." He walks off to join Marc.

I turn to where the signs for the bathroom are and walk slowly, needing the time to recover from the sensations hitting me.

After using the bathroom, I stare at my appearance in the mirror above the sink. I try to fix my wavy brown hair, using my fingers to comb the knots out. Then I check my makeup, adding ChapStick to my lips, instead of lipstick, because it might be too obvious I'm trying to impress Marc.

I straighten my blue top and black pencil skirt, and then stand back.

You can do this.

As I turn and walk out, I head straight to the boy's table. Marc's facing me, so he notices me first. A small lift of the corner of his mouth makes my stomach flutter once again, and I take the empty chair that's between them. Sitting, I notice the table is small, giving minimal room between us.

I pick up the menu and read it over, giving me time to avoid his gaze.

"Have you decided on what you'd like to order?" a waitress asks.

I lift my head, and we all say "Yes" in unison.

"Okay, what can I get for you?" She doesn't ask me, but Marc is quick to say.

"Gracie, ladies first."

I turn to her with a smile. "I'll take a latte with regular cream, no sugar. Thanks."

"And to eat?" the waitress asks.

"Can I get the turkey sandwich?"

"Of course." She nods, writing it down, and then I hand her the menu.

"I'll get the turkey sandwich and a long black," Marc says, but I don't move my gaze to him.

"Sounds good. I'll have the turkey too and a latte with one sugar," Mason says.

The waitress collects their menus and rattles off our order to check she got everything before walking away.

"So, as I was saying," Mason says. "My parents need Mat's help. The neighbor dispute was turned up when the guy patted his gun, that was nestled in his waistband, toward my dad. Mom's beside herself and wants to move."

"Yeah, so would my mom. I don't know how busy Mat is. We only spoke about the twins' antics. But just give him a call. I have his card here."

A card slides in front of my vision, and Marc's large, tanned hands reach out. I see his nice watch, but again, no ring.

I'm so confused.

"Thanks, I appreciate it. How are the boys?" Mason asks.

Marc chuckles, and I haven't heard it in a while, but I miss it. It's a deep, raspy sound. "Same old. You'd think the older they get, the calmer they would be, but I think it's the opposite for them."

I have no idea who these people are, but I stay silent until the waitress interrupts with the coffee.

I take the warm coffee between my palms, welcoming the liquid in my dry throat. It's a damn good brew. And I'm grateful for something to do with my hands, with the way my body is racked with nerves. The cup is saving me from leaving and running out of here.

CHAPTER 14

MARCO

She's sipping her coffee and avoiding looking at me. Again. Why?

Mason being here doesn't help because it means I can't talk to her. He's still chatting away like friends, and yes, we are, but my stomach drops at the thought of her feeling left out. Since Mason doesn't know we've met previously, I have to act like my brothers are all new information to her.

"I have three brothers, and two of them are twins," I say to her. And it works. She turns to face me, offering me a warm smile.

"And you're the oldest?" she asks, and I lean forward, excited this is getting her to face me and say more than two words to me.

"Yep, then Mateo."

"Ah," she says, sipping more of her coffee.

"Sounds like your life is never boring. It would have been great to have someone to grow up with," she says,

"I agree. I'm an only child, and it sucked," Mason says.

We laugh together, and the waitress interrupts to drop our lunch off, giving me a strange look before walking away.

Gracie begins to eat and some yellow mustard drops down the front of her clothes. She squeezes her eyes, and her lips move in a curse, causing me to smile. She's so adorable. Grabbing the napkin, she tries to clean it, but it smears, making it worse. She huffs and puts the napkin on the table, shrugging before turning to eat again.

I can't help myself. On instinct, I take my napkin and dip it into my water, then try to help clean it. When my hand hits her lap, I see she's frozen still, only her thighs are shaking under my touch.

Her breathing is heavy, and when I finish cleaning it for her, she breathes a soft "Thanks."

Sitting back, I put the napkin on the table and return to focus on Mason. Who's looking between Gracie and me with a puzzled expression. I don't want him to ask questions, so I change the topic to focus on him. "So, how's your wife, Mase?" I ask. They've been together since they were teenagers, and they have always been close.

He beams at the mention of her. I lean back in the chair with relief as he speaks. "She's great. Still teaching and loving it."

"Oh, I'm glad," I say.

"What year does she teach?" Gracie asks, and I'm trying to think, but I don't actually remember.

"Grade one," he answers.

"Oh, that would be tough," Gracie says, and I have to agree with her there.

"She tells me she loves it, but I agree with you. It sounds awful."

I check the time and see a couple of new urgent emails have popped through. I need to get back to the office and respond to them and make some calls. But I also want to spend more time talking to her. I'm stuck between two minds. But I have to put my business hat on.

"It was so nice to see you two. Thanks for letting me tag along, but I have to get back to work."

I stand, carrying my second bag of lunch for the day. Looking down at her, she meets my gaze, and I offer a warm smile. She smiles but looks back down.

"We shouldn't leave it so long to catch up next time," Mason says.

"I agree. It's so nice to see you again. And if you ever want a job, the offer always stands," I say.

He shakes his head and grins. "You're very persistent."

"Always," I say, leaving them and look over my shoulder one last time at her.

After seeing her yesterday, I'm more at ease going into the meeting. I'm prepared because I know she will be there, and I plan to talk to her afterward and find out why the sudden cold change?

She's ignoring all my calls and texts.

And I want to know why. I miss our chats.

I miss her.

I sigh and turn to move to the computer to have a final look at all my altered designs.

A knock on my door sounds, and Cassie walks in. "Your mail, and you have your meeting soon. I've organized the driver, but you told me to remind you."

"Yes, thanks."

I pack up the pile of papers and take my case to leave. I wanted to be there first to prepare for any opportunity I can get to talk to her.

Arriving in the meeting room, I begin working until I hear Jason's voice. "Marco. Good morning."

I lift my gaze off my laptop where I'm working to meet the clients awaiting their gaze. "Good morning, Jason." I shake hands, and then I see out of the corner of my eye, her walking out of the elevator with Mason. Her tight black dress is delectable, the way it cinches in her waist, giving me a tease of the memory of how perfect my hands fit around her and how soft her curves felt beneath my fingers. My mouth is salivating, so I swallow, and Jason turns to greet them. I openly watch her. The pretty pink lipstick shows off her plump, delicate mouth and beautiful smile, and I just want to kiss her again. She scratches at her neck, and it leaves a red mark behind. Is she nervous to see me? Or excited, like me?

When we were together, I could read her like a book. My hands felt her body's reaction, and her words would be full of encouragement. But right now, I can only read the subtle cues she's offering me, like the roll of her lips pinching together.

Jason moves away, saying, "Let's get started, shall we?"

I take my seat at the table, which is opposite of hers. But she wiggles around, and her gaze then settles on the back of Jason, just to avoid me.

Mason starts first this time, and they offer a few different options, and Jason makes a sound of approval with his throat. My stomach hardens. Mason looks down at Gracie and she's smiling broadly at him. I'm suddenly uncomfortable in my chair, and I need to move around. I don't want to see that. No, I want her to only look at me like that...like she used to.

I need to know what the fuck happened for her to be hot one minute and cold the next; it makes no sense and the nausea rolling in my gut from their exchange makes me see red. I don't get angry, so the way my body is vibrating, and my muscles tensing, makes me uneasy. And I want to return to my calm and controlled self at work.

When Mason finishes his presentation and takes his seat, he whispers in her ear, and her large smile and lit-up face make me clench the pen in my hand. Without realizing, I've snapped it.

I drop it to the table and keep my hands together on top. Jason says it's my turn, and both Gracie and Mason cease chattering to watch me. At least now she will have no choice but to focus on me, and they will stop whispering and smiling at each other. I trust Mason. He is a great guy. He's married. I just don't know what this tension toward him is for, but I know it involves Gracie.

I clear my throat and begin my presentation, going right back to my smooth and effortless business manner. When I finish, my gaze finds hers, and she has one of her broad warm smiles directed at me. My body hums from her attention.

As I take my seat, Jason begins talking, saying it will take a couple of days to decide before moving on to a different part of the design. My heart rate increases with the knowledge I'll have more meetings with her.

I've been packing up, so that after the presentation, she can't leave without talking to me.

The meeting ends and I take off to round the table in time to catch her, where we, would be far enough away for the boys to be out of earshot. I'm almost to her, and she sees me approaching. I watch her eyes widen. "Gr—"

"Marco," Jason calls. "I need a moment."

I suck in a sharp breath and clench my teeth together. I can't ignore him, meaning I have to give up the opportunity to talk to her. And it's like she knows, because her face softens and now she has a little smirk on her lips.

I smirk back.

Don't think I'll give up on you, Gracie.

When I want something, I don't stop until I have it.

CHAPTER 15

GRACIE

I watch him tear his gaze away and head toward the client. Letting out a long breath that I was holding. He was right in front of me with a look of determination. Jason interrupted, and I'm relieved. I don't want to talk to him right now. Not at work. He and Mason are friends, but it doesn't change the fact I'm trying to make a good impression.

When his name was called, I saw a flicker of pain hit his face, and I had to swallow the bit of guilt I was holding.

"You ready?" Mason asks.

"Yep."

Leaving the room, I take one more glance over my shoulder and run my gaze over his navy suit. Enjoying how he looks in one and imagining for a second what it would be like to peel it off. I let the fantasy play out in my head as I turn in the elevator and his gaze hits mine. Stealing my breath away. Definitely peeling a suit like that off him would be the best fantasy ever. I can imagine his brown eyes turning heavy with desire and him focusing on my movements, encouraging me with his dirty mouth.

"I think they liked your hint of blue the best." Mason's voice pulls me out of my head.

"Yeah, I thought so too. But why did they take Marc-o."

I almost called him by the nickname I give him. And I know Mason calls him Marc, so I'm sure he would have been wondering why I'm so casual, but I managed to save myself.

"Maybe they want him to tweak one of his. But I'm not worried. We provided what they asked, and they seemed happy, so let's wait and see."

I nod and wonder what will happen at the next meeting.

Will he try to talk to me again? And what will I do if he tries?

"I'm finished. I'll see you tomorrow." Mason pops his head into my office.

I look up and wave. "See you tomorrow."

He leaves, and I'm still finishing off my work. I'm half an hour past my usual finishing time, and it's quiet around here. Nora likes her employees to have a good work/life balance so they perform better, so I need to hurry and get out of here.

I take the elevator, my eyes so heavy and sore from the long day. I can't wait to order some noodle takeout and chill on my comfy couch that is screaming out my name.

I'm rubbing my eyes when the elevator door opens. Exiting the building I walk out mindlessly into the cool air. But I jump back when I see *him*.

"Gracie."

I shiver, not from the cold, but from the purr in his voice and the way he says my name.

"Marc, what are you doing?"

"Trying to talk to you. Please. Will you talk to me now?"

I try to take deep breaths, my throat constricting with the thought of him and me having this conversation. Peering around to make sure no one from work is seeing us, I nod. I need a drink. "Okay. But can we go somewhere else? I'm new here, and I don't want to make a bad impression."

He smiles. "I love your care for work. I wish you had told me when we first met. Maybe I could have helped you out. If it wasn't a conflict of interest, I'd love you to work for me."

I smirk. "Not going to happen, but where is a good spot for a drink?"

"Around the corner is a lounge, private, with good food and drinks."

I nod and follow him. We walk side by side, and I'm quiet the whole way. It reminds me of the bar, back when I struggled to speak to him. He makes me nervous.

"Are you okay?" he asks, turning to read my face, but I keep my eyes focused on the street ahead.

"Yeah, I'm just tired. It's been a long day." My stomach flips.

"Sorry. Did you want to go home and do this another time?" he asks in defeat.

I shake my head as he looks at me, and my expression softens. "No, I think it's best we talk. We will keep seeing each other at work, and it would be nice if we were on the same page."

He frowns, not understanding what I mean. We reach the lounge, and he grabs the door, holding it open for me.

"Thanks," I say and walk past him, straight inside. The hum vibrates through my body again.

"Just in here," he says, pointing to a more private booth.

I walk over and take a seat. Sitting down opposite him, even though I want to be right next to him.

"Good evening, what could I get you two to drink?" the server asks us.

He waits for me to order a wine, and then he orders a scotch on the rocks.

"Would you like something to eat?" he asks me.

I don't want to have too much pressure to stay longer than I feel comfortable, but I'm starving, so I decide to grab a quick meal.

"Yeah, maybe a burger and fries? I don't want to cook tonight."

He peeks over his menu at me with a warm smile. "I remember you said you don't like to cook."

"I don't," I say, scrunching up my nose.

"I'll have the same," he says to the waitress and returns his gaze to me with a wink. I can't help but twist my lips up into a smile.

The server repeats the order, takes our menus, and leaves us alone again.

"How was your day?" he asks, leaning back into the leather booth, his gaze focused on me.

"Busy, as I'm learning so much every day."

Even though I'm busy, a day in the office is still better than a busy night at the bar. I don't miss my old work. I'm definitely happier now.

He rests his elbows on the table, rubbing his jaw with his hand. "But do you like it?"

I have to rip my gaze from his jaw stroking, up to his blazing eyes to answer him. "I'm so grateful for the job. Nora and Mason and all the team are beyond nice. I've been welcomed graciously."

"They are a good team. Even though I think mine is better," he says with another wink, and it causes me to giggle.

"I heard you trying to poach Mason," I tease, feeling like a weight has been lifted slightly. I still need to talk to him about...I suck in a breath, knowing I'm avoiding it because it will surely ruin this moment. The moments like this are what I remember from the bar when I first had a conversation with him. I felt relaxed, like myself, and desired. But sometime soon, I'll be bursting the bubble and facing reality. For now, though, I want to hear his answer.

"I've even thought about buying the company because it's got too many workers I want for myself." He straightens in his chair, his tone serious, and my face falls as realization hits.

"You could buy it?" I choke out.

He chuckles darkly before narrowing his gaze at me. "I haven't tried to yet. But I'm leaning toward it now."

Shit, he has serious money. And the thought of him wanting me and doing anything to get me sends a shiver down my spine.

Crossing my arms over my chest, I ask, "How was your day?"

I hope he forgets about buying the company. I don't think I'd be able to concentrate on work if he was around me all the time. Plus, how would I get treated if I slept with the boss? I bet they would think I was just some young girl sleeping her way to the top. Nobody would stop to find out the truth, rumors would be ruthless, and I'm strong, but that might push me. So yeah, working at a different company is the right decision. I need to focus on the next twelve months of my journey, not on him. I want to be self-sufficient and not to rely on a guy. Look what happens when you open your heart...it gets stood on.

His mouth drops open, and he tries to close it, but seems surprised by my question. "It—"

The waitress interrupts us to deliver our drinks. I smile and wait for her leave before focusing back on him and waiting for his answer.

"It was busy, but it always is." He shrugs like that's the normal thing to expect, but I wouldn't know.

"What's it like to run your own business?"

"You're hitting me with a very unexpected question." He takes a big sip of his amber liquid.

"Sorry, I'm just curious."

"I get that. Um, well, it's a hard question to answer on the spot, but if I had to say something off the top of my head, I'll say exhausting, powerful, and rewarding."

He grabs his glass and peers over the rim at me as he drinks, and when his Adam's apple bobs, I feel it between my legs. I squeeze my thighs together to stop the ache and dip my chin, grabbing my wine and taking a big sip. He watches the way my throat moves when I swallow the liquid. And I can't help but let my imagination go into the past. Liquid and our bodies seem to be a potent sexual mix.

I need to get the conversation back somewhere safe. "The way you speak is so effortless, and I can tell you love it."

A big stupid grin sits on his face. "Thanks. I do very much. I hope you end up loving it too."

The server brings over our food and leaves. I stuff a fry straight into my mouth.

"I can't remember the last time I had a burger and fries. A long fucking time, and it's a shame it's so good. The way the salt and fat hit my tongue, damn. It reminds me of being a kid with my brothers and having this on Friday nights. It was a tradition."

I smile at the way he talks about growing up. A part of me is jealous. It wasn't the same type of childhood I had, but I wouldn't want anyone growing up in the abusive situations I did. This is part of the reason I don't want to date a man with a child. "Sounds like another fun, youthful time." I say smiling. "And I have burgers and fries all the time. What do you mean by a long time?"

He rubs his jaw, and as I watch the languid strokes, it's hypnotizing. I want to run my hand along his shadow.

"Many years."

"What?" I gasp with a horrified expression. "Why would you deprive yourself?"

He chuckles deeply at my reaction. "I just haven't. I don't know why."

I stuff another fry into my mouth and chew before saying, "You're missing out. Nothing better than a good burger and fries."

"I'll have to get you to take me, to some good fast food restaurants."

My soft face falls, and I cough from the fry getting stuck.

"Did I say something wrong?" he asks, picking up the burger and taking a big bite.

I do the same and welcome the beef patty and cheese with a special sauce that has me releasing a moan. "It's good, right?" I ask after I swallow, trying to push past the fact he spoke about taking me out on a date.

He nods. His nostrils flare, and his stare is both heated and conflicted.

I wash down the burger with some of my drink.

"You never told me you were coming here. Did you come to New York for me?"

I blush crimson and look down before meeting his curious gaze again. "Well, yes, that was part of it, but I did want a job as an architect."

He offers me a wide smile. "I do remember you saying that."

I nod, even though I'm still embarrassed. "My professor helped me get the traineeship. I was surprised and thrilled that it was here, and I figured it was a sign."

"But what's going on, then? You stopped texting and you seem different." His brow furrows as he searches my face for answers.

I lower my burger and dust my hands, my heart thundering inside with nerves. It's time to talk about it, and fuck, I'm panicking. I'm so not ready, but he needs answers. I need to explain and get him to understand why I didn't respond to him.

I take an audible breath and lean back, looking directly into his curious eyes. "I came to your house."

He sits up straight, a crease forming between his brows. "When?"

"Sunday."

"But I was home. What time did you come?"

"I can't remember, but yes, you were home."

He scratches his head, totally confused. "So how come you didn't knock?"

It's as if a bucket of ice was just poured over me. Do I have it all wrong?

"Your wife and child turned up."

"I don't have a wife. That would have been my ex-wife and daughter."

My face falls, but I recover quickly. Taking a sip of my wine, I pop a fry into my mouth and chew it. I need to think for a minute.

An ex-wife and child.

Baggage...

I drop my gaze to the table, then drag it slowly back to him. What does this mean for me?

I've never dealt with an ex-wife.

It was never in my future plan to take on someone else's child.

And now what?

I'm only twenty-six and just starting my life. And sometimes I think I'm a child myself, so how could I possibly be responsible for someone else?

It's still silent between us, neither one of us speaking for a moment. I'm lost in my own head, trying to figure out what I'm supposed to do.

"She remarried and had more children," he adds, obviously wanting to make it clear they are over. It seems to get my brain working again.

"Okay, so she is your ex-wife, but it still wasn't fun to see. It was a huge shock."

"I bet. I wish you didn't find out like that."

As I look at him, he stares back with hurt-filled eyes, and it kills me to see him like that.

But I have to ask. "Would you have told me?" Taking a sip of my wine, I wrinkle my nose.

He leans forward to grab my hand, and I look down at his large one covering my small one. "Of course. I didn't think a text message or a one-night stand was the appropriate time. Not yet, at least."

I pull my hand away and play around with a fry before eating it.

"How long have you been divorced?"

"Twelve years."

My eyes bulge and I rapidly blink before eating another chip. "So, what happened?"

"I worked too much and wouldn't change my work/life balance. I was barely home."

I nod but don't say anything and I worry for a moment. He sips his drink, waiting for me to ask the next question.

"So, she remarried and had kids...and you?"

He shakes his head vehemently. "Not even close. I worked more than ever when she left. And no one has made me want to give it up. Well, not until recently."

Trying not to get my hopes up, I just nod, not wanting to read too much into what he's insinuating. "And you share a daughter."

He smiles. "Yes. Aria. She is thirteen and my best friend. She stays whenever she wants to. Me and my ex have an open-door policy. So, if she wants to stay at my house for a week, she can, and vice versa."

It's what co-parenting dreams are made of, but most don't end up that way.

"That's a really good relationship you have." I smile, but it's not as easy as usual. I'm tight and not at all relaxed. Whereas he looks totally comfortable with our conversation; he's even undone his tie and top button. Usually, I'd find it hot where his exposed neck is on show for me, but I can't get my head out of the cloud it's found itself in.

"Yes, we all do. Including her husband and step kids."

"I'm sorry. This is a lot to take in," I say honestly, rubbing my forehead, feeling overwhelmed. The start of a headache forms behind my eyes.

He shuffles in his seat and leans forward slightly. The wide smile is tighter and his face even. "It really is, but I need you to hear everything."

"You're open to dating me, even though you have no work/life balance?"

"I don't want to repeat my first mistake again. I promised myself I wouldn't if the right person came along, and that person is definitely you. I think we have fun together and I'd love to date and see where this could go."

CHAPTER 16

GRACIE

The way my stomach is rolling with nausea, I'm scared I'll actually vomit. The nervous energy is all coming from the thought of him having a thirteen-year-old and what that means for me.

I'm not someone who dates and then the one that I do has baggage. The ex-wife isn't an issue; she has moved on, and has a new life, but they share a child, and now me dating Marc would involve her.

How would she treat me? Would she like me?

I just don't know if I even want children, but what if I do?

The way I grew up...an unpleasant shiver runs down my spine.

My family life was hurtful and cold, and then the streets with Ava were rough. I don't know if I want to bring a little piece of me through life. It's not always easy. But taking on someone's child isn't something I thought I'd ever have to worry about. He's also thirty-eight, so maybe he doesn't want to have any more kids, and then where does that leave me?

"There is a lot for me to think about..." I trail off and pick up my drink to take a large sip.

"So where does that leave us?" he asks, and it pulls my eyes from the food to his gaze. His expression is tight and pained.

But I need to be honest.

It's not always easy to tell the truth, especially when they wear a face full of pain and they beg you to be with them. Sometimes you need to be selfish to look after yourself, to take some time to think to make a proper decision without any clouds of judgment. He deserves a confident decision, and I deserve to give myself time to make the right one. If I am going to commit to him, it'll be without reservations, and I'll give him all of me.

"To be honest. I can't date you while I still need to think about what I want in my future."

His lips thin, and I think he is going to protest, as most men would.

"Even though that saddens me, because I wish I was part of your future, I want you to be sure about being with me. Because it involves Aria too."

"Exactly."

The nausea lessens, and I offer a small smile to him. His eyes are sad, but he smiles back.

We eat in silence, and when we finish our drinks, he asks if I'm ready to go. The heaviness in my eyes tells me I need to sleep soon.

"That would be great. I'm exhausted."

"I'll fix up the bill, and I'll walk you home."

"I'll pay."

"No, *Bella*. I'm a gentleman. I pay." His deep gravelly voice saying my nickname makes me tremor.

I nod, not wanting to argue. "Thank you."

Afterward, we walk outside and it's chilly, so I fold my arms over my chest.

"Let me walk you home," he offers.

I shake my head. "It's out of your way."

"It's dark, and you're alone in a new city. Please, let me do this." I turn to capture his gaze, and his eyes are pleading as he says, "Just humor me and let me do this."

"Okay," I say, returning to the safety of looking in front of me.

He places his jacket over my shoulders, and I grab the top to stop it from slipping off. The caring nature hits me hard in the chest. Why does he have to be so thoughtful? My mind is a jumbled mess...*but I need to give myself time.*

"Are you sure? Won't you be cold?"

He chuckles. "Not at all. I'm used to running in the very early mornings, so to me this isn't cold."

"How early are you talking?" I ask, sliding my arms into the jacket sleeves, and it takes every part of me not to pull it up and take a big sniff, but I don't want him to think I'm a weirdo.

His masculine spice hits me in the nose, so I subtly take a deeper inhale, loving his scent surrounding me.

"Five."

"That's awful. And you choose that?" I ask.

"It's the only time I have."

"I don't exercise. I think the only time I do is the constant moving I did around bar work, and now walking everywhere."

"You never workout?" he asks.

His unusual tone has me asking, "Why is that so hard to believe?"

"Your body's perfectly toned."

I grow hot from his compliment. "Well, thank you."

It's silent before I speak again.

"So you exercise because you're scared you'll gain weight?"

He laughs loudly. "No, and yes. I like to stay in shape, but it's also a mental thing. It keeps me focused for the day."

"I don't see how running at five in the morning for half an hour—"

"An hour," he corrects me.

My jaw slacks before I shake my head. "I don't even know what to say to that."

"Maybe you could try it one day?"

"With you?"

"Either that or by yourself. It's really good for thinking."

I half laugh, half choke. "Nice hint."

"Oh no, I didn't mean that."

"Sure," I tease.

"No, I mean it," he says, seemingly horrified.

I gently push him. "It's fine. I'm playing with you." He takes a breath, shaking his head with a small smile.

"I'm just up here," I say, pointing to the street ahead.

"Did you buy the apartment?"

I snort. "I wish. No, a friend of mine from Chicago helped me find it."

"Is she in real estate?"

"He, and yes."

He falls silent again after that, and we approach the door. I take the steps one at a time, and when I reach the top, I spin and gasp. Not expecting him to be standing right behind me.

My hands land on my racing heart. "Shit. You scared me."

"Sorry."

But he doesn't move.

I slip his jacket off and hand it to him.

"Thanks for letting me borrow this."

He smiles. "Any time."

I stand there awkwardly for a minute before grabbing the keys from my bag and opening the door. If I wasn't in the headspace of figuring out if I want to play house and take on a daughter or if I want children, then asking him in would have been a guarantee, but using my head this time, I say, "Thanks for walking me home."

"Of course. I'll see you at the next meeting?"

"You will."

He kisses my cheek, and my eyes flutter from his soft, warm lips. It was unexpected, but so nice. "Goodnight, *Bella*," he whispers.

"Goodnight," I say and watch him take the steps down.

"Oh, so will you respond if I text you again?" he asks, spinning around and pulling his phone out of his pocket with a smirk.

"Is that a good idea?"

"Of course, it is." He winks.

I roll my eyes, laughing. "Trust you to say that. Fine."

He beams, and I know it was the right thing to do. I may not have given him an answer he wanted tonight, but at least me agreeing to answer his texts again has made him happy.

As I turn and open my door, he stands there, unmoving, and I know he's waiting for me to go in first. Closing the door behind me, I watch him through the peephole as he smiles and walks away, staring down at his phone. When he's out of sight, I turn and rest my back against the door, touching the cheek he pressed a warm kiss on, and a large sigh slips past my lips.

My phone chimes, and I can't help but break out into a stupidly big fat smile. Grabbing it out of my bag, I open it to see his number, quickly reading it.

> **Marc:** My jacket smells like you now. I don't think I'll wash it...ever. Goodnight x

I clutch the phone to my chest and push off the door, needing a cold shower. He stirs too many feelings inside of me, one of them beating wildly under my hand.

"Have you ever had pickles in ice cream?"

"Ava, please tell me you're not eating that shit?" I say, sitting on the couch.

"It's amazing. You ought to try it."

"I'll pass. It sounds like a pregnancy craving, and I'm sure soon you'll never want to see a pickle or ice cream again."

"Not true."

"Mark my words."

"If I was a betting woman, I'd bet you I wouldn't."

"You won't bet because you know I'm right!"

"Untrue, but I'm not arguing with you. How come you're calling me so late?"

I get up from my couch and grab a bottle of water from the fridge before opening it and drinking some. "Well, I have some news."

"Yeah, what?" she asks.

"I had dinner with Marc."

She squeals, and I have to hold the phone away from my ear. When she calms down, I put it back. "Thanks for killing my eardrum."

"Sorry, I'm just a tad excited."

"A tad?" I tease.

"Come on, hurry up and tell me."

"After work, I was about to walk home when he was outside my building, waiting for me."

"Mm-hmm."

"I wanted to talk somewhere else because I didn't want them seeing me with their competitor. Plus, I didn't want people from work to see and ask questions I didn't have the answer to."

"Yeah, so where did you go?"

"This lounge where we had a drink and a burger and fries."

"Oh God, don't say that! Now I really want McDonald's."

I laugh at her cravings before I continue. "We chatted, but obviously, I had to tell him I came to visit him and I saw a woman and child."

"Ohhh...and?" she drawls.

"His ex and their child."

"At least not his wife."

"True, and they divorced twelve years ago, so that's fine. I'm not bothered by that."

"The kid?" she asks.

I sigh loudly. "Yeah, I don't know if I'm ready to take on a thirteen-year-old."

"Ouch. What do you want?"

"I dunno, that's the thing. I didn't think I wanted kids...you know, the past and all, but I've never indulged in thinking of being a wife and mother. Fuck, I'm only twenty-six, Ava."

She giggles. "It's not a big deal. Things happen when they are supposed to, so stop worrying about when and what. Just go with how you feel."

"I did."

"So, what did you decide?"

"I said I needed time to think about everything. I don't want to rush and make a decision. So, we aren't dating or anything."

"Damn it. I was hoping this was going to work out."

"Same, but if it's supposed to happen, it will. But he and I deserve the decision to be one hundred percent and with a full commitment."

"Stepmom Gracie."

My nose wrinkles at the thought. "No. Just no, Ava. I'm so not ready."

"How do you know? You said you need time, so how will you know if you want him or not?"

"I don't know. I'll figure something out."

"Oh! I know. Date someone else."

I roll my eyes. "That sounds like a terrible idea."

"Why?"

"It just is. And I can't be fucked getting dressed up or making conversation with a stranger."

"Bad luck. You need to figure out, if you want Marc or not, you need to go on a date with someone else and see how you feel."

"I'm not sure, Ava. I don't think I'm ready."

"You didn't think you'd ever want to date, and then Marc came along."

This is true. I stay silent, hating the fact she is right.

"Just let me settle into work first, then I'll tackle my love life. One task at a time."

"You can multitask."

"I never said I couldn't. I just want to take my time and give Marc a true answer. An answer from the heart."

"I guess I can't argue with that. I need to pee, so I gotta go. This pregnancy bladder is no joke. I've never needed to go to the bathroom this much in my whole life."

"Well, I'll let you go. I'll talk to you soon anyway."

"Yes, you will. I need regular updates."

"You're so needy."

"Shut up, you love me."

I laugh. "Always."

CHAPTER 17

MARCO

I hit the pavement a little harder today. Checking my watch, I can see my pace is my personal best. I make it to Max's house in record time, and he's just jogging down his steps.

"Morning."

He nods and grumbles, "Morning."

We take off on the usual path, and I'm desperate to ask. "What's wrong?"

"Just tired."

"Why? Big training week?"

"Nah, I went out last night, and I didn't get much sleep. It was hard getting out of bed this morning."

"I feel you. Some days, the cold mornings are worse than others. I could easily roll over and stay in bed."

"No. I don't mean that. I had to leave a woman in my bed."

"Oh."

We turn the corner to hit the park. The glow from the lights is the only light illuminating the path. The last time I woke up in the morning with a woman in my arms was with Gracie...and if she and I were asleep, I'd skip my morning run in favor of cuddling her.

"Well, I guess well done for dragging your ass out to come. Let's race, and we can get you home quicker to your awaiting woman."

He smiles at that. "I like what you're thinking." And with no warning, the fucker takes off.

"You shit," I say before sprinting after him.

We have been running for forty minutes, and as we turn the corner, I puff out a breath.

Jesus Christ.

I'm hallucinating, rubbing my eyes, thinking surely it can't be her, but nope, I know that shiny dark hair and pint-sized frame a mile away.

I slow, causing Max to stop abruptly. "What are you doing?" he asks.

I shake my head. "Nothing."

As I run past her, my gaze roves over her skin-tight outfit. Looks new, the leggings showing off her sinful curves, and the long-sleeve tight jacket fitting her like a second skin. I am glad she didn't come with me because I wouldn't be able to work out with her next to me. Not with her looking as sexy as that. I'm almost swallowing my own tongue.

Max's house is around the corner, so as soon as I drop him home, I race back to find her.

I see her frame speed-walking now. Her warm breath puffing clouds in the frosted air around her.

Jogging up beside her, I join her on the walk. "What a beautiful find on this fine Tuesday morning."

She laughs, more steam leaving her mouth. "I figured I couldn't sleep, so I'd try this exercise idea out for thinking."

"And you were hoping to find me."

I poke her ribs, and when she squirms, it causes me to smile. God, I just want to kiss the shit out of her, fuck her, and then, hold her in my arms. But I'm giving her space to take everything in; she clearly has a lot to think about.

"No, silly." She rolls her eyes, but an easy smile sits on her face. I'm glad I can help lighten her up...even a little bit.

"Well, is the walk helping?"

"No. All I keep thinking about is what if someone kidnaps me, what's that noise, and it's so damn cold, I should have grabbed a jacket."

I let out a deep, throaty laugh. "Let's walk you home and get you warm."

"I'm awake now, so if there is a place for a gingerbread latte and a bagel, I'd love that," she says, peering around, as if looking for a café.

Knowing this area like the back of my hand, I shake my head to say no. "You know what, there is a street not far from you that has the best bagels."

She begins running. "Well, the last one there is paying."

My jaw drops at her dare, and I take off and jog up to her. "I always pay, but let's swing past your place and grab a jacket."

She grows silent. And I worry she thinks I'm trying to push her when I'm not; I just want her comfortable.

"Relax, I won't come in. I'm just saying you can run in and meet me back outside."

She nods, liking that idea.

We arrive at her place shortly after, and she runs inside and grabs her coat before we walk to the cafe.

"I'm sorry I'm jumpy, but I feel like I can't make a decision and that I'm taking a while." Her voice is barely above a whisper.

A frown sits on my face as to why she's beating herself up. Did she think I was angry at her for some reason?

I run my hand down the back of her coat. "Hey." Her eyes slowly hold mine. "You take all the time you need. This is a big decision. I will wait for you as long as you need, and if you decide you can't do it, as much as it pains me, I'll accept it." I reluctantly pull my hand away from her back, instantly missing the contact with her.

"Thanks, Marc, I appreciate that. I would love nothing more than to jump right back to how we were in Chicago, but I'd be doing us both an injustice if I'm not 100 percent sure."

"No, I get that, and I want you to be 100 percent sure. I hope you getting that off your chest will help you will sleep better."

"Yeah, it will, and exercise is not for me, sorry." She gives me a cheeky grin, and I chuckle.

"At least you tried it." My heart thunders in my chest at the fact she tried something I suggested, as well as us getting to spend time together in the quiet early morning.

The next day, I'm standing at the front of the boardroom. I run my gaze over my managers. I want an update on all the projects we have open. The only way to keep the staff performing well is to regularly check up on them and make sure they get rewards for any outstanding work.

You win big jobs the bigger your reward, and if you're underperforming, I'll step in and see if I can help provide education or hire someone to work with the employee that's struggling. But the bottom line is that these meetings need to happen to keep this business as successful as it is. I didn't miss out on so much of my life for twenty years to have a sinking ship.

I take a quick scan across the room to make sure there is one person from each team, and when I'm happy, we start.

During the meeting, I find out one of the managers is working on a contract which would make the business a nice 110k in profit.

But unfortunately, one of my other managers is struggling on a project. After the meeting ends, I go back to my office and get Cassie to retrieve the file, and when she returns, I go through it with a fine-tooth comb. Once I'm satisfied, I've pulled it apart, I call down and get the manager to come up, then spend time working through the file and discussing how to turn it around.

When I'm alone again, I lean back and check my watch. *Shit.*

Because I spent so much time helping sort out that file, I'm running behind on my own work. I begin replying to emails and working on my back log and before I know it, it's seven-thirty.

I rub the back of my neck, trying to ease the knot that's formed there from staying in the same position for too long and pack up for the day. My stomach grumbles, and I'm too tired to cook myself any dinner tonight. Aria isn't coming over, so it's just me. I decide to go to the local Japanese place to pick up some sushi that's around the corner from here.

When I leave, Cassie has turned everything else off, so I don't have anything to do. She is seriously a lifesaver.

I move to her desk and write her a note for the morning, instructing her to scan and fix a file tomorrow. When I'm finished, I head for the elevator. And I'm interrupted when Mat calls me.

"Hey, Mat."

"Are you free to go to a gala?" Mat asks.

"When?" I grumble in response and hold the phone to my ear. I don't enjoy going to them, but for him, I'd make an exception because he doesn't enjoy them either. However, Romeo and Lorenzo love to dress up and mingle. They know how to schmooze people. Mat and I prefer to talk to the bare minimum and only for work purposes.

"It's Friday night."

"I can't. I have Aria this whole weekend."

"That's cool. And how is my niece doing?"

I smile. "Come over and find out."

"I might stop in. I haven't been around in a while."

"No, you haven't, but you've been busy." I don't want him to feel guilty when he works so much. Even though I'd love for him to see her more.

"I know, but she's getting so big. I need to make the most of it."

"Before she doesn't want to know us anymore," I say, finishing his thought. It scares me how fast she's growing.

"What's happening with Gracie?"

I blow out a breath. "She's still thinking about Aria."

"I wonder how long that's going to take."

"No idea, but I bumped into her yesterday on my morning run."

"That's good."

"Yeah, it was a nice surprise." I smile, remembering our easy conversation.

"Hopefully she'll come around."

"Sooner rather than later, I hope."

"You getting heavy balls, bro?"

"Exactly." I chuckle. My hand is going to lose its skin soon. With the amount I'm aroused because I'm thinking of her, it's unusual.

I would love to have her under me.

Yeah, that would definitely fix it.

"And every other woman—"

I cut him off. "Is off limits."

"Oh, you've got it bad."

I don't bother answering because he knows me too well to argue with him.

"How are you going with the boys' case?"

He groans. "The defense isn't making it easy on me."

"You thought they would?" I chuckle.

"No, but they keep providing more evidence."

"Ouch."

"Yeah. He will be a daddy after a one-night fling."

"Sounds like he needs sex education."

He snorts. "Even that won't help him."

"Maybe the baby will change him."

"Not everyone is like you."

"Yeah, but I was married. What I'm saying is that kids change you."

"You can only h—"

As I leave the building talking, I walk into the restaurant, my gaze lands on Gracie.

What is she doing here?

I'm shocked to see her sitting at one of the round tables, and she looks breathtaking. Her long hair is straightened, and her makeup is more dramatic. With her plump lips painted pink and glossy, and the green dress complementing her smooth skin. I clench my teeth, staring at the back of a guy with a shaved head.

I'm gonna kill him.

Who the fuck is he?

And what does he think he's doing having dinner with her?

CHAPTER 18

GRACIE

My eyes widen when I see Marc heading toward the table out of the corner of my eye. *Oh, fuck.*

His face is pinched and almost murderous. I freeze as I wait for him to approach. What else can I do when he looks like he wants to start a war?

I won't back down. I didn't plan this date. I'm going to kill Ava when I call her next.

She set me up on this blind date, and I couldn't say no when she suggested it by saying if I went on the date, I'll know if Marc's the one I should be with. Obviously, his daughter and my thoughts on having children in the future are still undecided. But I want to at least see if the ache in my chest and the burning sensation in my stomach for him is just a stupid fantasy, or if I'm unable to deny him and I need to accept that I want him.

But as he stands next to me, stiff and powerful, I swallow hard. God, he's sexy, even standing here all tightly coiled. I look over at my date, and he seems like he's seen a ghost. I almost feel sorry for him, but I also want someone to be able to stand up for himself, not be intimidated. I want to be protected. Like Marc protects me...

I stare up, appreciating the way his disheveled dark locks give off the fact he's been running his hands through it many times. The way the dark gray suit and white shirt sit on his body so perfectly, it shows off his broad shoulders, the tapered waist, and muscled legs that I know he's got under his pants.

He clears his throat, and I flick my gaze back to his as he says, "Gracie, what are you doing?" His tone is thick and velvety, and with his piercing eyes, I shuffle in my seat from the throb that's forming between my legs.

I can't be rude to this date. It's not his fault he's in the middle of this.

"I'm on a date, Marc."

When the words leave my mouth, he sucks in a breath and then releases it, causing his nostrils to flare. I'm not wanting to fight here.

I turn to my date. "I'm sorry. Could you excuse me for a minute?"

He nods. "Sure."

I peer back at Marc and say firmly, "Let's talk outside." I remove my napkin from my lap, putting it on the table before I stand. Walking around the table, I don't bother waiting for Marc to lead the way. He seems stuck to where he's standing.

Heading directly outside, my body trembles from him coming here tonight. Of all the damn places he had to walk into, it had to be here.

The universe is pushing us together. I can't deny it; I just want a little breathing room.

Heavy footsteps sound behind me, and I smile. Thankfully, he's following me and not traumatizing my date.

I push the door open and welcome the fresh night air.

Hugging my body from the cold, I look around for a spot to talk in private. But with not many options, I stand at the edge of the sidewalk, away from the door. I spin around and wait for him to stand in front of me. As he comes closer, he peels off his jacket.

"Is this your thing?"

His brow lifts in question. Clearly not understanding me.

I gesture to his gray jacket. "You give me a jacket every time I see you."

His lips twitch, but it goes back to a thin, hard expression instantly. He shrugs. "I don't like you standing out in the cold."

My stomach somersaults and this is exactly what the difference is...I feel every part of my being when I'm around Marc compared to my date. And the little things Marc does make him stand out.

"You don't have to worry about me," I say.

He moves to stand behind me, and I don't fight it. I take the jacket because I am in fact cold, and his jacket is covered in his aftershave, the manly scent doing something to me that I can't explain.

He doesn't move away, instead he whispers into my ear. "I want to worry about you. I enjoy taking care of you." I quiver from his gravelly voice, but the warm breath on my ear sends me into overdrive.

I try to speak, but my words are stuck in my chest. When he moves, I shiver from the cool air hitting my back.

Sucking in a deep breath through my mouth, I inhale him and shake my head to refocus.

"What are you doing here?" I ask, my voice uneven, giving away how unstable I feel, but he doesn't comment.

"What are you doing here?"

He stands toe to toe, not giving me too much space. I should take a step back so he can't invade my senses, but I love that he wants to be close to me. Because deep down, I want that too.

"I asked you first," I demand.

"I was grabbing takeout dinner."

I glance at the door, at a couple leaving, and then I focus on his deep brown eyes boring into mine.

He turns away to peer at the road. "Why?" he asks, bringing his gaze back to mine, and there is so much hurt swirling in them.

"Ava said that it was a good way to see..." I trail off.

"To see what?" he pushes, his tone growing frustrated.

I look away, needing him out of my head as I speak. "If you were the one or not. Because if I didn't feel anything for him, then it would at least answer one of the questions I have."

"What are the other questions?"

I bring my eyes back to him and frown. "I told you. If I want to be with you because you're a packaged deal and also, what if I want my own child in the future."

"I never said I wouldn't have a child with you."

"What?" I pull his jacket tighter around me.

"If it meant I'd lose you. I love my daughter, so kids are not an issue. It's just, I'm old."

"You're not old."

"Thirty-eight? Is still older, but children are not an issue. My daughter and the baggage, I get, but did you have to go on a date to figure that out?"

"No, that wasn't why I was on the date. It was to be sure these feelings were real and weren't just a memory from Christmas."

His hand goes to reach out to touch my face, but he pulls it back. I mourn the loss immediately. God, I wish he would have touched my cheek. I'd love to have his hands on me. He shakes his head and crosses his arms over his chest, as if to keep his hands to himself.

"It was real to me."

Fuck. The hurt look in his eyes is worse than before.

"It was real for me too," I say quietly. He's so close, I just want to yank his face to mine and kiss him passionately, and fuck it all, but I have to remind myself that I need to be 100 percent.

Why does being in a real relationship suck so much? Why can't shit be easy?

I have Marc right here, within arm's distance, and my date is waiting inside. I can't be rude. I need to go back in and end the date politely.

It's silent between us. I can only hear the blood rushing to my ears and my heavy breaths. I drop my chin and suck in a breath, then roll my shoulders back with new determination.

I'm about to say I need to go back in when he speaks. "And how does he make you feel? Do you want him?" He looks like he wants to say more, but he holds himself back, biting his tongue.

I know this is hurt talking because if I were walking in on him on a date, I'd be gutted. Fuck, it happened when I thought his ex-wife was a current woman. It tore me up.

I sigh. "No, I don't want him. But I still need a little more time to think."

He nods but doesn't say anything.

"I better—"

He cuts me off. "Get back to your date."

"Not like that, but I'm sure it's embarrassing for him, and it's not his fault he's in the middle of this."

"I'll let you go," he says, and adds, "Bye."

Fucking hell, this sucks.

He turns, and I reach out to grab his arm. "Marc."

When he looks back at me, his gaze goes to my hand on him, and I slide it down his arm and touch his hand briefly, loving the touch of his skin on mine. "Your jacket."

His face falls. Was he expecting something else?

"My jacket," he repeats before he watches me slide it off and hand it to him.

I stand here and watch him rest it over his arm instead of putting it back on, then he's walking away. I realize he never even got his dinner.

I can't seem to move my feet from the sidewalk until he disappears and I can no longer see him.

I sigh loudly and head back inside, ready to apologize to my date and explain I need to get home.

"You're home early. Was the date that bad?" Ava asks as she answers the phone.

"No. There was nothing wrong with him. But something happened."

"What happened?" she asks as she munches on something.

"So, we were sitting there, and he was nice, but there were no sparks or anything, you know."

"Oh, damn it. But at least you're back out there."

That makes me sit upright on the couch, clutching the phone. "Oh, no. There will be no more dates."

"Why? You need to try another guy. He might not be the right one."

"No. Marc is the right one."

"Oh, so you made a decision?"

"No, but guess who walked into the restaurant tonight?"

She gasps. "He didn't fucking follow you, did he?"

"No, of course not." I frown at her suggestion. "He was picking up takeout dinner, and he saw me."

"What did he do?"

I ease back onto the couch. "He came up to the table, mad as hell, and asked what I was doing?"

"No."

"Yep." I chuckle.

"Man, he really likes you."

"And I like him, but oh, that's right, so I told him we will talk outside. So I go outside, and he gives me his jacket because it's cold."

"Oh, swoon."

"Right, always thinking of me. But he said that he would have a child in the future, if I wanted one."

"Hang on. Don't tell me you agreed to have a kid with him? It's way too soon. I'll tell you now, it's not all sunshine and rainbows; pregnancy and a baby aren't easy."

"No, no, no. Not like that. But it came up in our conversation, and he said, if that was holding me back, he would happily give me a child. He just thinks he's too old." I rub my hand over my face, probably ruining my makeup, but I'm beyond caring after the disaster that was tonight.

"How old is he?" she asks.

"Thirty-eight?"

She snorts. "It's not old."

Exactly.

"I know, that's what I said. Anyway, he was so hurt, he was giving me these damn puppy dog eyes. It killed me." I slide down to lie on the couch. I'm getting tired from the night.

"But you said you liked him, so what's wrong?"

I kick off my shoes, but midway pause to answer her, shocked she needs me to remind her of this. "His daughter and my new job."

"Ah, yeah. They're still big things to take into account."

I return to kicking off the shoes and then curl up on my side. "That's what's holding me back. I don't want to just jump into his arms—"

"Or his bed," she says, cutting me off.

I laugh, even though it would be nice to be in his bed too. And then the laugh turns to a sigh…yeah, I miss him. "No, definitely not that either. I told him I'm still thinking."

"How did he react?"

"He didn't really say anything. But when he left, he just said bye."

"And what, did you want him to kiss you?"

"No." I giggle, though I remember how tempting the way standing there was, inches from me…I could have easily kissed him. "He just calls me *Bella*, or says something sweet."

"Oh, nicknames already. You two are screwed."

I grab the remote from the table in front of me and turn on the TV. "I know. I just need to figure out the last piece of the puzzle."

"He gave you his jacket. Did you keep it?" she asks. I screw up my face. "Why? That's weird, and he needs it to match his pants."

"I'm sure he owns hundreds of suits."

The money he has...I'm sure he does, but still no. "Maybe, but no, still weird."

"Plus, it would have been a good excuse to see him."

"We work on a joint venture every week, so I see him at least once a week."

"But that's for work."

That's true. Damn her for being right. I find a channel and put the remote back before getting comfortable.

"I have his number. I don't need any excuse to see or talk to him."

"Well, get sexting," she whispers.

I snort. "No chance."

As I sit on the couch watching TV, memories of him earlier haunt me. His tired, hurt eyes staring back at me instead of those big brown wide-set ones that stare at me with adoration. I miss those.

How do I get them back?

I try to change the channel to find something that can hold my attention, but I fail. Instead, I pull out my phone to send him a text.

Gracie: You didn't pick up your dinner.

It's only a couple of minutes when my phone chimes.

Marc: I'm not hungry anymore.

Reading those words hits me like a train.

Gracie: I'm sorry.

Marc: So am I.

I don't know what else to say. So I sit back and think about his daughter. But maybe I should find out more from him and see if that helps me make a decision.

Gracie: Tell me about her.

Marc: Who?

Gracie: Your daughter.

Marc: Why?

Gracie: I need to make a decision, and I think maybe talking about her might help.

Marc: Well, Aria is thirteen and the most fun-loving kid you'll ever meet. She loves a good movie night and thinks boys suck. (which, I'm not complaining about) She's kind, warm, and also very funny.

Gracie: Sounds like her dad. What's her favorite movie?

Marc: You think? I don't see how I'm funny, warm, and kind. Currently, when she visits, we are watching *The Hunger Games*.

Gracie: Yeah, maybe not funny, but you're warm and kind. I haven't seen it.

Marc: Maybe to you, but no one else I know would use those words to describe me.

Gracie: They don't know you like I do.

Marc: No, they don't.

I'm thinking of what else to say, when he sends another message.

Marc: She would happily have you here, so you can watch it with us.

I read the text line repeatedly.
Do I want to? How do I feel about that?
Pushing it away for now, I go back to find out more about her before I commit to a movie night. Even though that sounds like the best introduction if I decide to do this.

Gracie: Does she like school?

Marc: She does, but she has to if she wants to become a doctor when she grows up.

Gracie: A doctor. Wow, that's cool.

Marc: Yeah, she's pretty smart. That I know is from me.

Gracie: Tickets on yourself.

Marc: For intelligence, 100 percent.

Gracie: So what did you eat for dinner?

Marc: Eggs, toast, and turkey bacon.

Gracie: At least your appetite returned.

Marc: It did when you texted me.

Gracie: You made that while talking to me.

Marc: Yeah, and ate it too. I'm a master at multitasking.

I chuckle to myself before typing the final text.

Gracie: I better go and get ready for work tomorrow. Thanks for the chat.

Marc: Same. Goodnight, *Bella* x

That last word makes me smile. He's back.

CHAPTER 19

MARCO

I sit alone on my couch with three fingers of scotch. Sipping the amber liquid as I watch the football.

I wonder what she is doing. I haven't heard from her in a couple of days and this week's meeting was moved by the client, so I won't see her for another couple of days.

Bored and lonely, I pick up my phone to text her.

Marc: What are you doing?

Gracie: Watching *Real Housewives* on TV, why?

Marc: No particular reason. I'm just bored and thinking of you.

Gracie: You bored? Don't you have a business to run?

Marc: It's out of hours now.

Gracie: Still, I thought you never took time off.

Marc: I do at night. And when Aria comes.

Gracie: You actually take a weekend off?

Marc: Yes, why is that so hard to believe?

Gracie: I thought you were a workaholic...

Marc: Over the years, I've taken on less, so I have proper time off with her.

Gracie: What do you usually do on nights without her?

Marc: Nothing usually. I'm bored and lonely.

Gracie: That's cute.

Marc: What? Being bored is cute. How?

Gracie: No, silly. Just that without her, you're bored and lonely, so you obviously enjoy her company.

Marc: I do. And I enjoy yours too.

I smile as I hit send, wondering what she will think of that sneaky line.

Gracie: I enjoy yours too.

I sip the scotch and smile. Texting her was a smart choice.

Marc: It's so easy to just talk to you.

Gracie: You mean to talk shit too.

I chuckle loudly.

Marc: Exactly, but I could just sit next to you and say nothing and be content.

Gracie: Are you back to sweet Marc?

Marc: He never left. He's just waiting for a decision and giving you space.

Gracie: This is space?

Marc: I'm not pushing you for a relationship or an answer or to come to my house tonight. Even though I want it all.

Gracie: Greedy.

Marc: I'm so fucking greedy. You have no idea.

I drain my glass and wait for her response.

Gracie: Why do I feel like there is a hidden meaning to this?

Marc: There is. I'm so greedy for you. The things I'd do to you, you have no idea, but I'm waiting patiently...

Gracie: You have some very good control.

Marc: Don't worry, you will be punished, and I'll show you just how in control I can be.

Gracie: Marc...

Marc: Yes, *Bella*?

Gracie: We need to go back to the safe zone.

I sigh.

Marc: You got it.

I stand and pour another drink.

Marc: Do you have a favorite TV show right now?

I take the drink back to my position on the couch.

Gracie: Not really. I just watch any cheesy reality show.

Marc: Sounds boring.

Gracie: For boys, yes. For girls, no.

Marc: I watch thirteen-year-old movies. I'm sure I could sit through girly TV shows.

Gracie: Is that a challenge?

Marc: If it means I can hold you.

Gracie: Marc...

Marc: I better go because I keep slipping the longer we talk.

Gracie: Probably a good idea.

Marc: Goodnight, *Bella* x

Gracie: Goodnight, Marc.

I drain the glass and walk to my bedroom to strip and get into bed. Every night, I close my eyes and dream of her. And tonight is no different.

A few days later, there is another meeting with Jason. I sit and listen to him talk, occasionally peering over and catching a glimpse of Gracie. Sitting there in a pretty green top and a black jacket. Her hair is swept up into a bun, and it shows off her high cheekbones and tempting eyes.

"Okay, we made a decision for the first part," Jason says.

The picture of the winning design pops up and it's gray with blue undertones...it's theirs.

"Oh my god," Gracie mumbles around her hand that's covering her mouth. Her eyes are wide and glossy.

Mason smiles at her and says, "It's your design." And I'm no longer angry the competition won because it was her design. I'm fucking proud.

My face splits into a wide grin, and as she looks over, I mime, "Congratulations."

She mouths back, "Thanks."

Her face flushes pink, and then the client stops the celebration by changing the conversation to a new area for us to work on.

Using a new color pallet to work with the gray/blue of the sign.

The meeting lasts for an hour, and I pack up and leave. I want to catch Gracie to congratulate her properly, but Mason is talking to her. I follow them into the elevator, and I keep my eyes forward, not allowing myself to let them drift toward her.

Exiting onto the ground floor, I turn for my car and pull out my phone.

> **Marc:** Congratulations. You chose the blue, I heard.

> **Gracie:** I did. I'm still in shock.

> **Marc:** You deserve it.

> **Gracie:** Thanks. Aren't you sour because I'm the competition?

> **Marc:** Not if you chose it. I'm so fucking proud.

> **Gracie:** Oh, thank you.

Marc: Go work hard on the next part of the joint venture and see if your contribution wins again.

Gracie: I will. Game on, head down and ass up now.

I chuckle as I head back to my office.

CHAPTER 20

GRACIE

I carry a basket around the grocery store to pick up a few things for this weekend. Finding the snack aisle, I scan the shelves, looking for the right sweet treat.

I pick up my favorite Little Debbie Christmas Tree Cakes and Gingerbread cookies.

"Oh, what a mix." I turn to the sound of Marc's voice, but my eyes widen when I see his daughter Aria standing beside him.

"Yeah. Ah. I don't know which one to choose for the weekend," I say, holding up the two bags.

"I say cakes," Marc says, but Aria is shaking her head.

"No, cookies all the way."

I smile. "That doesn't help."

"Why not get both?" Aria suggests.

"I think I will." I put them both in my basket, and when I look back up, Marc's smiling.

"Are you looking for candy too?" I ask them.

"Yeah, it's movie weekend," Marc says, knowing he's explained it to me. "Aria, this is my friend, Gracie. Gracie, this is my daughter, Aria."

I smile. "Nice to meet you, Aria. So, what snacks and candy goes with your movie weekend?" I ask, flicking my gaze between the two.

"I like Snickers," Marc says.

"And I'm an M&M fan," Aria says.

"What flavor M&M?" I ask.

"Just the original chocolate."

"Good choice," I add.

My gaze holds Marc's for a beat and there is a shine to it. Clearly, he's enjoying this exchange and surprisingly, I am too.

"I better check off the rest of my list, and leave you two to shop for the movie," I say, shifting the basket in the opposite hand.

"Why don't you join us? We are watching *The Hunger Games*, and I know you haven't seen it," Marc says.

"You haven't seen *The Hunger Games*?" His daughter gasps and then her mouth hangs open.

I shake my head, my muscles freezing as panic swells up inside me. This is new for me, and I just don't know if I'm ready right now, so I brush it off. "No, I haven't seen it. I wouldn't want to impose on your weekend."

"Nonsense, you wouldn't. We would love for you to join us. Right, Aria?" Marc says, not taking no for an answer. I'm about to protest again, but as soon as I open my mouth, Aria interrupts.

"Sure. The fact you haven't seen that movie yet is a crime," she says, crossing her arms over her white sweat-shirt.

"Well, we can't have that, can we?" Marc says, offering me a wink. Both of them are watching me, as nerves rise to my throat and constrict me of breath.

What do I do...

I need to think quickly. If I say no, will that be an opportunity gone to get to know Aria? And will I lose my chance at winning his heart?

If I go tonight, it's only a movie, so there isn't a lot of talking and the movie will distract us. But at least it will be a good tester to see if this is something I can handle. The way my heart is in my throat right now, I don't know if that will be the case, but I don't want to lose him. So with that said, I could try? What's the worst that could happen? I hate the movie? Or choke on the popcorn and require mouth to mouth from him...

"If you don't mind, I'll be up for it. I just need to grab some food and drop it by my house. What time is the movie starting?" I ask.

I also want to run home and phone Ava. I need to talk this out with her. Hopefully, she has some good advice.

Aria looks at Marc and shrugs. Turning toward me, she says, "Whenever you come."

It shouldn't be too long...unless Ava distracts me.

"Don't rush. Whenever you turn up, it's fine," Marc soothes with the biggest shit-eating grin that reaches his eyes, showing the lines around them. He grabs Aria around the shoulders to guide her away.

"Okay, well, I'll go, and I'll see you soon."

"See you soon." Marc smiles, turning around, leaving the aisle, and I stay stuck into place, quivering but finally able to breathe.

When I finally get my legs working again, I stroll through the rest of the store, picking up essentials.

As soon as I get home, I unpack and call Ava.

"What's up?" she answers.

I blow out a breath and quickly explain. "I bumped into Marc and his daughter at the store before."

"Ohhh."

I love how excited she gets, even though I'm still racked with nerves.

"And he invited me to watch a movie at his place."

"Just you two? I hope you said yes."

I wince, remembering at first how I wanted to say no, but felt like they both wanted me to be there, so I couldn't.

"No, his daughter will be there too. I couldn't say no; his daughter was horrified that I hadn't seen *The Hunger Games*."

"You haven't seen *The Hunger Games*?" she exclaims.

I close my eyes and pinch the bridge of my nose. "Not you too."

"Everyone has seen it."

"Clearly, not everyone," I retort.

"So, you two and his daughter are all hanging out. You're nervous, and that's why you're calling."

I let out a nervous laugh while I stand in front of my wardrobe, looking at my clothes. "Yes, I'm freaking out. What do I wear?"

"What are you asking me for? You know how to dress yourself."

I step forward and grab my favorite comfy black acid wash jeans. Touching the soft denim before letting it go and stepping back again. "I know, but do I go in jeans or sweats?"

"Did you just seriously say jeans?"

I pause, frowning. What's wrong with jeans? They hug my curves in all the right places and when I sit for long periods of time, they don't dig in. "Yeah, why?"

"No, it's at his house for a movie night. Jeans scream *I'm trying too hard*. Wear sweats."

I pinch my lips together, still not certain, but I need to trust her. It's why I called, right? Advice, and that's exactly what she's giving me, so I'm best to follow. "Okay, I'll go through my sweats and find a nice pair."

"What time do you have to go?"

I lean over to pull open my drawer, sorting through them. "No set time, just whenever I turn up."

She groans. "That's the worst. It's like, pick a time so I can stick to it."

I pull a few out and toss them behind me to land on my bed. I laugh at her comment, knowing that's how I feel. I prefer set times and schedules. "I know, right? I think because I had to finish my shopping and get ready, they didn't want to put any pressure on me. Yet, I'm frantic."

I run my hand through my greasy hair. Another time-consuming task to do before I leave unless I use dry shampoo; but what if he touches my hair? I'll be thinking of how yucky my hair must feel. Nope, I can't have that, so I need to shower.

"Well, talk to me on speaker as you get ready. It will distract you."

"Good idea. But I need to shower quickly, so I'll call you right back."

"Yeah, freshen up in case, you know, things go well, and you better call me tomorrow. I need all the gossip."

I smile, knowing how excited I was when I got to hear about all of her and Josh's dates, so I get her enthusiasm. I just wish I was feeling more excited than nervous.

The food and essentials are all put away, and now I'm getting ready. I found a comfy yet cute matching pair of cream sweats. I braided my hair and popped a little fresh makeup on. Mascara, concealer, and gloss. When I'm ready and I can't stall any longer, I leave my house and begin the walk to his, bringing the cakes and cookies with me.

The closer I get to his brownstone, the more my heart rate increases. And the fear of Aria not liking me. And is this all too good to be true? I don't have enough time to dwell, though, because I turn the corner and cross the road, and I'm staring up at his wooden door.

Here goes...

I press the bell and wait for him to answer. But it's not him. Aria answers the door, wearing a pair of black leggings and a pink sweater. Her hair is in a messy bun on top of her head.

"Hi, Gracie," she says with a smile, opening the door wider. "Come in."

I smile back, my nerves still weighing me down heavily.

"Thanks, Aria. I brought the cakes and cookies." I step inside the house, and I immediately internally bug out. This is serious money. The dark brown wooden floors complement the cream walls, and the dark wooden staircase is lit with a warm glow from small lights trailing all the way upstairs.

"Oh, goodie," she says, distracting me from checking out more of the house. And I chuckle at her excitement. It makes me feel better that she seems happy I'm here.

She takes the stairs, and I follow.

Reaching the next level, I suck in a breath. It's gorgeous. The large cream couch is double the size of mine and looks way dreamier. I bet I could sink right into it.

He has the largest wooden table that seats eight, with black metal chairs, and I wonder if he has dinner parties to use all of them.

I keep following her until we reach the kitchen, and my jaw drops. It's massive. I've never seen one this big or beautiful. Movement flickers from the side, and I turn to find he's watching me, leaning on an entry wall. Aria has gone somewhere, leaving just us.

"Welcome." He pushes off the wall and comes to stand near me, and I realize my nerves have completely calmed, replaced with butterflies and warmth. Only he can do this to me.

"Your house is stunning. I've never seen a house like it."

He steps even closer until he's right in front of me, closing any distance between us. He's smiling so big, I can't help but smile too.

"Thanks. Would you like a drink?" he asks, his gaze on me, but his hand touches my arm unexpectedly and the warmth turns to heat as he softly strokes up and down, ever so gently.

"Yeah, a soda, please."

He raises a brow. "Alcohol? I have a bar."

My mouth pops open, and I leave his face to glance around the kitchen, not finding any bar in or near it. "Where?"

"Just behind this wall." He points to the entryway he was watching me from before.

I bring my gaze to his intoxicating eyes and smirk. "Maybe next time."

His face brightens and a matching smirk forms as he whispers with a wink. "Next time?"

I roll my eyes at his insinuation, and a small laugh leaves me. "A slip of the tongue."

His eyes flicker to heat, and I realize what I've said. I choose to ignore it, but then it gets the better of me. "I didn't mean it in that way."

"What do you mean?" He smirks, but there is a twinkle in his eye.

"You know exactly what I mean."

The butterflies turn into an ache that sinks into my belly.

"What are you talking about?" Aria asks from behind me.

I jump and slap a hand to my chest, feeling my heart beating hard behind it. When did she sneak up on me? And how much did she hear?

"Nothing, we were just grabbing sodas. Did you want one?" Marc asks.

I drop my hand and realize I'm still holding the bag of snacks. "Where did you want these?"

"I'll pop them in a bowl." He goes to take the food, and our hands touch, a buzz running through my arm from the brief connection.

"I can do it," I say with a smile. I need something to do. "Just point me to where the bowls are kept."

He turns, and I get a whiff of his sexy cologne, my body rumbling awake at the memories of that smell stuck to the sheets back in Chicago. I definitely didn't wash my sheets for a while. I probably shouldn't admit it, but it's true.

He grabs a bowl from one of the top cupboards. "Here you go."

I had been staring at him, as I was lost in a flashback, so I shake my head, trying to clear my thoughts. When I trail my eyes back to his, I see him wearing an amused look. *Busted.* He knows I was checking him out; I'm just grateful he can't read my mind.

"Thanks." I move to the counter and help. Our bodies stay side by side, and the feeling that runs through me is nice, almost domesticated.

"Are you ready?" He inclines his head with a grin.

I bite my lip. Disappointment from having to lose the moment of us alone mixes with excitement that there will be peace for an hour and a half, at least. My mind needs to do something that doesn't involve feelings; it's getting tired from all the work. I just want to recline in a comfy chair and eat snacks with him in the room. "Yep."

"Let's go. Follow me." He smiles, then dips his head and touches my upper back, guiding me. I love the subtle touches on me any moment he can. It's like he can't get enough of me, and it keeps the desire and the feeling that he wants me at the forefront of my mind.

I carry the bowls, and he holds the drinks as I follow him. The shiny wooden floors look almost new.

"How long have you had this house?"

"Ten years."

"Really? Wow."

He keeps it in such good condition. But I guess when you own a house this expensive, you can upgrade whenever you want. Have any problems fixed without waiting to save multiple paychecks.

I wonder what that's like.

With this new job, I have more money than from the bar. And the house I rent is better than anything I could have dreamed of. I just wish I could own a place like this.

We step into a room with cinema seats and a wall with the credits of the movie takes up a whole side. My mouth parts in awe.

"You have a projector?"

He gives me a smile. "Yeah, why?"

"Nothing."

Nothing at all.

"It seriously is the best. I don't think I could go back to watching a movie on a regular TV now. It's not a vibe."

I get that it would be hard to go backward after this type of lifestyle.

Aria sits down in one chair, and Marc sits beside her. "Come here." He pats the chair beside him, his eyes trained on mine.

The giddy excitement is back. But I also can't help but wonder if Aria thinks anything about it.

"Where do you want these?" I ask, peering around for a table or something.

"Hang on a sec, *Bel*—" He stops mid-talk when he starts to say my nickname, saving himself at the last moment.

He clears his throat and walks out to grab a low table, placing it down. Then he takes the bowls from my hand, brushing mine. It's brief and the soft way he touched me made me wonder if it was on purpose. It was nice and warm, and it triggers my memory of the way he held me.

How nice would it be to fall asleep and wake up with him holding me again?

Being here tonight made accepting a kid easier, which would help matters. But it's still early, so let's see how the night unfolds.

"Are you ready for the greatest movie?" Aria asks me.

I look over, and she's leaning forward, looking at me.

I smile and say, "Yeah, I can't wait."

"Oh, the popcorn. I'll grab it. Hold on, I'll be one minute."

He rushes out, leaving me and her alone. And the nerves return. I wet my lips and press them together as we stay silent and, thankfully, Marc is back quickly. I slump back into the chair, and the tension releases from my body.

The movie plays, and I really enjoy it. When it ends, I stretch out and yawn. These chairs are so comfortable, I could have slept, but the movie was surprisingly entertaining.

"What did you think?" Aria asks, leaning in and wearing an eager smile.

If I didn't like it, I would have a hard time telling her, because the cute way she is beaming at me, I couldn't break her heart. Lucky for both of us, I did. I nod and smile back. "It was good. I really liked it."

"There is more. So you will have to come back for *Catching Fire*," she says, licking her lips.

I flinch a little. Come back? Something I joked about in the kitchen earlier with Marc, but it's brought up again. With her head nodding rapidly, I find myself unable to say no. It's not that I don't want to come back; I'm still overwhelmed with getting to know her. She was kind and sweet, and I should have expected that because of who her father is, but I still did worry deep down that it wasn't going to work out. I didn't want to get my hopes up.

Every time I get my hopes up, I get crushed. Having low expectations or none at all prevents the pain.

Her little mouth opens into a loud yawn, and I know it's my cue to leave.

"That sounds like a deal. But I better get going."

"How did you get here?" Marc asks.

Craning my neck, I see him standing in front of his chair, running a hand through his hair, then over his face. He pops a brow when I haven't answered him.

"I walked," I rush out and quickly stand, meeting his gaze head on.

He stares at me and softly shakes his head. "You're not walking home alone. I'll call my driver."

He pulls his phone out of his pocket and is about to call, when I grab his arm to stop his movement. "Don't be silly, it's not far."

I've not been brought up with that help and availability. He's already been so kind, and I'm grateful, but I don't want to overstay my welcome or take advantage.

His face is hard and his lips thin. "No. You'll take my offer."

A snort comes from Aria, and I turn to her, still sitting in her chair. Her face is amused, and she looks up at me, saying, "Just take the driver, trust me."

I can't help but laugh at her, clearly knowing her father better than me.

"You, sweetheart, go shower and get into bed." He looks at Aria with a smile.

"I'm tired anyway. Night, Gracie. Night, Dad."

"Goodnight, Aria," I say with a warm smile as she waves at me.

She leaves the room and I go to take the empty bowls, but he touches my back, sending my pulse to rise. "Leave it, please. I'll do it later," he says softly.

I try to ignore how the one simple touch affects my whole body every damn time. The heat floods me where his hand is, and I straighten. When his hand drops, I miss the contact instantly.

"It will be done quicker if we do it together," I say with a breathier voice than usual.

"No, it's fine. I'm not tired."

His tone has me standing and not fighting with him.

"Okay, and I'll take the lift, but only because I'm tired. Work was busy this week."

"Let me call, and I'll walk you out."

We leave the cinema room, and he texts on his phone. We take the stairs down, and he opens the door. When we step out, I see the black car waiting, so I make my way forward, but I'm pulled gently back by the arm.

My face an inch from his, I watch his eyes drop to my lips, and it makes my mouth suddenly dry. He brings his gaze to mine, and there is a silent plea. Licking my lips, I try to moisten them, and the way his handsome face looks at me sends a swarm of renewed flutters into my lower belly.

"I want you so much. Do you know how much I miss you?"

"No," I breathe with a soft shake of my head.

"A lot. More than I should. But there is something unforgettable about you. And when you come here and spend time with me and my daughter, it hits me." He taps his chest before reaching out to grab my hand.

I glance down at our joined hands and watch him rub his thumb over the back of mine in circles. They are soft and hypnotic. I drag my gaze back to his face.

"I've missed you too."

He smiles and my heart swells. I love that smile on him. It's my favorite. It's soft and inviting. It totally melts me on the spot.

I reach out with my spare hand and grab his neck, stepping into him and closing the distance between us. And I don't wait a second more before crashing my lips onto his. He doesn't waste time either, kissing me back even harder and more passionately. Our joined hands disconnect so we can touch each other. Mine snakes around his neck to join the other one as I push my body flush against his. My breasts are heavy, and my nipples are peaked. Just being in his orbit again makes me horny. My tongue grazes his lips, begging for entry. And when he opens and tangles his tongue with mine, I can't hold back the little whimper that escapes me.

It tastes salty and sweet and totally him. I can't stop kissing him, even though I'm struggling to breathe. So I just inhale his oxygen.

He groans, and I can feel his hard, thick cock hitting my stomach through his pants. I can't help but move a little, bringing his sexy grunts back.

His hand moves from my hips to my ass, pushing me harder into him. Holding my hips, he grinds me along his length. This is dangerous. I'm so close to asking him if I can stay, but that can't happen. I still haven't decided if we should date.

The other issue is Aria being here. I still want to get to know her, and I need to respect her space.

I let him continue moving me over his dick, and even though I'm throbbing, I push down hard too. My hands are circling into his hair, trying to grip, and I'm totally lost in the feeling of us. When we pull apart, I'm panting hard. I try to suck some deep breaths of air into my lungs so I can speak.

"Oh, *Bella*, I want to take you back inside and spread you on every surface of my house and have my way with you."

A soft moan slips from me, imagining him fucking and licking me all around his gorgeous place.

"Imagine all the positions I could have you in."

I can imagine vividly.

"Marc. That was..." I struggle to form a full sentence.

He cuts me off with another breathless kiss, and I grab the back of his head and kiss him back once more.

His hand skims my lower back and grabs my ass to lift me. I accept and enjoy the way he holds me effortlessly, breaking the kiss to move my hands to the sides of his face. Holding him tenderly and laying a brief kiss on him that needs to be our last tonight.

"You're dangerous."

"And you're tempting. I am holding on to the last bit of restraint I have."

I swallow hard. "Aria."

"Exactly why I haven't already taken you to my bed. Because don't mistake me. I want you in it and I'll have you in it...soon."

I don't answer because I don't know what to say. I guess I agree.

But what does this mean now? His presence definitely has a way of clouding my thoughts.

"You are definitely winning me over; I can tell you that."

"So it's less of an issue now?" he asks, wiggling his brows at me.

I can't help but smile at his lit-up face. He's so damn cute. But I can't go running off into the sunset and get his or my hopes up. Baby steps.

"Well, I feel okay with it," I say, staring down into his dark eyes. Under the stars and the moon, I can see his eyes in a different light. Still drawing me in close to him.

His large smile is back. "That's all I can ask for."

With the way he's looking at me now, a wash of nerves and panic hits me. Does he think I'm all in?

I swallow the lump in my throat and hope what I'm about to say doesn't hurt him, but I need to be sure we are on the same page. "Just to be clear, we're still not dating. I have my job to consider." I exhale while looking up into his eyes. And as I watch his face soften, I breathe again.

"No, only when you're ready. I won't push you." His lips twist, as if trying to hold back a smile. "Much."

I giggle and peck him on the lips, but I pull away slowly. He lowers me to the floor, and being here like this as he holds me up, I feel young and free. No work or home life to think about.

Just me and him in each other's arms.

CHAPTER 21

GRACIE

I squeeze my eyes shut and mumble, "Please, Ava, answer your phone."

"Hey," she pants.

"What are you doing? Why are you out of breath?"

"I've been deep cleaning the kitchen."

"Isn't it too early for nesting?"

"I'm not nesting. I just feel nauseous seeing all the dirt."

I scrunch up my nose. "If it makes you feel better, then do it. Do you want me to let you go?"

"No. No. Talk to me. I'll just finish the stove while we talk."

"Doesn't Josh have a cleaner?"

I'm totally confused. Why is she cleaning if she doesn't have to? It's the worst chore, yet she is doing it by choice.

"Yeah, but I don't want her doing that."

"Why not? She's the cleaner? You hire her to clean."

"You sound like Josh."

"Because you're pregnant and we don't want you doing things you don't have to do."

"I know you both care and I love you both, but I'm fine. I'm totally capable of doing this."

"Fine," I mutter.

"Let's change the topic, and you need to tell me about the movie last night."A stupid grin appears on my face just being reminded of it. "Well, I'll start with Aria. She was cute and so easy to be around. Even in silent times when it should have been awkward, it was surprisingly okay."

"That's good, so you're warming to the idea of her."

I pause a beat. Really thinking deeply. How did it feel to be with them?

"Yeah, I am. Even sitting there, just the three of us, it was nice. We watched the movie, ate snacks, and it wasn't uncomfortable at all."

"So what does this mean? Will you date him?"

"I had two hours at their house, only speaking to them for maybe thirty minutes. I want more time, but I guess I'm leaning toward a yes."

"I say dive in and get to know them in time."

I shake my head at her eagerness. "He hasn't asked me out. And I don't know how it will affect my job. But I'll decide in the moment how I feel. But we kissed."

She gasps. "No way. When?"

"I was going to walk home, but he insisted I let his driver take me." I laugh. "You should have seen his face when I tried to argue with him. He wasn't having it."

"They have no idea about the streets, do they?" She laughs.

"No. We find comfort walking them. Not an ounce of fear in me," I say, with memories of my time with Ava and our small stint on the streets and in shelters.

"So, you obviously took the offer."

I smile, remembering the way Aria told me to take the offer, knowing her father is bossy. And I can't deny he was being all protective and cute. And who doesn't want that?

"Yeah, I let him win. I was tired from the week at work anyway."

"Now tell me about this hot kiss."

"I never said it was hot," I tease her.

"You said after Christmas he was the best guy you've ever been with."

Well, fuck, she got me there, didn't she?

"I did, didn't I? Well, he walks me out, and I kissed him. I was staring at him so close, and he is so fucking handsome, I just needed to. Probably a dumb thing."

"Why?" she asks, still not understanding my issue.

I groan loudly. I can forget my head if it wasn't stuck on. He makes me forget and want to be in the moment.

"Because I was close to sleeping over," I explain.

"Oh, then why didn't you?" She sucks in a breath excitedly.

"Aria," I remind her.

"Ah, yeah. That wouldn't have been a good thing." She laughs. And I shiver at the thought. Nope, I couldn't face her. I don't know how it works having sex when your stepdaughter is around. Is there like a dummy for being a stepmom book? Because if there is, I need it.

"Exactly. So I had to go home horny, but...um, at least I got one hell of a kiss." I feel a flush run up my neck and onto my face, and I'm so glad she isn't here to see me.

She whistles. "Good for you. At least someone is getting action."

"Why, what's wrong?" I ask, sitting up a little. Worried there is trouble in paradise and not being in the same state anymore has me fretting.

"Joshua keeps thinking he is going to poke the baby, so he doesn't want to have sex."

I laugh so hard and when I recover, I say, "He can't be serious. Take him to your next appointment and get the doctor to explain it."

"I will, but that's a couple of weeks away. What do I do until then?"

I think for a second about what she could do, and an idea pops into my mind.

"Oh, I know. Get a toy out and when he gets home, he can walk in on you using it. If that doesn't get him wanting to fuck you, I don't know what will."

"That's a really good idea. So clever."

"Glad I can help you. It seems you've been listening to my shit for too long. Giving me advice, so now it's my turn to help."

"That's what friends are for."

It's different at the meeting today. As I drink him in, I admire the fit of his navy suit and white shirt. He stares back at me openly, and I can't help but hold it for a few beats longer. I wonder if he's thinking about the kiss we shared a few nights ago.

I drop my gaze to his big full lips that taunt me. God, how I'd love a taste of them.

Moving my eyes back up, they collide with his heated gaze, and it sends a shiver through me. I know he's thinking the exact same thing.

Jason talking pulls me away from Marc's face and back to work. Exactly where it should have been, and I settle into work mode.

The new concept we have to design is the top floor. It's an office building, but this floor is the CEO's, with a bathroom included.

I scribble any bits that Jason says without thought in case it has any value to our design later on.

My phone vibrates in my pocket, and I can't look at it, but when I drag my eyes to his, there is a twist to his lips, and he lifts his chin to me.

He sent me a text.

The fact I can't open it kills me with anticipation.

The meeting goes on for another thirty-five minutes and the whole time my phone is burning a hole in my pocket.

When we are finished, I round the table, bringing us toe to toe.

"Good morning, Gracie."

"Morning, Marco."

His grin is mischievous, and I just want to know what he's thinking.

We step into the full elevator. He purposefully stands next to me, his shoulder touching mine. It's like he just wants to touch me, and I can't help but feel my heart flicker a bit.

I quickly remember the text I've been dying to read. The elevator hits the ground floor, and he steps away from me. I read his text with a full smile.

> **Marc:** You're killing me. Sitting there with those pink luscious lips that I'm desperate to taste again. When will you indulge me and let

me take you on a date? I want more time with you. Remember, I'm a greedy man.

I type out my response while I walk.

Gracie: I'll check my schedule.

Marc: Don't take too long.

Gracie: I'm just joking. I'm free any time.

Marc: Saturday night? I'll pick you up at six-thirty.

Gracie: Sounds good.

Marc: It's a date.

I laugh loudly and wear a stupid grin on my face for the rest of the day.

It's Saturday night, and I have less than twenty minutes to figure out what I want to do with my hair. The date is making me a little queasy. The bundle of nerves causes me to overthink everything. I had to ask Ava to help me decide on an outfit. She told me to wear my best lingerie, which was the only advice she provided.

I run the curling wand through my hair, and looking at the time, I realize I have less than five minutes. So, I add some pink lipstick and put my shoes on. Tonight's choice is black stilettos.

When I'm all done, I stand in my kitchen and check inside my bag. Adding the lipstick and a compact for touch ups and other than that, I stand waiting. Should I wait outside?

No. I shake my head. That seems too eager. I don't want to look desperate, so I'll wait here until the doorbell rings.

The sound echoes, and the rush of excitement hits me. He's here.

I grab my bag and slowly walk to the door. Before I reach the handle, I suck in a deep breath, trying to calm the adrenaline pulsing through me.

Finally pulling it open, I'm welcomed by the sight of him.

I've never seen him in jeans, so my breath is lost when I take him in. His black jeans are thigh-hugging, and he's wearing a shirt that's more of a relaxed cotton, rolled up at the sleeves, with a few buttons undone at the top. He's making me delirious with how deliciously handsome he looks.

The small amount of exposed skin I can see on his chest and neck makes me lick my lips. Yeah, tonight is definitely only going to end in one way.

His eyes shimmer under my porch light, making me get lost for a moment. There are no other worries; it's just me and him and tonight. He holds out his hand and smiles as I place mine in his. Closing our hands together in a tangle. They feel good together, and feel familiar.

"My goodness, you're a vision."

I offer a shy smile, feeling every bit of a giddy young woman. The lightness I feel when he compliments me has me desperate for more.

I've never received so many. And from Marc, it's everything.

He's everything.

He makes me believe they're true. Including appreciating my drive for the future and how he saw a bigger and better one for me that makes every kind word from him mean so much more.

"Thank you. You look very hot yourself," I say.

His smile broadens, making me smile bigger too. "Only for you." His dark eyes hold mine, then they slowly trail down openly over my body. My stomach flips from the way he hungrily looks at me, and I can't help but wonder if we should just skip dinner and go inside.

I shake off those thoughts. I don't want to miss out on the lovely night he has planned. "Well, thanks. I feel special."

"You deserve to. You're very special to me." He reaches out to touch my face, and I lean into it.

"Are we back to being cute and cheesy?" I tease, biting my lip.

He pulls my lip out from my teeth with his thumb. "Yeah, and now instead of texts, I'll tell you with words."

"You like your words," I say with a knowing grin.

He kisses me briefly, causing my eyes to flutter. "I love words. Especially yours." His deep voice turns down a notch, and I feel the sound between my legs.

Is it a longing that I'm feeling? Maybe he is dying to orgasm too? I wonder if his ache is as painful as mine.

He ushers me into his car and the driver takes off.

"Where are we going?" I ask.

"Somewhere private, but I want to keep it a surprise."

"How much time do we have?"

"Twenty minutes. Why?" He squints, eyeing me critically.

Do I?

Fuck it.

I lean in close to his ear to ask, "Can we get some privacy?"

He leans forward, hitting a button. The screen goes up and so does my heart rate.

But before I have a chance to move, his hand touches my thigh, skimming the inner most tender skin. My body quivers when he reaches down to my panties.

He twists in his seat and whispers, "I've missed you. I've missed this. Will you let me touch you?"

"Yesss," I breathe.

"You want one finger or two?"

Jesus Christ.

"Whatever you give me."

His fingers brush over the sparse piece of fabric covering me.

"More," I beg.

"Have you been with anyone else since?"

I shake my head. "No."

"Good. Neither have I."

His touch grows a little firmer, and his breath tickles my neck.

I lift my hips, moving against his strong fingers. The flare of heat hits my back, and this is good, but not enough.

"I'm going to fuck you with two fingers."

His breath on my ear is warm, and it causes a shiver to run through me.

"Right now," I beg.

He grunts, "Right now," biting my earlobe as he moves his hand under the lace, caressing his fingers through my slick folds and around my opening.

"So ready. And so fucking wet." His voice wavers, and I move my hand to find him rock hard and just as big as I remember him. He continues the up and down motion, but does not enter, and I'm growing frustrated.

"Please."

He rubs my clit in slow, tantalizing circles, then finally pushes through and enters me. I choke on a moan, only able to hold it back because of the driver. Instead, I bite his shoulder, muffling my sounds.

As he pulls his fingers out, I shudder. I miss the tight full feeling his fingers gave me. He doesn't make me wait much longer, before he's entering me again, and I'm widening my legs. I release my mouth from him as his gaze drops to my lips.

"I want to kiss you, but I also love the pink shade on your lips, and I don't want to ruin the rest of your makeup."

"I don't care."

"I do. I love the effort you put in for me. It doesn't go unnoticed. But maybe..."

He licks his lips and leans in, and I suck in a sharp breath. His warm lips caress my neck, and he kisses down lower until he hits my collarbone. I think he's about to stop, but instead he goes lower. He trails kisses over my chest and onto my breasts, my breathing increasing as I watch him. Then he's moving to the other breast and back up my neck before kissing just under my ear. I'm panting and feverish, more so with every kiss.

I'm so worked up, I could come in less than two seconds.

I close my eyes and just enjoy the heaviness in my breasts, the coiled tension in my lower belly getting stronger, and I chase the release. My legs quake, my breath catching, the tingle working its way through my core, right on the edge, and he slips his fingers out.

What's he doing? He uses my slickness to rub my bundle of nerves, and I try to get him to penetrate me again by shifting my hips. But he keeps rubbing my clit as his mouth moves to my neck, his teeth dragging against my exposed skin, and it's driving me wild.

I'm so horny and so damn close that tears spring to my eyes. I need to fucking come.

His mouth moves to my ear, and his hand retracts, my eyes snapping open with the movement.

"What are you doing?" I grit out through my clenched teeth.

"We're here," he breathes with a smug grin.

Mother. Fucker.

CHAPTER 22

MARCO

B ringing her to the edge and not letting her orgasm was one of the hottest things to watch. The way she clenched around my fingers, her sexy pants, her thighs trembling as she begged. I knew she was close. But holding it will pay off later when she comes so hard she'll see stars. It's a high I can't explain.

I bet after she comes tonight, she will crave that feeling again and again.

I help her out of the car and into the restaurant. There is a slight pinch in her expression as we enter an elevator, but when we step out, she sees the view of Manhattan at night. Her face slacks and she slowly looks around, taking it all in. Then she turns to me and her mouth opens to speak, but the waitress interrupts.

We follow her onto the rooftop, where the igloos are dimly lit with a blue hue. Gracie's hand goes to her mouth as her wide eyes take in the setup.

The night sky is the perfect backdrop for us. I wanted a romantic feel but with a touch of fun.

The waitress takes us to our igloo, even though I hired the whole place just for us. We have our own, so we can take in the city views and spend quality time together.

Stepping inside, we take a seat opposite each other on a white couch, and between us is a white table with a glowing light.

"The menus are there. I'll give you two a couple of minutes, and I'll be back to take your drink orders."

When the waitress leaves, Gracie speaks. "What the hell?"

I chuckle at her response. "So you like it?"

She smirks and softly shakes her head. "This is crazy."

"In a good or bad way?"

"Good, but over the top. Just us here?"

"Mm-hmm, I wanted time alone."

"Doesn't mean you have to hire the whole place." She laughs.

"You deserve it."

Looking around again, she says, "I do like the privacy." Her gaze holds mine, and she raises her brow and whispers, "Maybe you could finish what you started."

I smirk. "Not going to happen."

"Damn it." She giggles.

And it makes me chuckle too. "What would you like to eat?"

We pick up the menus and decide on the sharing plate option.

The waitress comes to take our food and drink order.

"You know, this is a little extreme. You don't have to impress me," she says when the waitress leaves.

"I do, and I want to know more about you."

"What do you want to know?"

I lean back on the white couch, cross my ankle over my leg, and rub my jaw as I think.

"First. Your family. I know you don't have siblings, but that's all."

Her face pales, and she takes a breath before meeting my gaze. A flicker of pain washes through them, and I shift in my chair.

"Well, this requires a drink." She laughs, but it's strained.

"Let's wait for them if you want." I don't want her to be uncomfortable. But worry swirls in my gut, and I hate that I have to wait longer for the information.

Our drinks come, and I encourage her to go on.

"I grew up in a not so nice house. I left home at fifteen and lived in a shelter until the bar owners offered me a place to stay and a job."

"What do you mean, not so nice?" I ask. My spine is straightened, and the blood is rushing to my head. The thought of her having a bad childhood is tearing me up inside. But it explains her mentioning not being held and her need for independence.

"Domestic abuse."

I swallow hard. Domestic abuse. I'm conflicted. One part of me wants to know more, but then I worry if I find out too much, I will want to hunt the fuckers down and kill them myself.

"That's awful, and I'm so sorry you had to go through that." I reach over and grab her hand. Giving us the touch we both need right now.

She looks at my hand in hers, and I wonder what she's thinking.

"So am I. I met Ava, my best friend, at the shelter, though, and my fill-in parents really are great."

"The positive still doesn't help. It shouldn't have happened."

"No, you're right, it shouldn't have. But it did, and I just try to move on and be grateful for every day. Like, look at this." She smiles, and it cracks my chest wide open.

I realize how this would feel to her and I just want to do so much more. She deserved better. But this also makes me even more proud of her for working so hard and getting her fresh start here.

"I'm really glad you like it. I just want to make you happy."

"You do, well, except in the car. I'm frustrated at that." She grins.

"It will be worth it."

"I don't know about that."

I chuckle.

She sips her drink, so I do the same, and then ask, "Do you miss home?"

"I miss my friends and the familiarity. But the adventure and self-discovery I'm having here outweighs anything."

I smile and take another drink, draining my glass. "Good, because I don't want you running back there." I reach over to touch her face, and when she leans in, I kiss her. Her wine-tasting lips are so drugging.

"I won't. I love this city," she breathes against my lips.

We kiss again before we sit back, staring lost at each other.

The food and more drinks come, interrupting our moment. We pick at the pizza and nachos. Between having our new drinks and music softly playing in the background, I want to have her close to me.

"Do you want to dance?"

"Like slow dance?"

I smile broadly. She is so innocently cute. "Yeah."

She shrugs. "I've never done it, but how hard can it be?"

If we're talking about my dick, it's rock hard. But I keep that thought to myself.

We stand and close the distance between us. My hand slips into one of hers, and the other wraps around her middle. While she holds on to my shoulder, I lead her around. She is soft and somber in my hands, and we dance effortlessly. Even though she's never done this before, she's a total natural. Or is it because we are together and everything with us is just so easy? I hold her gaze as we move. At some point, my face moves closer, and I lean my forehead on hers. I just breathe and soak in every second.

"This is incredible. To have you here in my arms was never something I thought would become real. But here you are, and I couldn't be any happier."

She pulls her face away from mine and tilts her head back, gazing up at me with a warm smile and a shimmer in her eyes. Her hazel eyes are so much brighter. And I'm so happy it's me who is putting it there.

"I'm so glad you walked into my life."

CHAPTER 23

GRACIE

The trip home becomes a rush of tangled limbs and passionate kisses. We manage to keep each other's clothes on during the drive back, but I sat on his lap and ground myself along his erection the whole way. The friction on my throbbing clit eases the pain, but as soon as I stop, the ache intensifies. I need him inside me, filling me. Now.

Arriving at his house, he grabs my hand, and we enter with a quick swoop. As soon as the door closes, he pins me to the back of it. The cold wooden door feels amazing on my heated body.

Little grunts leave my throat as his rough kiss captivates me. I'm losing my damn mind, and he's all calm. I need a little control, so I try my best to unravel him. I suck on his tongue and as he growls. Letting go, I take a bite of his bottom lip as I pull back. His eyes hold me hostage with a feral look, and I smirk, knowing I did that to him.

"Fuck." He lets out a groan before speaking again. "I've missed your hot mouth."

I capture his words again, repeating the sucking until he lets out a deep grumble. I've set him off, and I just hope he fucking lets me have it. I need to orgasm already.

Breaking our kiss, he grabs my dress at the collar and tears it straight down the front, the air causing goose-bumps to cover my skin. I stand in the prettiest teal, barely there lace set.

"This cannot be ruined. This set is fucking ravishing. I'm going to buy you every one I find in this color. I love it on you. It's almost a sin for me to remove it."

"Please rip it off me," I pant. Not caring that I'm now begging, and completely desperate with need.

He slips the bra off my shoulders and reaches around to unclip the strap.

"Do you want me to get you off? How badly do you want to come?"

I nod.

"Words, *Bella*. Don't forget, I like to hear your voice."

I can't find it. It's lost between the state of arousal and the bliss of what he's promising.

I swallow and breathe. "Yes...now."

He drops to his knees, still fully clothed, his hands grazing my panties. I'm quivering with anticipation as he drags them down my thighs. I desperately want to close my eyes and lean my head back to enjoy the pleasure, but fuck, I want to watch him eat me. The memory of the bar reminds me I don't want to miss the sight, and I know how much he loves me to watch.

He grabs the panties and tucks them into his pocket. I laugh, but it's trembling.

He really loves them.

Laying a gentle kiss on each thigh, he then moves to the top of my apex. My breathing is rushed as he stares up at me, pressing another kiss, but this time on the top of my hips. He pulls back and his mouth twists into a knowing grin.

Lower.

As he lifts one of my legs up onto his shoulder, I feel my wetness trickling down my leg. The air hits me, and I moan. Leaning forward, we lock gazes, and he licks my inner thigh, catching every drip of me.

I mumble, "Fuckin' hell." I'm forcing myself to not close my hooded eyes.

"So fucking wet. So fucking sweet. I've gone way too long without you. I've jerked off thinking of your pussy, but it's not the same. Your taste is something I need to have in real life."

I'm about to tell him to shut up and lick me. But then he does.

His thick tongue slides between my swollen lips and over my bud, and I convulse beneath his touch. Our earlier edging makes every sensation ten times stronger. The heat flaring from my lower back and into the front is like an inferno. I'm going to combust from burning up.

He moves my leg wider to stretch me more open, and then I feel his tongue enter me, slowly fucking me with it. After a couple of pumps and licks, I'm trembling and moaning, unable to keep my eyes open.

"I'm going to come."

He mumbles against me, "Come," then pushes on me harder.

And that's all the encouragement I need to arch my pussy into his face and ride it. All the while, he fucks me with his incredible tongue, and I quake from head to toe. The wave of heat racks my body, and I've never come as hard as I have tonight.

I'm sucking in short deep breaths, trying to collect myself. And he doesn't stop the whole time. He is still licking my tender pussy, and I'm still twitching from the sensitivity, but reveling in it all the same.

When he finishes, giving my clit one last sucking kiss, he slowly eases my leg to the floor, but continues to hold me up. My shaky legs, still trying to recover from the high.

"Are you okay?" he asks.

I open my eyes and a slow smile forms on my face. "Is that a trick question?"

He frowns. "No, I'm serious. Was that okay?"

"More than okay. I think I may love and equally hate you for bringing me to the edge earlier."

His face softens, and his chuckle erupts, and I laugh with him. "I told you it's worth it."

When I take in his disheveled hair and then down to his top, I point to it and say, "I ruined your shirt."

"I'll wear you proudly any time if I get to have you shatter like that in my mouth."

I bite my lip as a rush of blood tickles my cheeks. His words are so raw and unapologetic. It makes me blush, and I don't blush normally, but of course with him...I do.

I wander through his house behind him as we take the stairs up to his room. My body is lax from coming already, but it doesn't stop my stupid heart from flipping at being in his space.

The first step inside, and I'm hit with his scent. It's masculine, spicy, and clean, with a hint of? Pine.

It's unusual and so completely him.

His bed is grand, and the bathroom is off to the side with another door, which I could guess is his walk-in closet.

Black wooden accents adorn the walls and furniture, and navy trimmings make up his minimal décor.

When he turns to face me, wearing spots of me on his shirt, his room disappears, and I step up to him and unbutton it. With every piece of skin that's revealed, I lay a chaste kiss on in my wake. My lips hit his chest, and I love the feeling of his heart beating against me. For me. Its strong beats calm my own. He's so in control and not a flickering mess like me. With his buttons undone, I reach up to push it off him. As the shirt falls to the floor, his hands go to the sides of my face, and he tips my head back, kissing my lips in a soft, adoring kiss.

I trace my hands along his chest and down over each ridge of muscle, and when I arrive at his jeans, I unbutton and unzip them. Our lips break apart, and I look down, his face still close so I can feel his breath coasting over my lips. I shove his jeans down and they fall to the floor. He kicks them to the side, my eyes catching on his cock that's fully erect in his blue briefs. I push them down eagerly. When they are off, I swallow hard. His big erection is making me wet all over again.

"Sit," I demand, pushing him back until he hits the bed.

He follows, but mumbles, "Gracie…"

I don't answer with words. Instead, I lower to my knees and grab his cock, wrapping as much of my hand around him as I can and bring my mouth closer. Parting my lips, I eagerly take him inside. The salty pre-cum hits my tongue, and I moan, knowing how much he loves me to be vocal.

With a satisfying groan, his hand runs through my hair, grabbing the back of my head. I slide his length in as far as I can go, making his hand tighten and his cock twitch. I slide my mouth off him, sucking it at the same time, pulling a deep grunt from his chest. When I pull off with a pop and gaze up at him, his eyes are black, heavy with desire.

I keep my gaze holding his, smiling as I slide him right to the back of my throat again.

"Fuck, *Bella*. I'm not going to last long."

I can feel his length swell between my lips as his mouth hangs open, barely restraining himself. The way his chest is rapidly moving, I know he's close, but if one quick motion, he pulls me off him and lifts me onto the bed.

"Even though that was incredible, and I'd love you to swallow me, I haven't waited this long to be inside of you to not have you shatter under me. I've dreamed of this day."

"But I was having fun," I tease.

He hovers over me with a smirk. "You can do it again later, but for right now, I need you around me."

His cock hits my opening, but then he backs away.

"Where are you going?" I ask with a frown.

"Condom."

"I'm on the pill, remember?"

He smiles. "Good I want to feel you completely. Without any barriers."

He doesn't even finish the last word before he thrusts all the way in, and my breath catches in my throat.

My muscles clench around him, welcoming him.

He hisses when I do it again.

Laying a kiss on my lips, he grunts, "You keep finding new ways to torture me, and I'll have to do the same."

His thrusts become harder, and I lock my ankles around his back. The pressure builds and my walls squeeze against him.

"Come, now," he demands.

And I do, grabbing hold of his neck with a scream of his name. His cock grows, and he pulses inside me, letting me know he's coming too.

When he stops moving, I unlock my ankles and lay them on either side of his hips. I'm completely exhausted.

"Now, for the best part."

"Hold me," I say, finishing his thought.

"My pleasure."

He pulls the blanket from under me, and we both slip under. His arm snakes around my middle from behind, and his body scoots flush with my back.

"Get some rest, *Bella*," he says with a kiss to my neck.

The doorbell wakes us. And I blink rapidly, trying to look around, but Marc is still holding on to me tightly.

He's breathing heavily, and I can't believe he's not awake.

"Marc," I say loudly.

He stirs, mumbling, "*Bella*." But pulls me tighter to him.

"Marc," I say, wiggling in his arms, and he startles.

The doorbell chimes again.

He lets me go and sits up, rubbing his eyes. Peering around, I try to find the time.

With no luck, I ask. "What's the time?"

"Nine fifty-five."

What? I never sleep this late.

"I better grab the door."

We untangle and get out of bed. I slowly dress into one of his tops and pants, both of which I'm swimming in.

"Bathroom?" I ask.

"Just through that door."

"Thanks."

I freshen up before I trek down the stairs and hear talking. Marc smiles when he sees me approach. I spot Aria, and she turns at the sound of my footsteps.

Her face falls as she looks at me and then back to Marc, and she asks, "What is she doing here?" She tried to whisper, but I lip-read. I mastered it from working in the bar, with people slurring or talking quietly. I couldn't hear much over the crowd, music, or TVs.

My body freezes, and my stomach hardens. But she was so nice the other night.

"Aria," Marc warns. "Be nice."

"No. You didn't tell me she was your girlfriend. You said, *friend*. I'm not okay with a girlfriend."

I feel like my heart is ripping. His daughter doesn't want me. It crossed my mind once. But I never thought that it would actually happen.

"We are not talking about this right now. It's rude," Marc says.

Aria huffs and storms off toward the stairs.

I stand still, not knowing what to do or say.

Marc walks right up to me, grabbing the backs of my arms. His eyes are soft and pleading as he searches mine. "I'm so sorry. I didn't think she would mind."

"It's okay. It's probably a shock." I try to tell myself it's all fine, even though I feel anything but.

"Yeah, that would make sense." His shoulders lower and he looks down at the floor, and I know it's time for me to leave.

"Well, I should go..."

When he looks back up at me, it's with such an empty stare that it causes the backs of my eyes to sting. "Yeah, I'm sorry, but I think it's best." His tone is flat, not holding his usual sexy rasp, making me feel even worse. I hate that I'm causing both Aria and him pain.

I put a smile on and push away my hurt. All with the hope that him seeing me with a smile will help him not feel sorry for me. "I'm fine. I think it will be better if you go talk to her. You can make it up to me next time."

He strokes my face and runs his thumb over my lips, whispering, "Thank you."

As I grab my bag, he says, "I'll call the car."

I nod, not bothering to argue this time.

I'm shaking like a leaf, the threatening tears ready to come thick and fast as soon as I open that dam. I manage to keep myself together, trying to take deep calm breaths. When I get home, the first thing I do is call Ava.

She whistles as soon as she picks up. "I can assume the date went well, if you're calling me this late the next morning," she says with excitement.

I roll my head to ease the tension that's now built up in the back of my neck. Blowing out a breath, I make my way to the kitchen to get the bottle of wine out. Hopefully, a glass of wine will help. "Not exactly. It was until thirty minutes ago."

"Why, what happened?"

Opening the fridge, I spot a bottle, grabbing it and setting it on the counter as I answer. "Date and post-date were perfect. But this morning the doorbell rang, and his daughter turned up. And she wasn't happy to find me there."

She shrieks. "Fuck off. Why the change of tune?"

I turn to my cupboard and reach down to grab a glass. "No idea. He looked so gutted. So I told him I'd go and that he needed to talk to her."

I balance the phone between my shoulder and ear, opening the white wine and pouring a good helping into the glass.

"Good idea. You don't want to get in the middle of that," she mumbles.

"No, and I don't want her to hate me."

"Hmm, it won't last between you two if she does."

That's the fear that's been circulating in my head since I left his house. What will happen to me and Marc if she doesn't approve?

I guess soon I'll find out.

I lower down onto the couch and take a sip of the sweet and refreshing Moscato.

"Exactly. She stormed off into her room and you should have seen his face. It killed me. It was sad and broken." My heart is in my throat as I think about it again. I just want to help him, but this is as much as I can do right now. Give them space to talk, though, it just doesn't feel like enough.

"Why is he so cute? It makes me want to puke." She chokes and I frown, worried she may actually vomit.

"You're pregnant; isn't that the reason you want to puke?"

She hums. "Oh, yeah. You're probably right."

A text pings, and I see it's his name. He's probably just checking up on me, so I'll reply after I talk to Ava.

"You feeling okay?" I ask, taking another sip before I lower the glass to the table and bury myself into the back of the couch, loving the way it hugs to my body right now.

"Yeah, just normal pregnant woman stuff, nothing unusual."

I breathe a sigh of relief and lower down to curl up on my side.

"Good. How many weeks do you have left at work?"

"I don't know, but I'm fighting with Josh about staying until thirty-seven weeks."

I snicker at that, imagining her stubbornness.

"Isn't that late?"

"No. If I sit down at a desk, I'll be fine. What will I do at home? It will drive me nuts, sitting around waiting for labor."

"Well, good luck convincing Josh."

She groans. "I will."

"Anyway, I want to go shower and eat. I'll call you soon."

"You better, and hey..."

"Yeah?"

"Promise me not to stress about the daughter. She'll love you."

But I'm not worth loving.

"Mm-hmm. Okay, I'm going."

"Bye."

I hang up and read Marc's text.

> **Marc:** I'm so sorry about earlier. She apologized and said it was just a shock. Are you okay?

> **Gracie:** I'm fine. I bet it was. Maybe we should have said something earlier.

> **Marc:** Yeah, I said it was my fault. I should have said girlfriend, not friend. But to make up for it, I said you should come over to watch *Catching Fire* tonight?

> **Gracie:** Are you sure that's a great idea?

> **Marc:** I promise she was totally cool about it when I chatted to her. Please, I miss you. I didn't even get to enjoy snuggling with you this morning.

I don't know if it's a good idea. But I would like to smooth things over with Aria.

Gracie: I'll come, but I can't stay over. I have to get ready for work.

Marc: Okay, I'll take whatever you're willing to give me.

Gracie: I'll see you tonight.

Marc: Yes, and I can't wait.

CHAPTER 24

GRACIE

Taking the stairs to his house feels different tonight. The earlier behavior from Aria makes my stomach drop. I want to be here, so I hope he's right about it just being a shock and not her putting a wedge in the relationship that we just started.

I press the doorbell and tap my foot, waiting for someone to open it, letting out a breath when Marc comes into view. His hair is messy, and he's wearing a navy shirt and jeans again, but this time with bare feet.

I smile. "Hi."

"Hi, come in."

Stepping inside, I hesitate, not knowing how to act with him after the disastrous morning. But before I can think too much, he grabs my waist and pulls me against him.

"Oh," leaves my lips, then he's kissing me. I kiss him back, but I stop us before we get too carried away, not wanting Aria to walk in and be upset again.

"Come, I'm preparing a charcuterie board for us."

"You are?" I ask.

"Yes." He laughs. "I'm a good cook. I just don't get time."

"You need to work less and cook more," I say with a wicked grin, as if I'm not trying to tell him to cook for me. Because he was already perfect before, but his cooking is definitely another tick to marriage material.

Oh my God. I can't believe I'm having these thoughts.

"I'm trying," he groans with his gravelly voice.

We walk into his kitchen, and he rounds the counter, grabbing some grapes to add.

"I've worked for so long, and yes, it made me happy, and I'm very successful, but I'm still lonely, so what's the point?"

My brows rise and my mouth twists as I think about his words. "I can't disagree with you there. I think life is too short to only work, but I know my career is important to me right now."

He pours me a glass of wine, and I smile. "Thank you."

"You're at a different stage, and I'm sure you aren't working twelve plus hours a day, seven days a week."

Shaking my head, I take a sip of the Moscato, swallowing before answering. "No. Definitely not. I work nine to five, so I understand the balance you crave. I'd be tired working long days like that constantly."

"I am tired now, and I just don't want to live and breathe it anymore."

"That's fair enough," I say.

The sound of steps coming down the stairwell has the hairs on the back of my neck rising.

I swivel and wait for Aria to enter the room. Here I am, at twenty-six, scared of a damn thirteen-year-old.

Get a fucking grip, woman.

"Hi, Aria."

"Hi, Gracie."

Marc clears his throat, and Aria's eyes to flick briefly to his before returning to mine. "I'm sorry for how I acted earlier."

Her voice is a little estranged, and it comes across as forced. I hope Marc didn't make her apologize and pretend to want to watch this movie, because the uncomfortable well in my stomach will just continue to swirl.

I sip more wine and then say, "I'm ready for *Catching Fire*."

She smiles at that and goes to the fridge to grab a bottle of water. Marc carries the platter inside, and I follow him.

"I'll go to the bathroom quickly, but, Aria, can you set the movie up, please?"

"Yep," Aria says back, and as I watch him leave, I think of what excuse I can come up with so I can leave too. I don't know if it's safe for me to stay here with her.

Grabbing a cracker, I scoop it into the dip and pop it in my mouth.

"I think you're too young."

Sorry? I blink and bring my focus to her. What do I say back to that?

I swallow the food and answer with the only logical thought that pops into my head. "I'm twenty-six."

"I know, but he's almost forty, and won't have kids, so what's the point of being with him?"

I rub my forehead, trying to come up with a nice response.

Get the fuck back in here, Marc, and help me.

Clearing my throat, I try to respond the best I can. "I really enjoy his company. Your father is a beautiful man. I'm very lucky to be spending tonight with you both."

I avoid the topic of our ages and kids because he and I have already spoken about this, and I don't know if it's my place to go into all the details of our relationship. I don't have kids to know how much I can explain or what I can't. All I know is I'm sweating here, trying to figure out what to say.

"I didn't want you here. This was his idea."

All the air leaves my lungs as panic claws at my throat, and now my nerves are coming back in tidal waves, knotting my stomach.

"I'm sorry. I'm not here to make you uncomfortable. I was invited," I say with a gentle tone.

"Not by me." Her voice is shaky, and a flicker of sadness hits me. This is what I feared, and it's becoming a harsh reality. What can I say to make this better?

"Sorry, I'm back. Did I miss anything?" Marc interrupts before I can respond. My gaze hits the floor, my hands twitching.

For a second, I wonder if I should leave right now, but I don't want to cause a scene.

"No, all good. Let's watch the movie," I say with a small, very forced smile.

How is this going to work if she doesn't accept this? My mind is on overdrive as the movie starts. But I push any thoughts of Aria and how to win her over away and just focus on the movie. Only concentrating on things that make me happy and not the one causing me to want to run.

Chapter 25

Gracie

I decide to walk to the store to pick up some basics, but along the way, I get distracted. Finding a cute little boutique, I head inside to browse.

When something catches my eye, I grab the hanger and bring down the pretty blue shirt to have a better look. I run my other hand through the soft fabric, holding it up against my chest. Moving around, I decide I'll be taking this home with me. When I turn around, I see a familiar pair of eyes with long blonde hair staring at me.

"Not your color," Aria says with a roll of her eyes.

I look down and follow her gaze, swallowing roughly. My shirt. Yep, she definitely hates it, and right now I wonder if she hates me too.

After the movie ended, I left their house as fast as possible. I pecked him on the lips at his door and let his driver take me home. I never told Marc what she said that night because I didn't want to bring up drama, but I'm thinking now that maybe I should have, because she still seems very angry, and I have no idea how to deal with it.

"You think? I kinda like it." I say, just to see if I can get her to warm up.

"No, it's too dark, and it's a weird shape. I think it would make you look boxier than you already are."

I gulp some air.

What the actual fuck?

Am I boxy? I never thought about myself like that.

"Oh, okay."

I don't know what to do other than stand here, stunned. Do I put it back, or do I keep it? Bile is rising up my throat, and I swallow it down as I stare at the top, hoping for some answers.

"Did you find anything, sweetheart?" Marc's voice booms behind me, and my shoulders drop.

Thank God.

"Oh! Hi, Gracie."

"Hey," I say with a relieved smile.

He leans in and kisses my cheek, and my eyes widen when I see Aria's face. She doesn't seem impressed. No, she seems furious. Taking a step back away from Marc, I try to give a little space.

What I did to deserve this type of ice? What happened to the girl I first met? What can I do to get her back?

"I like the shirt," Marc says, but I don't respond because I'm in my head.

"Gracie?" Marc says, his tone firmer.

"You think?" I ask, twirling the hanger around, the fabric moving with it.

"Definitely. You should get it." He smiles, brushing my hair over my shoulder with the gentlest of touches.

And the panic from his daughter is melting away.

I take another peek over at her, and she still isn't happy. So, I move my gaze and keep them focused on him.

"What are you doing?" I ask, taking in his white polo and gray pant look.

"I played golf with my brother this morning, and now I'm taking Aria shopping. She wanted to have a look around and grab some lunch. Care to join us?"

His innocence warms me, but I can't do it.

Or should I just try again?

After looking into those deep brown eyes for too long, I get lost in them, and I say, "For lunch, sure."

If she still can't be nice to me after spending more time with me, I'm at a loss.

"Great. Once you grab that and you girls finish shopping here, let's go."

"I'm not done, Dad. I just got in here," Aria moans.

"Okay, well, I'll wait out front, and you two take your time." And I panic at those words. I think he imagines us spending quality time together, but he doesn't realize his daughter is attacking me every chance she gets.

I watch him turn and wish I could beg him to stay and save me, but I can do this. Pretend to act tough. Not let her win.

"Why would you come and ruin my time with him?" she sneers.

"Ah, I didn't see it as that. Sorry, I wanted to spend more time with you both. We haven't gotten to know each other much."

I desperately want to fix this before I have to mention it to Marc. If I can fix it without him, that would be great, but it's not looking like that at the moment. If I can't figure out quickly how to turn this around, I'll have to tell him. I can't lie.

"I don't want to get to know you." She pouts.

"If that's how you feel, I'm sorry. I can skip lunch. But how can I fix this?"

"Yes, you can tell him something came up and you have to leave unexpectedly. And there isn't. I don't like you—simple." She shrugs, but the flicker of pain that flashes on her face briefly makes me think there is more to this.

I shake my head. "I can't lie to him."

"Why? I don't want you there. He isn't going to love you. Just look at you."

Those words. Those same words my mother used to say to me. She used to blame me for my father leaving us. I wasn't loveable because "look at me." But what's wrong with the way I looked?

My mouth parts, my breathing turning shallow, the pain burning a hole in my heart.

I don't answer; the words won't come out. I turn and move slowly to the register, and I pay for the shirt on autopilot. Walking out of the shop, he stands there with the biggest, warmest grin, and I could cry.

He wants me, but she doesn't, and I can't get in the way. And I don't want to be hated. I've had a lifetime's worth of it. The memories still try to creep into my life, and I don't need venomous words thrown in my face by a thirteen-year-old.

I stand beside him, waiting for her to come out.

I stay quiet.

"How did she go in there? Did she find anything?"

Her mouth moving was all she was doing...But I don't say that. Instead, I say, "Not yet. I paid for my top and left."

A few minutes later, she steps out of the store with nothing.

"You didn't find anything?" he asks kindly.

"No. There wasn't anything that I liked."

Who is this girl? Definitely not the same one who talks to me. My back straightens with hurt and anger.

"Are we ready to go?" he asks us both with his smile on, his eyes bouncing between us.

She grins back.

I wish I hadn't said yes now.

"Great. Let's go." He turns, and I follow along, holding my new purchase tight.

We arrive at a cafe with a ten-page menu. Forgetting where I am, I say, "This menu is huge. I can't decide what to eat."

"I think you need the salad," Aria says.

"Their Cobb and steak one is superb," he suggests, not realizing his daughter is having a stab at me.

"Hmm," I pretend to deliberate.

"I think I'll get the burger and fries," I say with a grin. I like my food. Sorry, no salad being ordered today, kid.

Her gaze is fixed on me, and I feel it, but I don't look. I've had enough shit for one day. There's only so much I can take.

"I think I'll get the same," he mutters and closes the menu.

"What? You're ordering a burger and fries?" Aria exclaims.

"Yeah, why not? Sounds good. Right, Gracie?" he says with a cheeky grin.

"Sounds great."

Aria grumbles.

We order, and I sit back.

"Where are you off to afterward?" Marc asks me.

"I need to grab some food and do some laundry."

"Sounds boring," Marc jokes.

"It is, but it has to be done." I shrug.

"Why don't you leave it until tomorrow and come over tonight to watch another movie," Marc says.

I open my mouth to speak, but she cuts me off.

"I'm sure she's busy." She looks at me and then away, but not before I catch another glimmer of pain washing over her face.

She doesn't want me there. Because she probably wants her dad back. She's always had him there for her...someone to go to like a best friend. So sharing him with someone else wouldn't be easy. She's just a kid, and she's probably had a lot to deal with since her parents' divorce. I just need to help make this right, even if that means taking a step back.

I nod. "Yeah, I can't tonight. Next time."

"Okay," Marc says, looking a bit saddened, but I need to focus on how Aria feels. I'll be talking to Ava and seeing if she can help me find a way of figuring out how I go about tackling this.

Our food arrives, and we all eat.

"I can't believe you're eating that," Aria says.

He chuckles, and I can't help but grin, loving the sound.

"You will be seeing it a lot now." He winks at me, and I run my eyes over her before returning to my plate.

She's staring at me with so much hate.

Get me out of here.

When we finish, we get up, and I offer to pay. "Don't be offering me money," Marc warns.

I shake my head. "I can't have you pay every time."

"Don't argue with me." He kisses me, and I forget for a moment where I am, or should I say, who's around.

I sink into his gentle kiss, and when we pull apart, he dusts his thumb over my cheek. "Let's go."

I nod, and Aria's sour face hits us. He doesn't seem to pay any attention to it, but it makes my stomach roll.

He grabs my hand, and I don't want to pull away. I'm falling for Marc. He doesn't deserve hostility. I just need to sort out what I'll do about Aria.

How do I get her to like me?

Outside, I smile, and he pecks me again when I say good-bye. Aria offers me a fake smile.

When I walk away, my mind is a jumbled mess.

"What a little bitch," Ava says on the phone.

"She definitely is something else, but she's also just a kid," I say with a sigh.

"Kids can be cruel; I hope mine doesn't turn out to be."

I snort. "Let's see when he or she comes out. But anyway, I need help with what I can do to get her to change her opinion of me."

"You should bite back and see what she does," Ava says.

I groan. "Ava, you know I can't do that. She's a kid."

"You need to grow some balls." She huffs.

"I'm happy not to. But what should I do? You're really not helping."

"To be honest, I'd tell Marc. He deserves to know what a shit he's raised."

"I don't know…"

I trail off, rubbing my eyes, and sink back farther into the couch. A part of me wants to tell him, but the other part worries I'm betraying her, and that will make Aria more upset with me. And I don't want to make things worse.

"You can't keep going like this."

"Oh, I know that. I'm struggling to keep my face straight." I sigh.

"Maybe you should cool off?"

"What do you mean?" I ask, sitting up.

"Tell Marc his daughter has been vocal about how much she isn't happy about the relationship and until she is genuinely okay that you think it's best to cool things off between you two."

I nibble on my lip, thinking that over. It has crossed my mind.

"When she said he would never love me because 'look at me,' it was the final straw. I was done. It broke something inside me. It's just when he looks at me, or worse, kisses me, that I forgive her. Because she has these moments where she looks hurt, and I know there is something that reminds me of when we were that age."

"You are way too kind, and he sounds wonderful. I can't wait to meet him soon. But this is about you. You don't deserve to be treated this way. Remember, we walked away from abusive houses, lived in shelters, and did it tough, but it does not mean you go backward to accommodate her."

"Yes, and when she talks rudely, it's like I'm back there…"

"No," she snaps. "You're a fucking nice person, with the sweetest heart. Always welcoming people, and fuck it, his daughter can watch her dad be unhappy and see if that makes her feel better."

"I don't think that's what she wants. But I guess there is no other solution. Taking a break is really the only answer. I just feel like I'm punishing myself."

"No, you're just giving them space to figure out their shit and not drag you down. I won't be your best friend and see people do this to you. Thirteen or adult, it's unacceptable."

I sigh. "Yeah, you're right. Let's hope this doesn't blow up in my face."

It's Sunday night, and I'm hoping Aria's gone back to her mom's house. But despite that, I need to just make this call while I have the strength before the nerves take over and I back out.

Picking up the phone, I send a simple text first.

Gracie: Are you free to talk?

Marc: Of course, anytime.

My heart races as I hit the call.

"*Bella*, what's wrong?"

I laugh. "How do you know something's wrong?"

"Because you're asking if I'm free to talk and when women want to talk, it's never for good things."

He's got me there.

"Well, yeah, I guess you're right."

"So tell me what's wrong." His tone drops deeper, turning serious.

Here goes...

Nausea waves in my stomach, but I have to ignore it to get this out.

"Has Aria said anything to you about me?" I ask quietly.

"Hmm, no, not really, why? Should she have?"

"Well, um, she doesn't like me." My heart is palpitating from having to say this. I hate that I have to bring up a negative thing about his daughter. It's not a nice feeling, and it's probably why I'm feeling so sick.

"No. No way. She does," he says, brushing it off.

"Has she said that?" I ask.

He grows silent for a beat. The silence is not helping my racing heart that's skyrocketing with nerves. Then finally, he sighs. "Well, not in those words, but she hasn't said she dislikes you."

I take a deep breath. "Well, anytime you're not around, she makes comments."

"What do you mean, she makes comments? Like what?"

"Rude ones. I don't want to bring this up to you, but it's not getting any better, and I don't think I can go on..." My voice cracks on the last word, and my eyes blink rapidly, stopping the tears that want to leak.

The memory of Aria's hurt-filled eyes flash in my mind, and it plays push and pull with my emotions, reminding me why I am doing this.

"You can't go on with?" he questions.

"Us," I whisper. As if whispering will help it hurt less. But the tears I've been holding back run down my cheeks.

The line is now dead silent, and I can only hear my heartbeat in my ears.

"Because of how she treats you," he says after what feels like forever.

A part of me wants to retract and take it back, but the other side of me knows I need to stand my ground. I brush my cheeks and clear my throat, not wanting to sound how I feel—heartbroken.

"Yes. She obviously isn't as accepting of me as you think," I say quietly.

"I'm sorry. I didn't know." He sounds utterly defeated. "What did she say?"

"No, don't be sorry. But I don't want to go into specifics because that's not nice either. I think she needs some more time or a deep conversation with you. I don't know, but something isn't working, and I need to take a step back while you work on it."

He takes a big breath. "I wish you didn't have to, but you're right; something isn't right if she's lashing out at you. None of this is your fault." The sadness in his tone makes my chin tremble, my face growing wet with fresh tears.

A half smile hits my mouth at his kind words. Always so caring and thoughtful when he doesn't have to be. "I know, and this sucks. But you're such a wonderful father. She is so lucky to have you. I didn't have one growing up; he definitely didn't care about how I felt and how much pain I was in. So be the dad you are, and I'll be here when she's ready."

"You're so beautiful to put my daughter before yourself. You don't know what that means to me. But it's not forever. I can't lose you now. We've only just started."

I hope not.

"It can't be the end. We have a to-do list to check off together," I say, trying to ease the pain we are both feeling. I wish I could hug him right now and hear those words in person.

"Yes, the list. We have our list."

I have to go before I sob and make things worse for him.

"I better go," I croak.

"Okay, *Bella*."

I hang up and stare at the phone for a beat.

I did it.

I can't believe I broke my heart to save us.

Chapter 26

Marco

I take the stairs two at a time until I arrive at Aria's door. My heart feels like it's shrinking with the two women I care about in this world at war with each other.

I'm to blame. I should have spoken to Aria and treated her better by acknowledging that she needed to know exactly how I felt about Gracie from the moment she came to New York. Instead, I got swept up in my own feelings and let it cloud my judgment.

Now I'm in this position where I'm disappointed in myself, and I need to find a way to fix this. I just hope I can figure out Aria's problem before it's too late…just the thought has my ribs growing tight from the lack of breath. I shake my head. No, I can't lose her. I just need to make sure it's on Aria's speed, not mine.

I knock softly on the door frame before leaning my head against it, watching her sit at her desk, her blonde hair tied in a ponytail as she writes away on her computer, deep in thought. Well, until I knocked she was, and now her head has turned at the sound. And when I see her brown eyes look puffy, I momentarily forget to breathe.

Fuck, I messed up big time. She stops typing, but otherwise doesn't move.

Scrunching up her cute nose, she asks, "Dad, what are you doing here?"

I push off the door frame and slowly enter her room, taking a seat on her bed. She spins in her office chair to face me, her hands laced together in her lap, her face still scrunched up.

"I need to talk to you."

Her face softens, but there is a slight panic in her eyes that has me quickly saying, "It's okay, everyone is fine. I'm fine."

"Okay then, what's it about?" She leans to one side of the chair, utterly relaxed now. The complete opposite of me, who's sitting here with blood pressure that's unhealthily elevated, so much so, it's giving me a throbbing headache. But I stare at her delicate face for a moment, seeing my features, and take a deep breath.

We share the same eyes, and the same sloped nose, but the rest is all her mom. She definitely got the best of both of us, and I really didn't think any other female would fill my heart other than her, but things have changed. Therefore, sitting here, I know Aria's sweet face is dynamite to me, pulling on my heartstrings. But the other sweet and beautiful face I think about is currently hurting.

So I need to do this. Fix this and go get my woman.

"How you're treating Gracie, sweetheart." I give her a sad smile.

Her face falls, looking to the floor and then back at me before saying, "What do you mean?"

She kills me. I shrink inside, my heart hurting at the fact she just lied to my face.

"Don't lie," I say gently, with a slow, disbelieving headshake.

Now her eyes narrow, shooting me with a furious look as she asks with a sharp tone, "What has she been telling you?"

She's defensive, and it's so unlike her. I need to get to the bottom of this. I don't like that I've made this side come out of her.

"Unfortunately, she won't tell me the exact things you've been saying to her. I don't know why she's covering for you. But she's hurt by whatever you're doing, and it's unacceptable. She's not at fault. If anyone is to blame, it's me for not telling you right away."

"I'm not doing anything," she argues, but her voice croaks as she wilts a little in her chair.

I shake my head at her attitude. It's like she isn't hearing what I'm saying. As I speak, my voice breaks. "Please, Aria. I'm finally happy and you want to hurt me. I at least need to understand why? I at least need to know why you don't like her, or what's made you not be okay? I can't fix what I don't know. And I really want to fix our relationship. We've never fought, and I feel sick, and I hate it. Please, just let me in. Tell me what's going on." My hands clasp together in my lap and I wait, out of breath. I hope it's enough to get her to talk to me.

Her wide eyes soften, and she bites her nails before dropping them back to her lap, where she rubs them along her black sweats. "I don't want to lose you," she whispers, sadness dripping from every word, and I feel it tear a piece of my heart with it.

This is it...she doesn't want to lose me. Doesn't she know how much I love her? Have I had my head that far up in the clouds? I hadn't realized that she needed to be shown love too during this transitional time. She is my goddamn universe, and I will always love her, no matter what.

I shuffle to the edge of the bed to get closer to her and grab her hands in mine. She doesn't resist, and I'm grateful. I rub my thumb over the top of hers in a soothing motion. "What makes you think that?" I ask quietly, looking at her face.

Her gaze is watching our hands. "You've never had a girlfriend, and I love our time together..."

I nod and wait for her to finish.

"I just don't want her coming in and taking away our time." She looks up as she says this, and her eyes are glassy. My chest aches at the pain staring back at me.

I reach out and touch her hair. "Sweetheart, I'm not going anywhere. I promise. And Gracie wouldn't want to ruin our relationship. Trust me."

"How do you know?" A tear leaks and rolls down her cheek.

I push past the tightness in my chest and offer her a small smile as I think of Gracie's selflessness. "Gracie is so welcoming of you. She offered to take a break so I could talk to you and make sure you were okay. She didn't have to; she thought of you instead of herself and how she feels about me."

She stays silent, obviously thinking about what I'm saying. I stroke her hair one last time to offer comfort before I return my hand to hers, holding them as I speak. "Listen, you can set some boundaries and tell me what you want to do to ease into this."

I hold my breath and hope she at least will think about accepting Gracie. I know she has welcomed her stepdad with open arms, and she could do it for Gracie too. Gracie was right about going at her pace. I got all caught up and forgot about Aria. And including her in what life changes were happening around her, ones that would have a huge impact on her life.

Lesson learned.

"I want one day or night with just us two. No Gracie," she says quietly.

A small smile of relief spreads on my face. "Okay. What else?" I encourage, wanting her to keep communicating and getting everything off her chest. I can work with this. I can fix this.

"And maybe the next day or night we hang out with Gracie."

My heart swells at the thought of her accepting Gracie, and me being able to have both of them together hits me differently. My smile is taking up my whole face now.

"And you promise not to insult her behind my back?"

She shakes her head, her tears all dried up, but her eyes still red. "I won't do it anymore. I promise. But I am sorry, Dad. I did like her; she seemed fun and really nice."

I grin like an idiot who struck the lottery.

"Thanks, sweetheart. She is, you have no idea. You wait, I think you'll like her more than me." I wink at her.

And she laughs, disconnecting our hands and running them through her hair. "Yeah, I can't believe she got you to eat a burger and fries." She smiles at me with wide eyes.

I chuckle, knowing I can't believe it either, my grin growing. "I know."

She bites her nail again and peers at me shyly. I frown, wondering what she's thinking now.

"Does Gracie hate me now?" she mumbles nervously.

I sigh. "Not at all. You're a kid in a new situation. If anyone can understand being a teenage girl, it will be her."

She drops her hand away from her mouth, happy with my answer, and the beat of silence tells me the conversation has ended. But I urge her one last time.

"Is that all that's on your mind? You don't have anything else to say?"

She shakes her head before offering me a warm smile. "No, Dad, that's all."

"Okay. Don't stay up too late on that thing. It hurts your eyes, remember?" I stand and press my lips into her hair, and she leans in, welcoming it.

I'm mentally drained from the up and down of the day. I exit her room, yawning, my whole body feeling heavy. I pull my phone out to text Gracie but change my mind. I bring up the to-do list instead.

"Marc, your designs, please," Jason asks at the next meeting, pulling me from my daydream about the plan for Gracie I have set up.

As I sit across from Gracie, her pinched brows tell a thousand words. She's in pain. What she doesn't know is it won't be for much longer.

I stand and take the lead, showing my design concept of the meeting rooms.

When I take a seat, I glance at her, finding her biting her lip. When she sees me watching, she drops her lip from her teeth.

It's Mason's turn, and I listen to their concept, albeit a bit distracted, knowing after this I get my time with her. And I plan to soak in every minute I can.

When the meeting ends, Mason leans down into her ear and whispers something. Her eyes shoot to me.

Everyone leaves the room, and I ask with a knowing grin, "Are you ready?"

She wrinkles her nose, looking down to finish packing up, but Mason takes it off her. Her mouth opens and closes, not knowing whether to fight him or not. As soon as Mason leaves, and it's just us alone, the tension is palpable.

"I don't think this is a good idea." Her tone is quieter and less animated than usual. There's no enthusiasm, and a sense of worry washes over me.

"Why?" I ask with nerves.

"I'm...just...I—" She struggles to find the words, and panic tightens my throat.

I step closer to her, giving her a soft smile, and I keep closing the distance between us. She gives me a smile, but it wavers. Sweat forms on my brow at the thought of her walking away from us.

I stand toe to toe, inhaling her sweet scent and holding her eyes. "Tell me what you're thinking."

She hums instead of answering, her brow furrowed as she looks down at the floor. I reach out and tilt her chin up to keep eye contact. I need to see those hazel eyes boring into mine, even if they are shining with so much torment.

I hate this look on her beautiful face, and I need to fix it. I'll do whatever it takes to make her eyes glow bright again.

"I need your words," I say with a cheeky grin, my hand still on her chin. When I move to cup her jaw, she rests her head into it.

She gives me a small smile back, but a small roll of her eyes too.

"Did you just roll your eyes at me?"

"Maybe," she says, staring back at me with warmth that wasn't there a moment ago.

I turn back to serious. "Now, tell me, please."

She lets out a long sigh and straightens, causing me to drop my hand. She looks down, and I let her look away from me. If she needs to get this out without me staring at her, then I'll take it. I just want to know what's eating at her, so I can talk about it.

"I'm afraid to get hurt again. To get my hopes up, to only have my heart broken again. I don't know if I can do it." She peers up at that moment, and my heart squeezes at the red eyes staring back at me.

I hold her in a close embrace. Feeling her pulse thumping hard and fast, matching my own with conflicted feelings. I turn my face and whisper into her ear, "I can't promise to never make you mad at me or say we won't argue, but I can't live my life without you in it."

"Aria—" she says in my ear, as if I had forgotten.

I pull back to face her again and smile softly. "Is fine. I can explain it all, but will you come with me, please? I'm begging you."

"Okay. But I'm still nervous about Aria," she admits, and if my heart could grow any more, it would. I could explode with happiness.

"She is fine. I promise. I wouldn't be here if she wasn't. It wouldn't work between us if she didn't like you."

She lets out a heavy breath, as if it had been weighing her down. "You told Mason."

I chuckle. "Yep. He doesn't care. He's happy if I'm happy."

Her brows raise, wrinkling her forehead, and her eyes bug out with acute fear. "This won't affect my job, will it?"

I shake my head and peck those soft, pouty lips I have been dreaming of. "No, I'd never do anything to do that. You don't work for me, remember? Now that would be an issue, even though I want you to work with me just so I can have you all the time."

"Greedy," she whispers.

I lean into her ear and breathe. "Only for you."

She shivers, and I watch goosebumps cover the exposed skin on her neck. And before my mind drifts to taking her home, I remind myself that I need to get through the date before I can have my wicked way with her. It will be worth it.

We step outside, and the car is waiting. "Where are we going?" she asks curiously.

"Somewhere from our list." I grin.

CHAPTER 27

GRACIE

His kisses leave me breathless, and in those moments, the giddiness and butterflies of being with him return. But I need to keep myself a little weary in case Aria was only telling her father what he wanted to hear, or even him hearing what he wanted to hear. I don't want to be hurt in the process, so I'm a little unsure how to take this surprise.

We are standing outside the building and his face is shining in the sun, his open megawatt smile on display, and I can't help but smile with him. For the rest of the day, I'll keep an open mind and try to trust him that Aria really is okay with us, but I'll tell him I want to talk to her alone before we get back together.

"I can mark one off the list," he says, grabbing my hand and gently squeezing it.

I frown, wondering which one we've already done. As we turn the corner, he says, "Holding hands, and the second one is about to happen."

My lips part slightly, and my heartbeat quickens as I take a look around for a clue. My hand finds my mouth when I see it.

"Get coffee," I say, taking in the cute little café, and my dry mouth is very appreciative of the idea of getting a drink. Stepping inside, the wooden counter displays muffins and cakes, which all looking mouth-watering. The plants and pendant lighting are unusual, but so cozy and chic—I love it.

We approach the counter, and he orders our drinks and when they're ready, we go back to holding hands and walking the streets.

His hand in mine feels fitting, and it's not helping my racing heart at all. The nerves and excitement are mixed, and I don't know if I really needed the caffeine right now, but it's so damn tasty.

"What else is on this list?" I ask, peeking up at him, his profile enhanced by the sun. His high cheekbones, five-o'clock shadow, and full brows surrounding his brilliant eyes have me transfixed. He sips his coffee and then turns to me.

"You don't remember?" He raises a brow with a grin that goes from ear to ear.

Suddenly I feel embarrassed to confess. I bite my lip and whisper, "Not all of it."

"Well, lucky I wrote them all down." He winks.

"Really?" I ask, perking up.

"Yes, but I only want to do a couple more and save the rest for another time."

We stand at the lights, waiting to cross, and I face him. "I love that idea. But which ones are we doing today?"

"One, we are doing right now..." He leans forward, leaving a swift kiss on my lips, and I almost whimper. But thankfully, the excitement of guessing what we are doing makes me drop my plea for a longer and much deeper kiss.

I look around, sipping my coffee, and it clicks. "A long walk," I rush out excitedly.

"Yes," he says as he kisses my temple. We walk across the road, then along the park, and I wonder what Aria's up to.

"How's Aria doing?"

He smiles over at me with a dazed look. "She's good. Much better, actually. Our talk was really eye opening."

I look up at him with a small smile, but I'm still nauseas about the conversation I will have alone with her. I want to do it sooner rather than later if he wants us to progress. I just need to hear it from her for me to relax.

"When can I see her and have a chat?"

"Tomorrow? I'm sure she would love to come around to apologize, if that's okay. She's a little worried you hate her."

"Of course, I don't hate her." My heart drops that she would think that. I don't want to make her feel worse for apologizing. "She doesn't have to—"

His eyes narrow, and I close my mouth as he says firmly, interrupting me, "Yes, she does."

It's not like I can argue; it's his daughter. I sigh. "Okay, but I don't want her forced to do something she doesn't want to do."

"I wouldn't force her. She wants to do this. The reason she reacted to you like that was because she didn't want to lose me, but now she realizes I'll still make one-on-one time with her. And she's still my priority."

I turn to him and hold his gaze, and if I didn't like him enough before, I think I'm crossing the line from like to love.

The way he talks about her and makes her his number one is something I've always dreamed of, but it wasn't in the cards for me growing up. And watching him be so sweet with Aria warms the icy wall around me that holds memories I don't want to remember.

"Of course, you will. I'll never stand in the way of a relationship between the both of you. You two have a special bond, and I would never break that."

His eyes stare down at me kindly, giving my hand a big, reassuring squeeze. "I know, and I told her that. You are so kind-hearted. She just hasn't allowed herself to see that yet."

Hearing that makes a flush crawl up my neck and onto my cheeks. I smile bashfully before looking over at the stunning gardens surrounding us, totally lost in our lust bubble.

We stay silent as we continue to walk back to his place, sipping our coffees, hand in hand.

As soon as we hit the stairs, he glances down at me with his heated brown eyes. I smirk and kiss him. Before I can pull back, he grabs my face and kisses me hard, working around me to open his door.

We stumble inside, and I tear at his shirt, fumbling my way through unbuttoning it whilst not watching what I'm doing because I don't want to disconnect our mouths. But when I open his shirt, I'm gasping, trying to catch my breath as I rake my eyes over his toned chest and down over each of his abs to his belt. I swallow thickly, his breathing loud and labored, and when I slowly bring my gaze back to his face, he's amused.

"You like what you see?" His eyes are darker now and filled with desire. I nod and lean forward, kissing his exposed neck, and then move my mouth to his ear, and whisper, "I fuckin' love it."

And he growls, pulling back with feral eyes. Our hot mouths collide again, our tongues tangling, teeth clashing, and loud grunts sounding between us. This kiss is different. This kiss is full of deep longing, a *never letting you go moment*, both of our hearts pouring out into each other. It's making me unhinged and him just as much, and I haven't seen this side to him. But it makes the moment more exciting knowing he can't slow down or that he can't get enough of me either. The taste of his coffee mixed with the smell of his spicy aftershave is sending my senses into overdrive.

I can't get enough of him; I need him now.

My teeth scrape his bottom lip and tug it roughly. Needing some air, I'm gasping as if I have no oxygen left.

"So good. So fucking good. All for you," he rasps, and I smirk against his lips, loving the way he likes these little nips. And a humming sound leaves my throat, knowing he is saying he's all mine. Because I feel the same way. I want him to have all of me; my mind, body, and soul. My hands run over the back of his neck, messing up his hair and bringing my mouth back to his so we can kiss again. This time, when we pull apart, our breaths tickle each other's lips.

"Marc. I need you."

He kisses my forehead, then his lips touch my ear, and I shiver. "You got it.

Scooping me up, he carries me up the stairs as if I weigh nothing, while I sling my arms around his neck and snuggle in against him. Kissing his neck, I run my tongue along his salty skin, the word "fuck" rumbling from his chest and into mine. I watch his Adam's apple bob as he swallows hard. I do it again to torment him, and in response, I get another sexy growl.

Every step toward his room makes the thrill of what's about to happen accelerate. I can't wait to run my hands over his skin and have him show me how worthy I am. I love how he shows me with actions how much I mean to him.

He lowers me to the bed, and I reach out to run my hands up his back and through his unruly dark hair. Pulling his head closer to mine, I brush my lips against his. I can never have enough of his lips.

"I added something to our list...something I want to try."

I swallow thickly as he stares at me with determination. Licking my lips, I ask, "What is it?"

He grins wickedly before shuffling off me. I groan that the heat from his body is gone, and he chuckles. "*Bella*, I'll be right back. I'm not going anywhere. You're very needy tonight."

I hum. "So needy."

"Fuck," he mumbles as he walks to his closet, disappearing for only a few seconds before walking back out and bringing me a box. I frown, and he hands it to me. I rest it on my lap and lift the white lid to see a pink vibrator staring back at me.

I roll my lips before biting them, peering up at him with amusement. "This is on your list?"

"Yes. Move up to the middle of the bed and lie back. I want you to part those legs and show me your pretty pussy."

I put the box on the floor and scramble up the bed eagerly, lying back and opening up for him. I expect him to follow, but he only moves a few steps to the end of the bed, a hungry expression sitting on his face.

"Are you going to join me?" I ask as my lower belly quivers with nerves.

He smirks. "No, *Bella*. I want you to grab your new friend and put it on your clit. I want you dripping before I fuck you."

A throb hits my center and I breathe out, "Oh God," closing my eyes briefly before reopening with a dazed look. My breathing increases, and I know it won't be long before I'm panting through a climax.

I put the vibrator on my clit, and he growls, "Good girl."

I've always been independent, so to succumb to his orders is freeing and more of a turn on than I could ever have imagined.

"That feel nice?"

My mouth opens to answer him, but the tingle from the light vibrations makes it a struggle.

"Move the vibrator around in slow circles."

My eyes close, and I just enjoy the feeling this gives me. The idea of him watching and telling me what he wants me to do is exquisite.

"Now lift the vibrator and rub your hand through your wet lips. Show me how wet you are."

I peel my heavy lids open and see the hard lines on his face, his chest rapidly moving up and down and his eyes fixed on my center. As I run my hands through my slick folds, my sex clenches, but I follow his order and hold his gaze. Then I hold my hand up to him.

"So good. Taste yourself. Tell me how you taste."

I bring my hand to my parted mouth and lick slowly over my fingers, and he groans. "Mm," I murmur, sucking my flavor.

"I want you to come. Put the vibrator on a higher setting and push harder on your clit." I peer down and see his erection, and I love how much this is affecting him. I can't believe how much restraint he has.

Grabbing the vibrator, I put the settings up and lower it back down onto myself. The delicious vibrations running through my clit have my back arching and my toes curling through a moan.

"Pinch your nipple with your other hand." His heavy breathing helps me climb closer to a climax.

I pinch my nipple softly, a feral sound leaving my throat. "You have such pretty tits. Squeeze it, feel how beautifully soft your skin is, how full your breasts are."

I pant and squirm, trying to get to my climax, my heat needing more. "Touch me," I beg.

"You're so pretty when you beg. I can't wait to watch you come. You look so beautiful when you come for me."

And his words break me. The wave of pleasure slams into me hard, and I moan out his name so loudly, my head falls back, body tightening and releasing as I come hard.

I didn't hear his footsteps, so I'm surprised when I feel his warm touch on my thigh, moving my leg to open again. He climbs over me, naked, so he's kneeling between me, with his erection thick and heavy. I stare up at him while I try to catch my breath.

As he hovers over me, our eyes stare at each other with such a burning desire that I haven't seen before. "I'm not done with you yet. I'm going to make you come again."

Then, before I have any time to think, he thrusts himself inside, and I cry out. "Marc!"

My eyes roll to the back of my head, my back arching as he fills me. It's perfect, just like him. My walls spasm and when I've caught my breath back from a moan, he pulls out and then rocks deep into me again. The way we fit together doesn't help my growing feelings. He makes me feel treasured, adored, and seen.

He continually thrusts into me, and I grip his back as the wave of heat rolls through me all over again. I can feel him grow thicker inside me, and I know he's close. He comes first, calling out my name in the most guttural groan, and my orgasm hits me at the sight of him coming undone. Only a long deep moan and my nails digging into his back let him know I'm coming, but the way his cock pulses only one more time lets me know he's finished.

I go limp and my back melts into the mattress. As my eyes flutter open, I see his perspiring forehead, a piece of his dark locks stuck to his face. I lift a hand and push his hair back with an adoring smile.

He offers me a lopsided grin. "That was amazing. Is it possible you're getting better?"

I bite my lip before saying with flushed cheeks, "No, I think we just explode with passion whenever we are together."

He kisses me briefly. "We are definitely explosive, but there is something different about you. Something magical and beautiful. And the best part of me is you."

We are in his kitchen making dinner. I'm more of the observer and cleaner because, let's face it, unless he wants a burnt dinner; he's best to do the cooking.

The smell of roast chicken and veggies fills the air. It feels very homey and domestic with us in the kitchen working together and having a hearty home-cooked dinner.

"Come taste this," he says.

I put the dish I just finished on the drying rack and step over to the stove, where he is stirring the gravy. He picks up the spoon and blows on it before bringing it to my lips.

I taste it, and the sweet onion hits me immediately.

"Mm." I lick my lips.

He tastes it too.

"It's good, right?"

I nod. And I go to step away, but he kisses me briefly.

"What was that for?" I ask.

"I just wanted to."

I smile as the doorbell rings.

Here we go...

The hair on the back of my neck raises, and I return to the dishes, needing to do something. I need to focus on something other than if tonight will be the same as it was.

"I think the plate is clean enough," Marc whispers behind me. His hand touches my waist, and he kisses the back of my head. "I've got you."

I don't bother denying that I'm nervous. I don't want to lie to him, so I just nod as he walks away to answer the door.

I can hear voices and the heavy footsteps across the wooden floors let me know they are close.

Wiping my hands dry on the towel, I wring them together with white knuckle force.

"Hi, Aria," I say with a smile, pushing past the way my heart is beating in reaction to seeing her.

She offers a warm smile back. "Hi, Gracie. What are you cooking?"

"Well, I wouldn't say I'm cooking." I laugh. "Your dad cooked. I observed and cleaned up."

"You can't cook either?" she asks, moving to stand behind the counter, and I can't help but admire her olive-green sweats and how the color complements her blond hair and complexion.

I shake my head with a knowing smile. "Do you burn everything too?" I ask curiously.

Aria looks at Marc, who's grinning. "Yeah, I'm not really allowed to cook."

The pink cheeks and the way he's grinning make me want to find out more.

"Why's that?" I push, lifting a brow.

"I once left a pot of water on the stove and completely forgot about it until the fire truck turned up."

I wince, covering my mouth with my hand. "Oh no. I think that may beat any of my accidents, but at least not having to cook means less mess to clean."

"Oh, dear," Marc mutters, but Aria just laughs, and I wink at her.

Finally, we find something to connect over.

"Well, lucky for you two, I can cook. But maybe I should sign you both up for cooking classes." He wiggles his eyebrows at us.

I shrug. "I'll do it for you. But there is no guarantee that I can be helped."

Aria leans on the counter with a quirk in her brow. "Same. Sorry, Dad, but I do well in grades for school, but this may be one area I suck."

He steps closer to us and waves his hand, as if we are being ridiculous. "Never. I have faith in both of you girls. I'll find the best teacher."

I look over at Aria, who's shaking her head. I'm enjoying the lightness of this conversation; my stomach isn't churning with nerves like it was before. As soon as I saw her glowing eyes and relaxed face, I took a long breath. We aren't going to have a bad night.

Wanting to make myself useful, I go to set the table for dinner while Marc's at the stove.

I'm more humming to myself as I'm laying the forks down, when Aria asks, "Can I help you?"

Peeking up, I see she moves toward me. "Sure. We can't burn anything in here." I smile while handing over the spoons.

She giggles and takes them from me, helping to finish the place settings. It's silent between us for a minute, and I don't feel one bit of tension. It reminds me of the first time we met. She was sweet and kind, so it's nice to see we can go back to there.

"Gracie, I'm really sorry for being rude to you. I didn't mean anything I said." She talks in a low, brittle voice, and it causes me to stop what I'm doing and look up at her. She's paused and is already looking at me too.

Holding her gaze, I can see she's being genuine. She is wringing her hands and her mouth is opening and closing, so I just give her a moment to see if she is finished.

"I just wasn't expecting you. It felt rushed."

I nod, trying to give her a gentle face so she knows I understand. "I'm sorry you felt that way, and I'm sure it would have been a shock. We should have been more honest. I've known your dad for a while now."

Her nose scrunches up. "Since when?"

I pull out the chair and sit down, and she copies, sitting opposite me and leaning her head in her hand.

"I used to live in Chicago, and he had a project there. And then I ended up getting a job here, and we just started the relationship recently. It's all very new, but we still could have handled it better." I ease back into the chair.

She tilts her head and drops her hand away from her chin. "It's okay. We all made mistakes."

I really want to get to know her too, so I ask her something about herself. "Your dad said you want to be a doctor. What type?"

That has her wiggling in her chair and rubbing her hands together with a glow on her face. "I do. A pediatrician."

I smile, loving how she knows exactly what she wants to do. "That's awesome. I wish I knew what I wanted to do when I was younger. I've only just started my dream career."

She frowns. "What did you do before?"

"I worked at my parents' bar."

I swallow the lump, since having a deep conversation about my upbringing with her seems inappropriate. It's something I'll mention at another time.

"And now?"

"I'm doing a traineeship in architecture."

Her eyes widen. "So, you work for my dad?"

I shake my head and laugh, but I'm cut off.

"No, I wish. She works for my competition." Marc enters the room, carrying a tray of food.

"Ohhh, I'm surprised he is letting you," Aria says with a roll of her eyes.

I laugh again before explaining why I won't. "It's a conflict of interest to date the boss. So, this works out for both of us."

It would also be way too distracting to have him at work. The number of times I'd be going into his office for *work* would get me hated real fast by the other employees. It's definitely better if I stay where I am.

He grumbles and leaves the room.

"He likes to wrap us up in cotton wool."

I giggle. "I secretly love it."

"I know, same, but shh, don't tell him that."

"Tell me what?" He walks back in with the sauce and bread.

"How good this dinner looks," I say, winking at Aria, who beams back at me, clearly grateful for my save.

CHAPTER 28

MARCO

Four weeks later

I just ran my usual route around the park, but instead of five and for an hour, it was seven for a half hour. I made it a quick one this morning. It's the second time since Christmas Eve I've slept more than six hours...and it's all because of *her*.

I'd give up my five-a.m. run for her any day. Heck, I've already cut down my working hours just to be with Gracie. Waking up and having her warm curves wrapped around me isn't something I want to give up. If it wasn't too soon, I'd happily have her move in permanently, but I need to take baby steps and not rush in like the horny teenager I've become.

Taking it slow is best on all three of us.

After I shower, I walk out to cook a big breakfast, but I see Aria and Gracie have already started.

I run my hand through my damp hair and grin. I don't care how bad this breakfast tastes, because the way the girls are smiling and dancing to the music that's blaring through speakers makes me smile too. Leaning against the doorframe, I silently observe them.

These two have become fast friends, making me feel like I'm the third wheel sometimes.

The smoke coming off the stove has me wanting to close my eyes, or worse, step in and take over, but I cross my arms over my chest to stop myself. I need to let them learn because how else can either of them improve? I thought breakfast was a meal that couldn't be fucked up, but of course these two are currently out to prove me wrong.

"I love this song," Aria singsongs, and when she dances, she notices me, pausing mid-spin. A blush hits her cheeks in record time.

I have a big fat smirk on my face, and I pop my brow as she stares blankly at me.

"Why are you being a creep over there?" she asks.

I push off and step into the kitchen, moving to the counter to grip onto it while I watch Gracie try to move the pan off the stove. I'm ignoring the panic clawing at me and just let them destroy the food and pan instead. We can just order in if we need to. I refocus on what she said to take my mind of it.

"I'm not a creep. I finished having my shower, and I was coming to cook for us. But it seems you two are one step ahead of me."

Aria nods, but my gaze flicks to the sexy brunette in my kitchen, standing in her sleepwear that's hiding sinful curves. The way she's biting her bottom lip is causing my cock to come alive all over again. I'm holding myself back from taking her inside my bedroom and having her for breakfast.

Luckily for her, Aria is here, but it's bad for my cock that's trying to tent in my pants at how perfect she looks in this house with my daughter. It's funny, because ever since they made up, Aria has wanted Gracie around more and more. Aria was also the one to make Gracie sleep over the very first time, creating my new morning addiction...Gracie.

"Can I help with anything?" I ask with humor dripping from my tone. I'm staring at Gracie, totally lost in how beautiful she looks after having just woken up. Her hair is in her signature messy bun, random pieces hanging loosely around her face.

She clears her throat and moves her gaze from mine and answers. "No, take a seat and we will serve."

"Okay..." I say with uncertainty, but take a seat.

Taking in the already set table, I can't help but be stupidly happy at how hard they are trying today. For me. This sudden burst of love is hitting me like a tidal wave. I'm drowning in love and contentment.

I pull out the chair and sit, and it isn't long before it's time to eat. I almost want to laugh out loud when Aria carries both plates in, and I get a look at the food. My choice is either the undercooked pancakes, or the *very* overcooked ones. I decide to eat the burnt ones, which are unpleasant, but I pretend it's at least edible.

But I've made my decision. After breakfast, I'll be going into my office and phoning up a friend to get these two into cooking classes stat. I don't know how much longer I can pretend to enjoy their food.

After breakfast, dishes are cleaned up and packed away, and we take our seats on the couch. I'm reclined back in my sweats with Gracie curled up on her side next to me, while Aria is on the other. I'm drawing circles on both of their backs, paying them equal attention as we watch some reality show. All I know is the mother has named all her kids starting with the letter K. I think if I had another...

I pause for a moment, wondering why my thoughts are drifting to another child.

My heart races, knowing I would have a baby tomorrow with Gracie if that was what she wanted. Would I call the next child something that begins with A?

I don't know because, if I'm truthful, I'd let Gracie choose the name and go along for the ride just to see her happy. Her smile is infectious, and I'll do anything to keep her looking at me like I make her day. She has no idea how much of a highlight she is in mine.

I know the pain of her past still bothers her, and I don't think it will ever go away. I bet it lingers there in the back of her mind, so anything I can do to ease the stress is what I'm going to do.

She's constantly on the phone to her friend Ava, who is panicking about being a mother, and it shocks me because it's not the same calm and collected woman I've heard about.

Is that hormones, or is it fear?

Gracie has opened up to me a bit about Ava and her struggles growing up, and I understand how and why they are so close, almost like sisters. The fact some parts of their pasts are similar scares me. I can't lie and say I'm not a little worried that if she were pregnant, would Gracie have the same terrors as Ava?

I hope not...

I think she would be the best mom, especially after seeing her with Aria. I don't take it for granted for one second, knowing it will take work and not just for a couple of weeks. But I'm willing to put in the work because they are worth it.

"Hey, slacker, keep up the tickles." Gracie rolls over so her eyes catch mine, and the mischievous pair sparkling back at me makes me want to kiss the cheeky grin off her face.

"Sorry, I was thinking," I reply.

"Of what?" Aria asks.

I don't want to share everything, so I say what's in my heart. "How lucky I am."

Aria groans like it's the most disgusting thing she's heard, whereas Gracie stares at me with the biggest wide-set hazel eyes and an even bigger lopsided grin.

She gets me.

She really fucking gets me.

The credits roll and I check the time on my watch, seeing it's almost time for Aria to go to her mom's. So, I shuffle out and up off the couch. "Aria, your mom will be waiting, we need to leave soon. Can you go get your bag ready?"

She sighs then mutters, "Okay, I'm going," as she stands.

"Do you need a hand?" Gracie offers her.

And she gives Gracie a smile. "No, I'm good. Thanks, anyway. Don't start the next episode without me."

Gracie smiles back at her with her hands up. "I promise, I won't."

Aria is packing upstairs, so when I find Gracie cleaning at the sink, I can't help but sneak up behind her. I snake my hand around her waist and bring my nose into her brown hair, inhaling her scent before moving my lips to her ear and whispering, "Shh, or Aria will hear you."

Her body has turned rigid in my arms, and I watch her chest rise and fall with fast breaths. My hand moves to slip beneath her sweats and inside her panties, and I don't waste any time. I need her coming on my hand like that time in the bar. Rubbing her clit in hard circles, her back arches into me at the sensation.

"Marc," she rasps.

I grin into her neck where I kiss her repeatedly, nipping and sucking her sensitive flesh. I lower my hand and slide my fingers between her wet folds, entering two fingers easily. Her pussy is wet, warm, and so ready for me. I hear a little sexy grunt and her head drops onto my shoulder. She's holding back a loud moan. And my already hard cock is now throbbing. But this isn't about me; this moment is all about her pleasure.

Her warm pussy clamps down hard at the intrusion at first, before her body relaxes under me.

"Does that feel good?"

She nods and mumbles under my hand.

"I can feel how close you are, but you need to stay quiet."

Her body quakes against mine, and she falls apart beneath my touch. It's so damn sexy, and it's only the start. She has no idea what I've got planned for her later.

Afterward, she spins and her lust-filled eyes stare back at me and my lopsided grin. She shakes her head, unable to believe I just did that, and truthfully, neither can I.

"Are you two almost ready?" I call out to my girls.

My girls.

CHAPTER 29

GRACIE

"I can't believe you're really here," I say, hugging Ava at the airport.

"I've missed you so much, and you weren't coming to me." She pulls out of my hug and gives me a dirty look.

I can't help but laugh at how dramatic she is.

"I was for your baby shower," I say, looking down at her beautiful bump covered by a white, long top. Her makeup still done perfectly, but her normally outdone hair is swept on top of her head in a bun.

I have missed her so much and I'm so glad she's here.

"That's not for a couple of months," she argues. "But anyway, I'm here now."

"You are. Where to first?" I ask, linking my arm through hers and walking in the direction of the car.

"Food. I'm getting nauseated. I eat every couple of hours to keep it at bay."

I scrunch up my nose. "That sounds awful."

She shrugs as if it's not a big deal. "It's not that bad."

"You haven't been in labor yet."

"Yeah, but I'm asking for all the drugs if I need them."

I laugh at her directness and no fucks given attitude. I do envy how she puts herself and her happiness first. "I have a feeling you won't need them. Your pain tolerance is high."

I think she has forgotten how I almost fainted in the room when she got her nipples pierced. I don't think she needed me there because I did not help at all. I was pale and sweaty in the chair in the corner as I watched. And afterward, she asked if I wanted one. "Hell no," was my response. I don't care how good it feels, I have no desire to get them.

"But I've never had a baby before and a watermelon coming out of my *you know what* doesn't sound fun."

I giggle, but the vision of a watermelon has horror dawning on me. "No, it sounds awful."

We get inside the car Marc arranged and grab some take-away.

My phone chimes, and I pull it out and see that it's him.

Marc: Did your friend arrive okay?

Gracie: Yeah, she's here with me now. We are picking up food.

Marc: Nice. Well, have fun and I'll see you both soon.

Gracie: I can't wait x

Marc: Me too, *Bella* x

Arriving at Marc's house with Ava makes me feel stupidly giddy.

I hit the doorbell as she whispers, "His house is big and fancy, isn't it?"

"Yeah, it's stunning," I say, holding the food in my hands.

"Am I going to be asking Josh to upgrade my house?"

I shake my head, knowing how nice Joshua's place is. "No, his house is big enough."

"But it's not big enough for more than one child."

"Well, that's true, but don't worry about more than one for now; you still have to get through this one."

She stays silent for a second, clearly thinking about that. "This is true."

My heart explodes when Marc opens the door in his navy top and dark-wash jeans and bare feet. I feel the heat hit my cheeks from the flush he gives me. The handsome man standing there is all mine.

"Holy shit, Gracie." Ava hits my arm playfully.

I giggle and whisper, "Told you."

She gapes at me and softly shakes her head. "Damn. Good for you. You deserve this."

After the way I grew up, I know she's right. I do deserve him and this life I'm living.

"I just wish you lived in Chicago still," she adds.

"I know, but this is home now," I say, stepping into his house and kissing Marc.

He's my home, my orbit, and I'm not leaving for anyone or anything.

EPILOGUE

GRACIE

"Where are we going?" I ask, touching the silk blindfold.

"A surprise."

I pout. "That's no fun."

"It will be worth it. I promise."

He grabs my hand, and I sit back in the leather seat, trying to relax in the car. His scent is so much stronger now that my sight has gone. It makes all the other senses work so much harder.

A little while later, the car stops, and he unbuckles my seat belt and takes my hand to help me out.

When I stand, I dust my dress down, hoping I'm all in place. I can't see it, so I can only judge by how it feels.

"Let's take this off," he says, his hands grazing my temples as he slides the blindfold off.

I blink and adjust to the light. He stands in one of his navy suits and his white shirt with a navy tie. As he grabs the door, I notice the diamond cufflinks are ones that I recently bought him as a birthday gift. He is one of the hardest people to buy for and luckily this year, he was only thirty-nine. What will I buy the guy who has everything for his fortieth?

Inside the restaurant, I see a large wooden bar. The high ceilings in New York are my favorite part. This place is exquisite, the roof being all glass. And the chandelier hanging over the middle screams expensive. Marc walks us to the bar, and he pulls out one of the tall wooden and gold stools for me. I still don't know what he's doing as we both take a seat. Are we having dinner here?

The bartender comes over and asks us what we want to order.

"I'll get two whiskey sours, please," Marc says, and I smile.

The bartender walks off and Marc faces me.

"What are you doing?" I ask, tilting my head.

"We're at a bar, having drinks." His smirk makes me wonder what his plans are.

The bartender brings the drinks and Marc asks for nachos, hot wings, and fries.

I chuckle to myself and whisper, "Are you trying to replay our Christmas Eve together?"

He leans in close to my ear, whispering, "Well, it is Christmas Eve."

I shiver from his warm breath on my neck. "It is," I say, picking up my drink to cheer him on. Needing the cool liquid to calm my scorching body.

"To us. May every Christmas Eve bring us more love and good times." He holds my gaze with a longing look, and the way it makes me feel has me biting my lip.

His words send a warm feeling running through me.

We clink glasses, and I take a sip.

"I haven't had this since last time," I mumble before adding, "This could be dangerous."

He looks at me with the same desire, and I know he's thinking back to that night at the bar and what happened after we drank these.

"Same." He sips, and I can't help but watch him drink it and appreciate the bob of his Adam's apple.

I lick my lips, tasting the residue. "I forgot how good it was."

He nods, but his eyes narrow at watching my tongue. I suck in a breath, expecting him to kiss me with the way he's staring at me like he wants to eat me.

"So, are we going to play truth or dare?" I drink more, needing a slight buzz to calm the nerves. But also, this game could be fun.

He tips his head back and laughs before standing to shrug out of his jacket. Showing me his white shirt that hides his taunt toned body that I can't wait to touch tonight. I wish we could skip dinner and go straight to dessert. And this bar is full, so here is not an option.

"If you want." He stares at me with mischief. I don't want to seem too keen, so I shrug. "Why not?"

He rubs his chin, his gaze fixed on me, before dragging them over my body. "Only one problem. I know a lot about you."

"I guess dare needs to be used more tonight, then." I move to cross my legs, my foot brushing his calf, and the simple movement has my skin prickling with goose-bumps.

He shakes his head, but he looks down at my foot, totally transfixed by the movement. "This could be a really bad idea." His voice sounds strained, as if the soft strokes are affecting him, and it gives me the confidence boost I need.

"Are you scared?" I raise a brow, but my lips want to widen into a large smirk. I love teasing him.

"No. But let me order another round." Gripping his drink tightly, he throws it back and swallows.

He waves down the bartender and orders us another round. I watch in awe at how even the bartender is focused on him. You can't help but be sucked in by his presence. He demands your attention without you even realizing.

We get our drinks, and I take a big sip before asking, "Did you want me to go first?"

He runs his hand through his hair, messing his perfectly styled locks. "Yeah."

"Dare."

He shakes his head and then looks around before focusing on me. "Ask someone to take our photo when we are kissing each other."

I find a woman in her twenties as I slide off my stool, and I just know she will know how to take a cute picture. This dare is a good one. A minute later, the photo is taken, and we thank the woman.

"Your turn," I say with a smirk, and he sips his drink, unexpectedly leaning toward me and whispering in my ear, "Dare."

I tap my lips with my finger, seeing his phone sitting on the bar, and it gives me an idea. A wicked smile spreads on my face as I speak. "Write a love letter to me and post it on your socials."

"Easy," he says, grabbing his phone.

There's no hesitation as he types away. Then I get to read it only a moment later.

Bella

I love you from the very depths of my heart. There's nothing in this world I wouldn't do to keep us together. You have shown me what it means to be loved and love with all of myself in my most sincere form.

I love you beyond words, and the best is yet to come.

Marc

"Marc," I breathe through a constricted throat. "That's so..."

I don't even have a big enough word.

Sweet? Kind? Beautiful? No words feel big enough.

"Thank you." I drop my quivering chin, trying to dry up the tears sitting on my lashes.

Clearing my throat, I take a drink.

He strokes my shoulder and lays a kiss on it, then lays another to my neck. "Are you okay?"

I lean my head against his, closing my eyes as I enjoy his attention.

"Gracie?" he asks, pulling me from my daze.

I open my eyes, but don't move my position, so he continues his trail of kisses. The heat gives me the promise of what's coming later. "Yeah, let's keep playing."

He lifts his mouth from my neck, and a moan leaves me at the loss. Narrowing his eyes at me, he looks between the two, trying to read my face. "Are you sure?"

"Yes," I say, smiling. I'm so happy in this moment; I don't have many words to describe it.

He turns to sip his drink, and when his mouth returns to my neck, I gasp, feeling ice coldness. I swallow hard as he drags it slowly up and down, and I can't believe he is doing this here. I squirm when he hits my ear, chewing on the ice as he asks, "Truth or dare?"

"Truth," I choke out, unable to speak evenly. My thighs quiver with need and the ache from my chest hits me between my thighs. I just want to get out of here and be together before holding each other until the sun rises.

"What part of your body do you want to be kissed again and again?" He bites on my earlobe, and I hiss.

I sit there watching him and think about it.

Touching my neck just under my ear, I remember how much I shudder whenever he kisses me there. And how I miss his mouth already, even though he's been kissing it for ages. I still crave it more, so the answer is easy.

"Here."

He leans forward, and my breath hitches when his lips hit that exact spot. And he whispers, "Here?"

I mumble incoherent words. Knowing my neck is getting sensitive from his beard, and I'm flushed from how he makes me feel. The combination is indescribable. But he sits there, unaffected, while I'm a hot mess. I need to put the conversation back to a safe zone in order to get through the night.

"Truth or dare?"

He answers with amusement in his eyes, and I see a twinkle of heat. I bet his mind is there, but what he doesn't know that whatever he chooses, I'm going for fun. "Truth."

I'm laughing before I begin speaking, and watch as he scrunches up his face up, confused. I try to take a deep, long breath to steady myself. "Have you ever tried to lick your nose using your tongue?"

He grabs his drink, laughing. "No, and what kind of question was that?"

"What? Never?" I say, ignoring the other part of the question. I'm sure if I told him I was horny, he would throw me over his shoulder and take me home, but I want to have fun tonight.

He shakes his head in a no.

"Well, come on, and try now," I say, trying to do it and failing miserably.

His face drops, and a chuckle comes out. "You are crazy." But for me, he tries and also fails.

We chuckle loudly together, and both take a drink, draining our glasses.

"Last one, and that's it," he warns, and the way he says it sends a shiver through me.

I rub my finger over my bottom lip, and he watches it with hungry eyes. "Dare."

"You're ending on a dare?" he asks with wide eyes and a smirk, and I smirk back.

"Yep. So, make it good."

He looks around before he finally holds out his phone toward me and says, "Call my parents and ask permission for our marriage."

My jaw drops. Surely not? I feel my heart drop and then my stomach flutter because I know I'm going to have to do it, but I need to stall. "What?"

"Go on." He grabs his phone, swipes it to unlock, and waves it in front of me.

I drain the glass of my drink, and he brings up his parents' phone number. I hit call, taking a deep breath. I can do this. No big deal, right?

And when his mom answers, all the blood rushes to my toes as I say, "Hi, Mr. and Mrs. Giordano, um, I'm calling to ask if I could have your blessing to marry your son?"

Marc is watching me with the biggest grin on his face. And I'm glad one of us is amused because it isn't me. I'm a ball of nerves, and he is happy as a pig in mud.

"Really? That would be an honor, love," his mom gushes, and I can finally breathe, though the stomach flutters are still there. Why was asking that so hard to do?

"I better go, but thanks for the blessing," I rush out, still in disbelief that I just did that.

I hang up and hand him the phone.

"That was so nerve-racking. And why did they say yes? I've met them once," I say, horrified. Aren't in-laws supposed to be like parents and give me a hard time?

"Why? They love you. I talk about you all the time. But let's get going." He checks his watch and stuffs his phone in his pocket as he stands and holds out his hand.

I freeze momentarily. He talks about me all the time and they love me? I never expected it, but I feel a small swell in my heart. How kind they can be toward me, yet they barely know me. My own parents knew me for years and would only treat me with such venom.

I slide off the stool and take his hand in mine. "Where are we going?"

He lifts my hand up and kisses the back of it before squeezing it and tugging me toward the door. "A surprise."

I narrow my eyes and try to keep my lips pursed, but they break free into a big grin. "Don't blindfold me this time."

"Okay, but..." He leans and whispers, "Only if I can use it in the bedroom on you tonight."

I shiver at the idea. Oh yes, please. Even the idea to blindfold him...yes, an even better idea. A wicked grin sits on my face as I say, "Deal."

"You didn't even hesitate. And what are you thinking? *Bella*? You're looking a little too pleased with yourself?"

We step outside, and I keep my eyes forward on the car as I pull him inside. "Come on, I want to get home."

He swats my behind as I'm about to get in. "We have a stop along the way that I'm sure you'll love."

We walk from the car to the beach. I kick off my stilettos and carry them.

"We are ticking watching the sunset off our list?"

"Yep."

We get to a spot on the sand that looks perfect to watch the sunset. He rolls out a blanket, and I smile as I take a seat and curl up beside him. My head rests on his shoulder, and as the time passes and the sky settles in a spot that radiates a beautiful hue of deep yellow and red, he shuffles, and I lift my head off.

Moving in front of me, he's kneeling, and his hand disappears into his pocket before he opens a ring box. A shiny cushion-cut diamond stares back at me. The white gold details make me gasp. It's so pretty. I've never owned something so delicate or expensive.

My heart is racing inside my chest, and my eyes are glued to the ring until he speaks.

"Gracie, I want to thank you for making me a better man. Since I met you, I've felt more centered, more at peace. Not only do I have something new to work for, but someone to share this life with. Please, do me the greatest honor and become my wife?"

I'm staring at him in awe. I can't move or say a word. There are no tears, my body just twitching in shock.

He's still holding the box, and I've still not moved or answered him.

"I'd give anything to hear the word *yes* from you now," he says with a soft smile.

Him and his words.

I nod, and then choke out, "Yes. Yes, of course I'll marry you."

Want to read how Gracie tells Marc she's pregnant in a Bonus scene?

Click Here and read it now

Ready to meet my final man in the Gentlemen Series?

Arrogant quarterback playboy Benjamin Chase is the hottest player on the team.
And guess what...he only has eyes for me.

But I finally landed my dream job as a club doctor and have no intention of falling for a guy. Especially one who wears his jersey like a second skin.

He thinks I'll swoon for his athletic body, those piercing blue eyes, or his charm like most women. But I'm not like most. I keep a wall around my heart because someone once showed me that what men do best is leave.

But when an old knee injury makes us work one-on-one, we exchange our banter, lingering touches, and secret kisses. And suddenly it's what's underneath that jersey that has my heart racing and the ice melting.

I try to resist him but his end-game is chasing me.

Pre-Order Resisting Chase Here

Have you read Josh and Ava's tension filled love story? If not, click below and read it now.

Read Bossy Mr Ward here

Also By

Gentlemen Series

Accidental Neighbor

Bossy Mr. Ward

White Empire

Saffron and Secrets

Resisting Chase

Standalone

Doctor Taylor

Preview of Bossy Mr Ward

PROLOGUE

J oshua

Staring across an old wooden desk into my father's gaze, my head thumps inside my skull as I watch my dad's small, thin lips move. I can't understand his words; it's as if he is speaking underwater. I scrunch my forehead, trying to concentrate on reading his lips, but I can't for the life of me lip-read.

I shouldn't have drunk so much scotch last night at the party. It was a regular boys' night that quickly got out of control. As usual, I let myself get loose. With no work commitments or girlfriend to answer to, I don't know when to stop. I'm not complaining. I love my easy, free life. But the hangovers every week are getting harder to bounce back from.

I'm slumped in one of his worn office chairs. I watch as he rubs his eyebrows with his hand, rests his elbows on top of the desk, and blows out his cheeks, frustration written on his face. I haven't had the best relationship with my parents. They wanted the so-called perfect child, not the rebellious party boy they got.

If they gave two shits about me, they would have talked to me. But I was invisible to them. I think I was born for the society picture, not out of love.

Love—what is that?

I wouldn't know what it feels like to be truly loved. People see the outside, the pretty face, the family money, the carefree attitude I put on, but underneath the façade is darkness. Deep loneliness hidden deep under layers.

I scan the office, noting the mess, the papers piled up on his desk. I shrug it off, blaming my drunken state that I must be seeing shit.

Rubbing my hands over my face, I say, "Dad, what did you call me here this early for?" Irritation is laced in my voice.

He rises, snatching his glass full of whiskey off the desk and taking a big swig. "It's eleven in the morning, for god's sake. Look at the state of you. Every week, you do this to yourself. You need to grow up."

I sigh, leaning back, taking in his profile. He looks out the window, talking to it instead of me. He barely looks at me. I shake my head. He seems to have aged, his gray hair more white, his black suit a little big for his small frame.

My head throbs and I snap. I would rather be on my couch, recovering, than sitting here. "What did you call me here for?"

He picks up a piece of paper and shoves it out to me. I move a little too quick and wince. I want to get the fuck out of here. I snatch the paper from his hands.

I peer down and my brows furrow. *What the fuck?*

I blink rapidly. *Surely not.*

It's a contract.

For the business.

The family business.

He transferred it.

Into my name.

Joshua Ward.

Effective immediately.

My mouth slacks and I try to think of what to say, but nothing is forming coherently in my mind.

I thrust my hand to the back of my neck and squeeze the tension that's building up, hard and fast.

I clear my throat. "Why?" I whisper.

I want to say more, but that's all I can think of right now.

My heart is beating erratically at the news and the contract that I'm currently glaring at. "Why?" The words leave my mouth again as I lean back into the office chair in shock and take in my old man. I squint as I try to read his face for answers.

"It's time, son. I'm not young anymore. I can't do this forever." He continues looking at the window and not at me.

Lie.

He is hiding something. I'm certain. I lean into the right side of the chair and rub my hand along my chin, trying to figure out what it is. As if glaring at him long enough will make him spit it out. *I wish!*

I lift my chin in a sudden thought. "It's sudden. Effective immediately? Why not prepare me—show me how you run the business?"

My dad stands and rounds his chair to the drink trolley. He turns and lifts the glass into the air in a silent offering.

Bile rises in my throat. I shake my head. *Fuck, that hurts.* I cease immediately and he shrugs before pouring himself another large helping of whiskey. He takes a large gulp of the amber liquid.

He cradles the glass as he returns to his chair. I notice his eyes appear red and dull.

Maybe it is the right decision. I just wish he hadn't thrown me into the business like this. A little warning would have been nice.

"Your mother and I are taking a trip for six to twelve months. Change of scenery." He stares out the office window and takes another large sip. Something is on his mind.

I shift, sitting up in my chair. Raising a brow, I say, "You're serious?"

His gaze meets my hard eyes. "What is your issue, son? I thought you would be happy taking over the business."

I think about his question. Am I happy? I sigh. "Of course I am. Just not like this. And this soon. But it's not like I have many choices. How much time do we have before this...trip?" I ask.

"Six weeks."

I slap my hands on my thighs, not giving a fuck about my head. "You expect me to learn everything in six fucking weeks? You're crazy, old man...Gahhhhh," I growl, sitting back in my chair.

His body straightens and his eyebrows draw close together as he says, "Do not speak to me like that. You will show some respect. You will be fine. You're young; you will find better and new ways to run the ship."

My jaw thrusts as I hold back another outburst. We don't speak as he drains his glass. I watch him stalk toward the alcohol trolley and lower his empty glass. He swings around and walks over to me. He stands beside me, resting his right hand on my shoulder, and squeezes. "I'm tired. It's time I get home. Your mother will be expecting me."

I nod, scared that if I open my mouth, I'll disrespect him. And I'm not wasting my breath. My sore head is quickly turning into a migraine.

I hear him walk to the door. It creaks open before I hear the click shut. *Asshole*.

I inhale a deep breath through my nose and stalk around the desk, dusting my hands across the top surface. Papers fly in every direction.

I take a seat in my new chair, scanning the room. Old white paint, dark brown carpet, and a small window looking outside at houses. It's a small, run-down building. The computer needs an upgrade desperately. My dad insisted that upgrading was a waste, but I don't agree.

Now that I am to take over, things need to change.

As I scan the office, I think about the recent projects we have lost to our competitors. My gut twists and I need to dig deeper.

I tear open the drawers and pull the paperwork of all our current jobs out and pile everything onto the desk. Some papers hold on top of the pile, but a few slip straight to the floor.

Once all the papers inside the office are on top of the desk, I sift through, making two piles. Keep or throw. My stomach grumbles, reminding me I skipped dinner with a fling I have been seeing this week.

It's close to two in the morning by the time I finally get ready to leave the office. I've been here all day, trying to make sense of everything, and I pick up one final paper that had slipped off the desk and landed on the other side.

I crouch down and scoop it up. As I stand, I scan the contents. "You asshole," I say out loud. So this is what he wasn't telling me; I knew he was hiding something... Scrunching the paper in my hand, I pull out my phone and click on James' name, bringing the phone to my ear. It doesn't take long for him to answer.

"Josh?" His voice is gravelly and I wince.

"Shit. Sorry. I didn't even think about the time when I called you."

"No, no. It's fine. What's up?" he asks.

"My dad left me with the family business, effective immediately. The asshole is going on a holiday in six weeks for six months, maybe a year. I don't know how to run a business, James—a failing one at that." I squeeze my eyes shut at the last statement. The paper in my hand has angered me further.

"It's okay. I got you. I'll be there in five minutes. You at the office?"

I sigh loudly. "Yeah."

I hit the end button and shove the phone back into my pocket.

I step to the drink trolley and pour myself a good three fingers of scotch, the one thing he still had—expensive liquor.

I move over to the chair and pull at the drink, the amber burning my throat before my head reminds me I'm still hungover.

I lower the glass to the table and sit down again while I wait for my friend James. I crinkle the paper and stare at the eviction words. Staring back at me. Mocking me.

Fuck!

Chapter 1
Ava
Six months later

My desk phone rings, scaring the crap out of me. I work as a receptionist for a printing company. "Good morning. Ava speaking. How may I help you?"

"Ava, it's David. Could you see me in my office when you finish with the orders?"

"Of course. I won't be too long," I answer.

"Take your time."

I hang up. I've been working with David for a few years now; I enjoy the peace of the small town I live in. And there are only a few of us who work here, so I can be myself.

Twenty minutes later, I rise and wander over to David's office. I knock on his doorframe.

He looks up from his computer with a half-assed smile. Uneasiness churns in my stomach. "Ava, come in. Please take a seat."

I frown at his comment. He doesn't ask me to sit down. Ever. Sweat forms on my palms and I rub them quickly down my ripped blue jeans.

"Okay." I step inside and sit down on the chair opposite him. I sit straight, waiting for the reason for his call.

He rubs the back of his neck before gazing at me. *Shit. He looks serious.*

"Ava, I'm so sorry to have to say this, but we have to close the business."

My hands cover my gasp. "What. Shit. Why?" I mumble through my fingers.

He hangs his head. "I know it must shock you, and trust me, I tried to avoid this, but financially the company is now in the hands of administrators."

I blink rapidly, trying to process his words. *What the fuck am I going to do for money now?*

Feeling my heart beating in my throat, I try to concentrate on breathing in and out, trying to calm the panic that's rising. My breaths are shallow yet audible. I'm unable to talk, my mind going over the same thoughts. How am I going to get through this? I can't go back there.

"Are you okay, Ava? Would you like a glass of water? Ava?" He asks again, louder this time.

I would rather have alcohol, but I know we don't have any here in the office. I nod slowly. His chair drags across the floor as he rises, and heavy footsteps walk to the water fountain. The water trickling sounds like my bleeding heart. The footsteps begin again as a shadow appears in front of me. I slowly raise my head to see David has the cup held out in front of him. Grabbing the cup slowly out of his outstretched hand, peering down at the clear liquid, I raise the plastic cup and chug the water back, draining the cup. The cold water coats my warm throat. *So good.*

David steps back around to his chair.

I offer a small smile and talk in a quiet voice. "Thanks." I continue to concentrate on breathing in through my nose, out through my mouth, feeling my shoulders relax with every breath and my heartbeat regulating.

He clears his throat, gaining my attention. "I'm giving you two weeks' notice. If you find another job before that, I will understand. You're a fantastic worker and I'm happy to be called as a reference."

My lips tip up. "Thanks, David. I appreciate that." I hesitate before adding, "What will you do?"

He takes a deep, audible breath and leans back in his chair. His gaze meets mine. The sadness there makes my cold heart break.

"I don't know, Ava. Truthfully, I don't know."

"Well, shit." A nervous smile appears on my lips.

He laughs, but it's not his carefree laugh. It's a broken cackle. "I will miss you. You kept this place in order. Hell, you kept me sorted. I just couldn't keep this place afloat. I'm sorry."

His eyes return to his computer and I swallow. "You are a significant person and boss. I'm sure something better is out there waiting for you."

He raises his chin to glance at me, offering me a genuine smile. The surrounding air is quiet, so I stand. "I better get back to work."

He nods and also stands, walking around the desk and toward me. I instinctively take a step back, not wanting any physical touch. I cross my arms, spin around, and wander back to my desk, lost in my thoughts about my future.

The next few hours drag. I work, but it's not as productive as I usually would be. Not like I have to try very hard now. I will be jobless in two weeks. *Fuck. What will I do*?

A few hours later, I clear my desk and make my way home. I pick up the cheapest bottle of wine from the store, not giving a shit that cheap wine causes the worst hangovers. I need alcohol tonight. It might help this numbness I'm feeling disappear. That, or it will help me sleep.

As soon as I enter my apartment, a lump forms in my throat. I hate that I could be looking at moving out of here. *My home*. It's a warm and safe place. Entering the kitchen,

I pull open the cupboard and scan the contents. I don't have the energy to cook a fancy dinner, nor do I have the funds.

I spot a packet of noodles. *Bingo*. I grab them and begin preparing them. While they cook, I connect my phone to the Bluetooth speaker so I have music playing softly in the background, then I open the bottle of wine and pour myself a decent helping. Taking a sip, I scrunch up my face. *This shit is awful. Fuck*. I stir the noodles, which are almost done, and take another large mouthful of my shitty cheap wine.

My phone rings as I lower the glass and choke on the awful shit, then twist the volume down on the speaker so I can answer the call. Pulling out my phone, I check the display. Mom's name is flashing. Even though I hate myself right now, and I hate that I could disappoint her, the need to tell her about my day has me answering it.

"Mom, your ears must have been burning. I was going to call you tonight." I step back to the kitchen.

"Oh, no, they weren't, darling. What did you want to talk to me about?"

Raising the wine, I take another large sip, needing the liquid courage. I stir my dinner before flicking the stove off. "Are you sitting down?" I ask quietly.

"No, but what happened?" Concern is laced in her voice.

A sour taste hits my mouth. I am hating how I'm about to let her down, that David sacking me is a disappointment to her. A heaviness enters my heart and I blow out a breath I hadn't realized I had been holding until she speaks.

"Darling, tell me. You have me worried sick here," she begs through the phone.

I squeeze my eyes shut, then open them. "Sorry. I was turning my dinner off. David called me into the office today and said he is closing the business." I hear her gasp. Tears form behind my eyelids. I'm glad she isn't here because I would be a basket case.

"Oh, darling. I'm so sorry."

"It's not your fault, Mom." Pinching my lips together for a moment, I finally say, "I have two weeks to find another job."

As I glance around my one-bedroom apartment, my heart hurts. I love this place. I'm settled here and my paychecks keep me living here independently.

"No wonder you're upset, darling. But there is a reason. Things happen in your life for a reason. There is a better opportunity out there. I believe that," she offers.

My eyes fill with tears. I still don't believe this is happening. I love how she always believes in me, but right now, I'm feeling numb and not optimistic.

Desperate to change the subject so I don't start sobbing on the phone, I say, "Thanks, Mom. I hope you're right. Anyway, enough about me. What are you doing?"

"I was going to see if you wanted to come for dinner Sunday night? Darling?"

I am having trouble responding; my mouth is opening but no words are coming out. After a beat, I sigh, "Yes. That sounds good." I would rather be by myself. Alone. But then all I will do is think about my jobless situation. And she would insist she comes to visit. At least this way, I won't have to cook.

"Okay, good. I'll cook one of your favorites."

I close my eyes at her sweet gesture. Any food is my favorite, but there are definitely a few dishes that stand out.

I feel weak, like I need to sit down. "Mom, I better eat my dinner before it gets cold."

"Good idea. Are you sure you will be okay tonight? Do you need me to come over?" she offers.

"No thanks; I'll be fine. I'm tired and will crash soon."

"Okay. Call me if you need anything. I love you."

My heart thumps at those words. "I love you too...Bye." I hang up and retreat to the stove to serve my noodles. Scooping up my bowl, fork, and glass of wine, I carry them into my living room, lowering my butt to the floor, my food on the coffee table and wine beside it. I stab the noodles with the fork. I try to eat but my throat thickens, making it hard to swallow. Deciding against eating, I push the bowl aside and drink the wine instead.

A few glasses of wine later, my veins are now filled with alcohol. It's warming me from the inside. Feeling hot, I peel off my sweater, leaving me in my tank top and leggings.

I search the television, looking for a show or movie to watch tonight. Scrolling aimlessly through the stations, I find nothing. I flick it off and open my mom's old laptop. I power it up and continue to drink. By now I have had too many, but I'm cradling my last glass as I scroll through job ads. I stop on one that sounds simple enough. I sit up straight and the wine sloshes around in the glass and over the edge. *Fuckin' hell.*

I lift my finger up the glass and wipe the wine up, sucking the residue into my mouth. I don't want to get this over my white couch or rug.

I squint as I read the job description.

Personal Assistant required for an expanding electrical company. That sounds easy.

I shrug at myself on this cozy night. Scrolling through, I read each duty.

Able to work as part of a team

Facilities management and maintenance

Schedule management and meeting coordination

Coordinating and organizing project manager

Office management including stationery, mail, greeting clients, couriers, and more

It all sounds easy enough. I can support a project manager with daily tasks. *Piece of cake*.

Feeling a little buzzed, I set the wine down on the coffee table. A little smirk plays on my lips. I fill in a new version of my résumé. I'm smiling to myself as I add some cheeky extra words and side tasks. I have never done them, but it makes me sound more experienced.

I need money and a job desperately. With no other options and only two weeks to find something new, I laugh at how ridiculous I sound on this résumé. But the website has nothing else that's suitable.

An icy shiver runs through my spine. The thought of getting kicked out of here has me hitting send. I close the laptop, drain my glass, and my eyes become heavy. Unable to concentrate on the TV, I switch it off and climb onto my sofa, snuggling in as my exhaustion takes over, and I pass out.

***

When I move the next morning on the couch, my head feels like it's about to explode. I groan out loud at no one. *Fuck. I feel sick. Stupid cheap wine*. Without lifting my head up, I reach for my phone.

I can't remember a thing about last night. I seem to have lost all recollection of events. My fingers touch my cell. *Yes. Found it.*

I lift it up in front of my face and squint as the light from the screen blares back at me. *Ahh, so fucking bright.*

I blink rapidly until my eyes adjust. My thumb moves aimlessly over my socials and I catch sight of my email icon, showing one new message. Frowning, I click on it and open my emails, sucking in a breath as I read the subject line to the one email.

Job Interview from Ward Electrical and Infrastructure.

I rub down my face, trying to wipe away the sleep and foggy brain. *What?*

Shifting my weight on the couch, sitting up a little, I try to understand if it's a spam email. I need a closer look. I haven't applied for any jobs. *Right?*

I open up a browser and google the company's name. Sure enough, a website pops up. And as I scan, it seems legitimate.

So, the next question is how?

I rub along my brow, trying to remember and finally deciding to check my sent emails. I have a niggling feeling in my stomach. *Did I apply last night?*

Clicking the folder, it opens up and sure enough, there is the application I sent off. *Fuck.*

Moving back to the inbox, I reopen the email and read the contents. Job interview means I'll need to look professional. I groan. But my stomach grumbles, reminding me I also need money for necessities. *And better wine.*

As I continue to read, I see a comment stating it's a phone interview. *Thank fuck.*

The interview is scheduled for ten a.m. on Thursday. If I'm successful, I start Monday. Maybe Mom is right about her signs. If I get this job, then I'll know for certain that it was meant to be...but at the moment, I'm not convinced. Surely someone is going to come busting through my door and tell me I have been punked.

My shoulders drop and I relax back onto the couch with a loud sigh.

Closing the application, I swing my legs off the couch and sit up. I grip my head with both hands, wincing from the movement. Waiting for the waves in my head to settle, I stay still before getting up and sorting myself out with some food before work.

***

Thursday arrives, and after work, I sit at my dining table, waiting for the phone to ring. I chew the end of my pen. I hardly slept last night, tossing and turning. Not having much experience with interviews, I was mulling over all the questions they might ask me. I stayed up and googled all the standard interview questions, as well as the business.

My pen repeatedly taps on the paper, my stomach fluttering with nerves. The phone rings. *Shit. It's time.* I pick it up and stare at the screen, not answering until a few rings. I don't want to seem desperate, even though I *need* this job.

I swipe the pad of my finger across the phone, bringing it to my ear. "Hello. Ava speaking."

My tone is the sweet professional one, not my regular, relaxed tone.

"Hi, Ava. This is James calling from Ward Electrical and Infrastructure. How are you?" A deep voice speaks into the phone. It's rich, confident, and sexy. I'm still nervous, but now a tad of excitement shrills through me.

"I'm good. Thank you for asking. And you?"

"I'm excellent, thanks. Now, I'm calling about the job for the assistant position you applied for."

"Yes," I say back.

"Are you okay if we begin the job interview now?"

"Sure." I shuffle to the edge of the chair and twirl my hair around my finger. I stare down at my paper. My heartbeat picks up speed.

"Why do you want this position?" he asks.

My mouth drops open. Straight to the point, no bullshit approach. I like that. I like it a lot.

"My previous company is closing. Having previously worked for them for the last eight years, I need a job and I'm experienced in the position you require."

"You are, and you have had no other workplaces?" He seems to be taken aback.

"No, my previous employment was the one and only. Oh, and the odd jobs when I had spare time."

The add-ons to my résumé have returned to haunt me. I really could kick myself for making that shit up right now. Hopefully, I don't get caught out by the lies. Surely I would have been interviewed on my work with David alone. I don't know why I lied. *The booze, you idiot. This is why you don't drink so much. And especially with no food.*

"Very good," he mumbles. I can hear the faint scratching of a pen gliding across paper.

I sit back a little, my shoulders still tense and sitting up around my ears. I'm waiting for the next question.

"What do you think you can bring to the company?"

I answer, "I'm creative, timely, and organized."

A pause and then he chuckles, "Perfect. Thomas, who you will potentially be reporting to, needs that. A lot," he drawls.

Oh god. I hope this Thomas isn't a slob; I'm not a cleaner. I can organize the office for a better system for working. But I don't want to be cleaning up after a male. I shake my head at the thought. *Gross.*

Luckily, David was tidy and understood my quirks.

"What do you know about the company?" he asks.

I hear a rustle of papers in my ear. When it stops, I answer.

"Ward Electrical and Infrastructure specializes in the electrical design, cabling, project management, information technology, and technical services. They provide these services to the construction industry, public transport, and the corporate sector," I answer without a pause.

"Impressive," he mumbles. "Are there questions for me?"

I rub my brow with my free hand, not expecting that question and feeling a tad stupid for not being able to think of anything. My brain is coming up blank. "Ugh, no. Not at this stage, thanks."

"Well, you sound like you would make the perfect assistant to Thomas, so congratulations. I'll email you now with a formal letter of offer and more important details about the company. If you can come to the address on the date provided, someone will welcome you in."

An enormous smile appears on my face. *I did it. I found a new job.*

"Wow. Thank you," I breathe.

My mouth opens and shuts, but nothing else leaves it, so I just slam it shut again. I wish I could talk, but I'm shocked by how I scored a job quickly after David sacked me.

"You're welcome. Goodbye, Ava."

"Goodbye." I rip the phone away from my ear, hanging up and staring at it out in front of me. I take a few big deep breaths as relief washes through me. Then I call Mom.

To keep reading Click Here to continue...

Acknowledgments

My husband you're my rock, I love you. And my two blessings, my children. Thank you for allowing me to write and watch you grow at the same time.

All my beta's, friends and family, without each of your support, I would be awfully lonely. I'm so happy to be supported by a tribe. Just know, I will be forever grateful. Love you all.

My readers, thank you for supporting me and purchasing my books. You are supporting my dreams and without you, my career wouldn't exist.

Thank you.

Afterword

To keep up to date with my new book releases, including title's, blurb's, release date's and giveaways. Please subscribe to my newsletter via my website.

Want to stay up to date with me? Talk book boyfriends and come hang out?

Come join my Facebook reader group: Sharon's Sweethearts

This is a **PRIVATE** group and only people in the group can see posts and comments!

ABOUT AUTHOR

Sharon Woods is an author of Contemporary Romance. She loves writing steamy love stories with a happy ever after.

Born and living in Melbourne, Australia. With her beautiful husband and two children.

http://www.sharonwoodsauthor.com

f www.facebook.com/profile.php?id=100082849748945

BB bookbub.com/profile/sharon-woods-4299d99d-9666-4633-aa7f-32ae2aad1506

O http://www.instagram.com/sharonwoodsauthor

♪ tiktok.com/@sharonwoodsauthor

www.ingramcontent.com/pod-product-compliance
Lightning Source LLC
Chambersburg PA
CBHW061515020726
47502CB00006B/2089